TIME EXPOSURE

By

Lynne Kennedy

Also by Lynne Kennedy

THE TRIANGLE MURDERS
PROVENANCE
THE COVENANT

ISBN-13 :978-1479331505
ISBN-10 :1479331503

Acknowledgments

I'd like to give thanks to the people who provided me with the resources to make this novel as authentic as fiction allows: Will Stapp, National Museum of Photography, Film and Television, Bradford, England, previously at the Smithsonian, first for getting me interested in Civil War photography and then for furnishing background detail on the Civil War photographer. Will, I hope you get to read this, wherever you are.

Joel Snyder, University of Chicago, for his critical wit and photographic expertise in both the nineteenth and twentieth century processes; Michelle Anne Delaney, National Museum of American History, Smithsonian Institution, for her guidance in the early photographic process; Kari Lee Chipman, Digital Creative Imaging, for her patient demonstrations of digital software; Larry Dale of the San Diego Police Department for valuable information on photographic enhancement capabilities in the area of crime detection; Arthur Olman, former Executive Director of the Museum of Photographic Arts, San Diego, for imparting his knowledge of nineteenth century photography, and helping me enlist the services of other experts; Hetty Tye, also from the Museum of Photographic Arts, who showed me original nineteenth century works, albumen prints, ambrotypes, tintypes, carte de visites, and stereographs; and to the many knowledgeable rangers at the National Battlefield Parks of Manassas, Antietam, Gettysburg, Petersburg, Spotsylvania, The Wilderness, and Fredericksburg.

To my first editor and advisor, Mike MacCarthy -- thank you helping me find my voice and for keeping me on the right path. To my final editor, Terry Wright, thanks for great suggestions throughout but most of all to a dynamite ending! And to my current, long term critique group: Ken Kuhlken, fearless leader, who always has something nice to say, Dave Knop, Barbara Hopfinger and

Maynard Kartveldt. Thanks for sticking with me! I hope it was worth the agony.

Most of all thanks to my patient and loving husband, John Kennedy, who read and re-read drafts of this manuscript ad nauseam, and provided me with invaluable insight.

I must also thank Alexander Gardner, master Civil War photographer, for poignant commentary accompanying his images taken at Antietam, Fredericksburg, Gettysburg, and Petersburg.

I wish I could take credit for the poem excerpt that begins the historic "Joseph" section, however, I must profoundly thank Walt Whitman for these precious Civil War mementos.

Lynne Kennedy

August, 2012

To my dearest girlfriends
Margaret, Pam, Melinda, Susan and Aly
for reading, critiquing, and encouraging.
Oh, and thanks to Bruno and Rosie,
for lowering my blood pressure.

Maggie

Chapter 1

Georgetown, Washington, D.C.

Wednesday, June 5, 2000, 5:30 p.m.

Maggie Thornhill turned her ten-year old Beemer onto Dumbarton Street and hit the brakes. At the far end of the block, blue and red lights flashed atop two police cars, their reflections mirrored in the wet asphalt. An ambulance siren cut off in mid-wail as it careened past her, and the static hiss of police radios radiated shivers up her arms.

Across the street, people clustered, advancing closer to the police cars, hungry for a news bite. She didn't recognize any of them but then she'd only just moved into the neighborhood. The crowd parted for the Medical Examiner's van as it drove unhurriedly to its final destination. Her house.

She bailed out of her car and bolted down the street in a panic-fueled run. Her brain scrutinized the tableau in front of her. No fire engines, so no fire.

A uniformed officer was rolling out yellow tape between two trees. As a digital photographer with law enforcement, a crime scene was familiar territory to Maggie. But she had never imagined her house being taped off. Hot bile singed the back of her throat. What the hell was going on? Her heart beat double time as she pushed her way through the crush of neighbors. Finally she reached her front steps and rushed at the uniformed officer.

"That's my house." Maggie tried to maneuver past the cop but he stood firm as a pillar of stone. "Let me through. What are you doing? I live here."

"Sorry, Miss, you'll have to stay back."

She recognized a man coming down the steps of her brownstone. A short, wiry homicide detective with thinning blond hair. He wore his usual tan jacket, button-down shirt, and no tie. Frank Mead.

"Frank," she cried out.

"It's okay, Officer, let her through." Mead stepped toward her. "Been trying to reach you."

"Did you try my cell?" She rummaged through her pockets, pulled out the iPhone. The display was dark. "Battery's dead. Goddammit."

Mead blew out a breath. "Um hmm."

"What's going on in there?"

"We got a call from Carlos, uh, something. . ." Mead flipped through his notes.

"My contractor called you?" She rasped out the words.

"You're renovating this old place?"

"I inherited it," Maggie said. "Been in the family over a century and a half. Carlos was checking the basement for mold and dry rot or whatever they check basements for. . . Frank, what are you doing here? The ME too. Did something happen to one of Carlos' men?"

Mead took her arm and ushered her up the steps to the front door. "They're all fine."

"Thank God." She could breathe again.

He opened the door and turned to the neighbors gathered below. "Go home, folks, everything's under control. Nothing to see. Go on."

He led Maggie inside.

"Then what the devil happened?"

"Carlos and his boys were doing their job when they found a body behind a false brick wall."

"A body? My God. What false wall?" She pressed fingers against her forehead as if she could force this new information into her brain.

Mead led her through the kitchen to the open cellar door and started down. "Good thing the lights are working down here. You could break your neck."

Maggie followed him down. "Can't believe. . . a body? Hidden?"

"Yeah, but not just *any old* body."

"Whose body?"

He didn't answer.

She glared at the back of his head and frowned. He wouldn't give her answers until he was ready.

At the bottom step all she could see were dingy brick walls, chunks of mortar, layers of dust, cobwebs befitting Dracula's castle, and old bottles and boxes leaning precariously on tilted shelves. Four generations of detritus she'd have to clean up.

Mead pointed to a part of the wall that had been dismantled, brick by brick. "This false wall was constructed after the house was built."

"It doesn't look new."

"Carlos says it's nearly as old as the original walls."

"Someone walled up a body in there?" She turned to face him. "But not just *any old* body?"

"Have a look." He walked over to the false wall, now only three feet high and shined a flashlight into the dark space.

"It isn't *any old* body," he said. "It's a *very old* body."

Maggie leaned in. She found herself staring at what remained of a human being. A human being who hadn't been alive in a long, long time. The skull and skeleton were shrouded in a thin layer of mottled brown, leathery skin, eye sockets long empty, mouth open in a silent O. What was left of the clothing were only strips of fabric, riddled with insect holes and crusted with dirt. Her throat constricted, choking her voice to a whisper. "Oh my God. It's a mummy."

*

Within minutes of Mead calling up to the street, the ME thudded down the rickety steps. "Whatcha got?"

Mead pointed her toward the mummy. "You might want to suit up, it's pretty. . ."

The Medical Examiner, Doctor Jemena Wooley, an African American woman of shorter than average height and wider than average weight, had already squeezed her bulk into the cramped space behind the wall. She eyed Maggie as she pulled on her surgical gloves. "It's Maggie, right? I've seen you at the Forensics Lab. I didn't think you actually took crime scene photos."

"I don't," Maggie said. "I analyze them. This is my house."

"No kidding?" The ME ducked down into the space and began her examination of the corpse.

Minutes went by. Mead tapped his foot. "Jemmy, what've you got? "And don't give me that *wait 'til the autopsy* shit."

"Male. Dead a long time. Long time."

"That's it?" Mead said.

"Wait for the autopsy." Jemena stood up with a groan. "Man oh man, I've got to go back to Weight Watchers." She brushed dust off her sleeves then called out to the crime team who were awaiting instructions.

In minutes they swarmed the basement. Without disturbing the body, they took photographs and gathered whatever evidence they could vacuum and scrape up. That crew departed and Jemena and an assistant readied the body for removal.

"Is there a special protocol for removing mummies?" Maggie asked.

Mead was about to comment when they heard Jemena shout. "You should see this."

Maggie darted to the wall, looked over. The corpse had been lifted onto a stretcher.

"The body camouflaged this." Jemena shone a flashlight onto an old satchel. "Let's get some photographs here," she called.

Mead pulled purple surgical gloves out of his pocket and handed Maggie a pair. Both snapped them on. When photos and evidence were gathered, Jemena handed the satchel to Mead. He laid it on the floor. Maggie angled a work light on it.

They crouched over the faded blue canvas bag, about sixteen inches wide by twenty inches long and four inches thick. The leather shoulder strap was almost worn through. The flap was cinched to the bag with a large rusted buckle.

"Could it be an old mail bag?" Mead asked.

Maggie turned the satchel over. She felt a trickle of sweat run down her back. The musty smell of earth and time attacked her nostrils. She wrinkled her nose, held in a cough.

"Are those initials on the flap?" Mead said.

She ran her fingers over the threads of the letters. A tiny whimper escaped her lips.

"What are they?"

"J.A.T."

"Who's J.A.T?"

"Joseph Andrew Thornhill."

"The famous Civil War photographer?"

"And my great, great, great grandfather." Maggie looked up from the satchel and stared at Mead. "What in the name of God have we found?"

Chapter 2

Smithsonian Institution

Sunday, June 9, 4:30 p.m.

Maggie stood in the great hall of the Smithsonian's National Museum of American History, her favorite place on earth, second only to her brownstone on Dumbarton Street. Because she was descended from a famous Civil War photographer, she'd spent countless hours over the years visiting the exhibits on the Civil War and attending lectures on Civil War photography. The study in her house was dedicated to memorabilia from that time period and Joseph Thornhill's photographs. It was, indeed, Joseph's work that had inspired her to become a photographer.

Now, a chill ran through her as several chords of the national anthem were struck and the wall at the far end of the room began to rise, revealing an American flag that had flown over Fort McHenry in 1812. The flag was kept out of the public eye in temperature and light-controlled conditions. It was only displayed on special occasions such as this one: a fundraiser for the Museum with special guest, the United States Senator from Massachusetts, Fitzhugh Morley Wade. Fitz, as his friends and constituents called him, was always willing to help the museum raise private funds.

He approached her, handsome in a dark gray suit, a sky blue shirt that matched his eyes, and a *Save the Children* tie. “Hello, Maggie. Don’t you get goose bumps whenever that flag is in view?”

“I’m glad you were able to arrange a viewing tonight.” She tilted her cheek for Fitz Wade to kiss. “Where’s T.J.?”

“He’ll be here any moment,” Fitz said.

Maggie thought how much father and son looked alike. Maybe she’d marry T.J. someday and become Mrs. Thomas Jefferson Wade and the wife of an up and coming federal prosecutor.

A woman’s voice, “Maggie, dear, so glad you could come.”

“Dorothy, it’s been a long time.” Maggie clasped the older woman’s hands in hers. As always, the Senator’s wife looked like she stepped out of a Neiman Marcus window. Not a blond hair out of place, crimson lipstick contrasting with even white teeth.

“We don’t see enough of you these days,” Dorothy said. “Although I don’t wonder with the mischief you’ve been up to.”

Maggie arched her eyebrows. “Mischief?”

Fitz said, “Imagine. Maggie Thornhill, my future daughter-in-law, makes the Washington Post.”

Maggie’s face blushed at the reference to daughter-in-law. “Discovering a body in my basement is not how I hoped to claim fame,” Maggie said.

“But a mummified body,” Dorothy said. “Incredible. Any idea who it might be?”

T.J. arrived and interrupted the conversation. He put an arm around her shoulders. “The press had a field day with Maggie’s story. Turned it into a series. Pictures of the old house, history of its occupants, plus background on how bodies turn into mummies, crime scene forensics, all kinds of gory stuff. Nothing on the other find, however."

"What other find?" Dorothy asked.

A short, round man with eyeglasses thick as the window glass in her attic edged his way into their group.

"Speaking of the Civil War, hello, Homer." Fitz turned to Maggie. "This is Homer Catesby, professor at GWU. He's an expert in Civil War photography, written tomes on the subject. In fact, he just won an award for--"

"Ach, never mind, Fitz." Homer grinned at Maggie. "Don't bore the woman to death."

"I'm familiar with your work, Professor." Maggie offered her hand. "I'm Maggie Thornhill."

"She's the young woman from Dumbarton Street," Fitz said.

Homer bobbed his head and gripped her hand with the exuberance of a baseball fan. "Oh yes, yes, I've been reading about you, Miss Thornhill. In my opinion Joseph Thornhill was the best Civil War photographer of them all. Far better than Brady and Gardner and Sullivan."

"I agree, Professor." She reclaimed her hand from his tight grip.

"So fascinating," he said. "Have they identified the remains yet?"

"No, it's much too early," Maggie said.

"I imagine it will take some time to date it as well, discover if it's someone from the Civil War," Homer said. "Good God, what a find that will be."

A waiter brought a tray of champagne and everyone reached for a flute.

T.J. spoke. "We do know it's a male, at least."

"Is it possible the body is Joseph?" Catesby asked. "Or is that too far-fetched?"

It seemed to Maggie that everyone was waiting for her answer.

"Maggie?" Dorothy said. "Could it be Joseph? He lived there, didn't he, with his wife

and son?"

"A number of Thornhills have lived there since, Mother," T.J. said. "It could be another ancestor."

"Perhaps." Dorothy looked skeptical. "Maggie, you never said what else you found in the basement."

"There was an old satchel," Maggie started.

"Under the body," T.J. finished.

She cast him a sharp look. "Will you let me tell the story?"

T.J. grinned. "Sorry, go ahead."

"Under the body was a knapsack with the initials J.A.T.," Maggie said.

"Joseph Andrew Thornhill," Catesby said. "Then the body could--"

"The satchel might be Joseph's, but we don't know who the body is." Maggie said. "Yet."

T.J. jumped in again. "We'll know once the DNA comes back."

"Ahh," Fitz said. They took some of your DNA, Maggie?"

She nodded, feeling her blood fizz like the champagne in her glass at the thought of the possibilities.

"What about this satchel," Dorothy said. "Was there anything inside? Were--?"

"Inside were letters between Joseph and Sara, his wife," Maggie said.

"Love letters?" Dorothy said. "Oh, Maggie, how romantic. Anything else?"

"Joseph's journal. From his days on the battlefield. Think of it. The War between the States. In Joseph's own words as it happened.

Gives me chills just thinking about what he saw and thought and felt."

"A journal, Holy Christmas," Catesby said.

"Have you had a chance to read any of it yet?" Dorothy asked. "What's in it?"

Before she could answer, Catesby asked, "Maggie, were there any photographs in the satchel?"

"Yes, Professor, there were photographs."

"Photographs. From Joseph Thornhill," Catesby said, sloshing champagne out of his glass in his exuberance. "That no one has ever seen. Lord. Tell me more. Please."

"Yes, Maggie, tell us," Fitz said.

The group surrounded her like she was suddenly a celebrity.

"When I held that bag in my hands there was no sleep for me that night. . . or much since, for that matter. I had to begin reading Joseph's diary right away. And then, I couldn't stop."

"And the photos?" Catesby asked.

"Between reading and typing notes from the letters and diary, I did a quick examination of the photographs."

Catesby leaned in as if to capture every word.

"Although they are brilliant in their depth and breadth," Maggie continued, "some of the figures in the pictures need more clarity, more definition."

"Is there anything you can do to sharpen them?" Fitz said.

"Of course, she can do it," T.J. said. "She's the director of the Georgetown University Digital Lab, isn't she?"

The band launched into the national anthem again and the wall at the far end of the hall began its journey downward. The American flag disappeared, sealed once more in its environmentally controlled chamber until its next appearance.

Fitz Wade's chief-of-staff stepped up. "Time to say goodbye to everyone, Sir."

"I expect to see you soon, Maggie, at the Plantation." Fitz always referred to his stately colonial home in Arlington, Virginia as the *Plantation.* The chief-of-staff hustled him away.

"Bye, Dorothy," Maggie said as the senator's wife strode off behind him.

Maggie remained in the Great Hall with Homer Catesby, waiting for T.J. to return. Her thoughts were like a thousand jigsaw puzzle pieces waiting to be assembled into a final picture.

As if he could see inside her mind, Homer said, "You can't stop thinking of the diary, can you?"

"No."

"Can you tell me a little about what Joseph wrote?"

"It's like I was with him on the battlefield. I smelled the sulfur of gunpowder, the rank odor of blood and decaying flesh. I saw the torn bodies, bent and twisted, like so many tossed marionettes."

He nodded, eyes wide.

"I pictured the landscape, burnt and scarred, damaged by the ruined redoubts and rifle-pits, blasted stone bridges and outhouses." She paused, gazed out into space as her mind relived Joseph's words. "And the pain. I felt it. I hurt."

Catesby continued for her. "The terrible loneliness and fear that the soldiers experienced. Makes me shiver."

She looked at him. He was someone who understood.

"Can you. . . will you let me work with you on your photographs and documents?" he asked.

"I can and I will."

Homer broke into a toothy grin. "Thank you. And will we help the police identify the body and solve the mystery?"

Maggie's thoughts flitted back to the body and the satchel. Joseph had lived in the house. The satchel bore his initials. But her experience in working on criminal investigations proved that things weren't always as obvious as they seemed.

Homer interrupted her musings. "The body could be someone more recent than Joseph, you know. Maybe a relative or even just a workman, a house boy who got himself murdered."

"When the DNA results come back, I'll at least know whether it was a family member."

"What do you think?"

Maggie steadied her gaze on him. "I know what history tells us about Joseph. So do you."

Catesby nodded. "One story says he died of a strange illness and was buried in a secret grave. Another purports that he abandoned his wife and child and ran off to the Orient with another woman."

Maggie felt Catesby's gaze on her. "We might never know the truth but one thing we do know. Joseph Thornhill vanished one day without a word at the end of the War."

Joseph

This dust was once the man,
gentle, plain, just and resolute,
under whose cautious hand,
against the foulest crime in history
known in any land or age,
was saved the Union of these States.
Walt Whitman, The Civil War Poems

Chapter 3

Washington City
July 9, 1861

A bell rang in the darkroom alerting Joseph Thornhill that a customer had entered the gallery. In the dim crimson light, he groped for a towel. The bell rang again.

"Jeb?" Joseph called out. "The Gundersons are here."

He poked his head through the door and looked down the hall. "Jeb?"

Joseph wiped his hands on the towel and threw it aside.

Why did he have to do everything?

He unrolled his sleeves and stomped down the stairs one level to the entry hall of the Mathew Brady Photography Gallery. He was glad to open the door if only to stop the persistent ringing bell.

The door burst open and three round pudgy children stampeded past.

"Whoa, now, hold on."

"Tut, tut, Mister Thornhill," said the obese patriarch. "They're just exuberant at the prospect of having their portrait done."

"Ahh, yes, of course. Do come in, Mister and Missus Gunderson."

Jeb, his assistant, gray and grizzled with stubble on his chin, arrived, an apology spilling out. "Sorry--"

"Never mind," Joseph said. "Is the blue room in order?"

"Yes, Joseph. This way, Ma'am, Sir, if you will." Jeb led the way upstairs to the studio where skylights provided the necessary lighting. Joseph followed.

They passed through the second-floor waiting room, a handsome and functional room with dark oak wainscoting, leather chairs and a Persian rug embellishing a plank floor.

One of the Gunderson children stopped at the main attraction of the room. The other two gathered around him.

"What's this?" the boy asked, his eyes shining with curiosity.

"That's a stereoscopic view box," Joseph said.

"What does it do?"

"Let's take a look." Joseph smiled at the opportunity to show off his prized possession. "Slide in one of those cards," he indicated the nearby box of stereo slides, "and see what happens."

The child selected a card and with Joseph's guiding hand, inserted it into the view box slot. He pressed his eyes to the viewer. "Yipes, it looks, it looks real, I mean not like a pitcher."

"You mean picture. Exactly," Joseph said. "That's a magic box. Makes the picture look three-dimensional."

They all took turns looking into the viewer, ooing and aahing. One of the children knocked over the slide box and the slides scattered across the floor.

"Careful, don't. . ."

The little girl raced to pick them up, stepped on one and Joseph heard it shatter.

"No, it's all right, I'll get them." Another child rushed over.

All of the children were grabbing at the slides.

Joseph heard another one crack.

"All right, now, children." Mister Gunderson shooed them toward the staircase. "Upstairs for our photographs. Upstairs."

Joseph gathered up the stereoscopic slides and stacked them back in the box. Two were broken and he growled as he tossed them in a rubbish bin. Jeb would handle the family now, thank God. There were three more sittings scheduled for the day, but at least they weren't bankers' families. They were soldiers.

Joseph thought back to three years ago, when he was a photographer's apprentice. He cherished it, couldn't believe his good fortune to land at Mathew Brady's Gallery and train with the best. Brady himself and Alexander Gardner. Alex, his mentor and dearest friend. Alex inspired him to love the craft of photography. Alex just hadn't taught him to abide the portrait sittings of society matrons, pompous bankers and their persnickety brats. Joseph sighed.

It was a good thing Alex had the foresight to order the extra *carte de visite* cameras. Otherwise, they'd never been able to accommodate the hundreds of newly commissioned soldiers who wanted photographs. Soldiers who arrived daily from all over the North.

It had been just three months since Fort Sumter. Joseph almost enlisted in the army. Too many excuses stood in his way. He couldn't leave Brady a photographer short. He needed the income. And he couldn't leave Sara. Lovely Sara Kelly, whom he'd been courting all that time. But even Sara couldn't help him dispel this disquietude about spending the rest of his life taking pictures of God-awful dull subjects.

In truth, it was more than restlessness with his current occupation, more than mere ambition to move on. This was his country and he yearned to defend it the best way he knew how. If not as a soldier then as a photographer, documenting the conflict for history.

Something had to change or he'd go mad.

At the very thought of madness Alexander Gardner careened into the waiting room like a tornado. As always, his bow tie sat askew under his beard and his elbows poked through holes in his brown nubby jacket. He grabbed Joseph's arm and forced him into a divan.

"Good grief, Alex, what on earth is going on?"

Alex flopped down beside him and sucked in a deep breath.

"I've had a special offer I must consider, and you, my friend, are an important part of my decision." He played with his beard.

"Speak then, for heaven's sake. I've got work to do."

"Aye, aye. I've told you about me dear friend from Scotland, Allan Pinkerton?"

"The detective?"

"The very same. He's working for the government now in the Secret Service."

"Secret Service? I didn't know there--"

"You said, speak, so let me finish, man. Pinkerton wants to appoint me to General McClellan's staff as a photographer for the Secret Service."

Joseph sank back in the divan, his heart thrumming. “What does that mean?”

"I will be responsible for photographing maps and charts and for taking photographs to identify spies or enemy agents for the Federal Army. Whenever there's suspicion of spy activity, I'm to take random photos of crowds and gatherings and Pinkerton's men can use the images to identify spies."

"How on earth will they do that?"

"Based on intelligence provided by scouts and Federal agents."

A buzz of excitement shot up Joseph’s spine.

"Photographers also record potential battle sites,” Alex went on, “to help commanders prepare their divisions or take pictures of bridges, railroad tracks and the like for the Corps of Engineers.”

Joseph looked at his friend, really looked at him hard, seething inside, not with anger but with envy as sharp as a nail in his stomach. How wonderful it must feel for Alex to know he would work out in the open air, the green fields, photographing the conflict for history, serving his country. He was astonished at his feelings and even ashamed.

Alex seemed not to notice. "I expect this sounds more exciting than it actually is, but t'will give me the chance to photograph the battlefield. Which is what I really want to do." His eyes glittered, sparking Thornhill’s jealousy like the fuse of a bomb.

“I would like you to accompany me as my assistant, Joseph. Mostly to take field photographs, but occasionally," Alex lowered his voice, "occasionally, to work on Secret Service missions. I have already obtained permission from Pinkerton, though you’ll need to have a formal interview with the man.”

The air seemed to have been sucked from the room.

“Me?” Joseph said. “Talk to Pinkerton?”

Alex laid a hand on Joseph's. "There is no other man I trust or respect more."

Joseph blinked.

"Think on it, man." Alex threw out his arms expansively.

"A chance to photograph history in the making. To help your country track down spies. Be a hero."

Oh God, here is my chance to get out of here.

"Remember what you were saying not too long ago about being sick and tired of studio portraits?"

"But me? A spy?" *Dare I say yes?*

"You'll be serving your country."

"Have you told Brady yet?" Joseph asked, the thrill of adventure building.

"No, but you may recall he's the one who originally jumped on the opportunity to photograph the battleground. He's already obtained his license to follow the Union troops."

"Hmm. I wonder how his failing eyesight's going to hamper that decision."

"Sure 'n it will make a difference if the war goes on a while."

"Most people think one brief and bloody skirmish will end the war quickly."

"Aye, that may well be. For now, I want to maintain my position with the Brady Gallery, so I will request a sabbatical, if you will. And you could too." Alex stood and placed a hand on Joseph's shoulder. "Please, Joseph, come with me."

A loud crash from upstairs followed by Jeb's hollering, reverberated through the gallery. Joseph flinched.

"Timing is so important in decision-making, don't you think?" Alex grinned. "What do you say?"

Joseph studied his friend and his brain wrestled with a decision. At once, he felt an overwhelming sense of relief, though a tickle of fear crawled up his arms. A vision of Sara Kelly's face appeared before him--the russet hair, emerald eyes, enchanting smile--and briefly he wondered what she'd think. He knew in his heart, soul and mind that she was his one true love. Sara would be distressed by this news but he prayed she would stand by his decision. She must, for he had no choice.

"We could get killed, you know," Joseph said.

"Aye, that we could."

"How quickly can you get the licenses?"

Gardner reached into his pocket and waved two small pieces of paper between his fingers.

Joseph burst out in a boisterous laugh.

Chapter 4

Washington City, The Ebbitt House

January 12, 1862

Samuel Quentin Lindsey approved of the Ebbitt House, partly because it was a popular meeting place for local businessmen, politicians and diplomats, but primarily because it afforded him a modicum of privacy in an elegant setting. And for a meeting such as the one he was about to attend, privacy was of the utmost importance.

He savored the cushioned booths, softly lit by gaslight sconces and delicate candleholders adorning the tables. He sniffed with pleasure the strong mix of tobacco, liquor and wood scents, all of which added to the comfortable ambiance of the roomy interior.

Lindsey joined two men already seated at a booth in the back corner of the establishment--their customary booth. He adjusted the vest beneath his dark waistcoat and smoothed back his steel gray hair.

Conversation ceased while the barmaid set the last of the drinks on the table. The moment she left, Porter Cranston Hobbs, the older and stouter of the two colleagues, said, "I hear that Simon Cameron's been removed from his position in the Cabinet and offered the post of Minister to Russia. Russia, imagine."

“Doubtful he’ll accept,” Lindsey said.

“Still, this means we'll no longer have easy access to information from inside the

White House."

"Now what do we do?” whined the third man, Harlow Knox, a tall emaciated man with frizzy red hair. “How the hell will we find out what's going on?"

"You're drunk, Harlow," Lindsey said. "Your drinking has brought you to a new low and it's getting the best of you.” Lindsey realized any mention of his sister, Violet, would send her husband, Knox, into paroxysms of dread, aptly stifling his foolheadedness. “Does Violet know your nasty habit is reeling out of control?”

Knox licked his ragged lips and skulked back into the cushions.

Hobbs fingered his muttonchops mustache and shifted his bulky weight in the booth. "He's right, you know, Samuel. There'll be no more inside information regarding the Executive investigation."

"Gentlemen,” Lindsey began. “This is precisely why I asked for this meeting. There’s no need to be concerned about Cameron. It's true, he’s out of the picture now but I've other resources to provide us with any information we need." He leaned over the table, clasping his hands together and lowering his voice. "What have you heard regarding this investigation?”

“I heard the Army’s been complainin’ about their guns, the artillery, the--,” Knox began. “That Union General, McIrvin?”

“General Irvin McDowell, idiot,” Lindsey said.

“Yeah, McDowell. He’s been whinin’ ‘bout the arms that we, er, I mean Concord Armaments is sellin’.”

“What exactly is he saying about the arms?” Lindsey said.

"That some are coated with rust, that the sights are outta plumb. That 'munition boxes were labeled wrong, like .577 caliber mixed up with .54."

"Hmmm," Hobbs said. "Those are not big problems. Could happen to any gun manufacturer. Now if he complained that the muskets showed a significant loss of velocity and accuracy, well then--"

"He did," Knox went on. "In a way. He said the guns would blow up in the soldiers' faces."

"Gentlemen," Lindsey huffed. "Concord Armaments was created at the behest of our dear friend, Vice President Johnson."

"Concord Armaments. I like the name," Knox said. "Better than Concord Utensils. Guns and rifles are more prestigious than pots and pans."

Lindsey shot Knox a glare. "The United States government has engaged our services to provide guns and ammunition to the Federal Army. We converted our manufacturing plant to do just that. They demand quality and quantity, but they also demand these goods with undue alacrity. There are limits to this speed and the government knows that. Certain concessions must be made to meet those needs. Sometimes defective pieces slip through."

"Right, and how else will we make a profit?" Knox offered then withered at Lindsey's icy expression.

"There's no way they can prove these defects are deliberate." Lindsey looked at each man in turn, thought of their complicity in the shoddy manufacturing business they were in. "You should be proud, my friends. Concord Armaments supplies the government with the latest in innovative arms for warfare. Muskets with rifled barrels on par with the Enfield. Supplied cheaper than the Enfields *or* the Springfields, for that matter. After all, war is our business. We are patriots."

"Patriots? I say, that's a good one." Hobbs gave a blustery laugh. "Next we'll be running for Congress, eh?"

"What do you propose we do about this government investigation then, nothing?" sputtered Knox then downed the last of his beer.

"*If* there's an investigation," Hobbs said. "It's just speculation and rumor now."

"But what if--?" Knox said.

"I've given it a good deal of thought," Lindsey said. "The government will have a difficult time proving that there is indeed a problem with arms. The investigators must first get out to the field, ferret out the complaints, verify them, no easy task--"

"True," Hobbs said. "After all, how will they know the guns weren't damaged during a skirmish?"

"Indeed," Lindsey went on. "Then they must report the complaints. Reports get lost, couriers get killed, all sorts of delays in a war, if you get my meaning."

"What if they do find out we're cutting corners," Knox said.

Lindsey trained his eyes on Knox. "I propose we hire an associate to deal with the situation."

"What associate?" Hobbs said. "Deal with it? You mean kill the agents?"

"If necessary," Lindsey said.

"But how . . . who? Do you have something in mind?" Hobbs said.

"A hired gun," Knox whispered.

Lindsey lowered his voice. "I realize this is a bold plan, and it will take a bold man to carry it out. I've chanced upon a most suitable man for the job. He's a southern sympathizer, smart, young and likable. He could slip in and out of the different regiment encampments disguised as a civilian messenger. No one will suspect him of any wrongdoing. I've had some preliminary discussions with him, and . . . no, no, I didn't mention any names, just feeling him out, testing his mettle. He's definitely interested in handling our problem."

"This, er, associate," began Hobbs, jowls beet-red. "Why would he do this, I mean, assassinate government agents? That's pretty damn risky. What does he want in return?"

"That's the beauty of it," said Lindsey. "He does have a fee, a small one, mind you, to cover his expenses, but his real motivation is in wreaking havoc on the Army of the Potomac. He loathes Lincoln and the Republicans and wants to see the southern states as sovereign entities. In fact our needs and his desires match to perfection."

"They do?" Knox asked.

"Harlow, we make guns, right?" Hobbs said. "We don't want the army shutting us down now, do we?"

"Right, but--"

Hobbs sneered at Knox, shook his head. He turned to Lindsey. "Who is this chap?"

"He calls himself Cade. Jack Cade.

*

Samuel Lindsey left the Ebbitt House about midnight and headed in the opposite direction from his Georgetown home. A frigid night, whirling flakes of snow fell to the street making the walk treacherous and his shoes squeak. The wind whistled in his ears. He pulled his cape collar up around his throat with one hand while pressing his flat-topped Derby on his head with the other.

As he approached the old carriage house, currently used as a storage shed, he looked around quickly to be sure he wasn't followed and slipped inside. He felt the comfort of a small derringer in his coat pocket. The interior, dark and still, seemed warmer, although not much, than outside. Lindsey peered through the darkness and made out the shapes around him--wagons, crates, barrels, and tack hanging from pegs on the far wall. He assumed he was alone until a hand reached out and touched him on the shoulder. He jumped and wheeled about.

"Good God, are you trying to frighten me to death? Creeping around the shadows."

"Sorry 'bout that, Mister Lindsey."

"You ought to have enough sense not to sneak up on a man," Lindsey spat, still shaken. "Haven't you got any damn light around here? I don't want to be talking to a ghost."

Abruptly a match was lit and a lantern brought up and held in front of Lindsey's face. As the lamp grew brighter Lindsey considered the man--slight in stature bearing sharp, uneven features, a wide, flat nose with flared nostrils. Maybe he had some nigger in him. Dressed in a cheap brown suit and bow tie, his attire befitting a clerk in the office of a prominent cabinet member. Lindsey knew from former dealings that this man had no qualms about selling restricted information. "What news have you got?"

The informant grinned. His protruding yellow teeth caused Lindsey to recoil. He held out his hand, palm upturned. "Yer still owe me from last time."

Lindsey pulled an envelope from his coat pocket and handed it to him, avoiding skin contact. "All right. Now what news?"

"President's gonna send out that special task force to investigate ordnance in the field, probably begin training operatives late spring or early summer."

"Hmmm. So it's true."

"Here's a list of names and details of the investigation."

Lindsey plucked the paper out of the informant's hand and skimmed it briefly. "This gives us some time, at least." He looked down at the list. "Who's this Colonel Sanford Baxter, the man in charge of the field operation?"

"West Point officer. Dedicated to the Union, thorough, absolutely no sense of humor. And, of course, he'll be workin' with Pinkerton."

Lindsey smoothed his mustache. "Allan Pinkerton? Why Pinkerton?"

"Pinkerton's the man that heads up the Secret Service."

This shed a whole new light on the future. Pinkerton was the best. His men were the best.

"Pinkerton's men will be out in the field with Baxter."

"Out in the field?" Lindsey said.

"Spying, assuming roles--"

"Assuming roles?"

"Kind of like theater. They pretend to be someone they're not, so's no one will know they're spying."

"Ahh, acting," Lindsey said. "What else?"

"They'll be taking photographs, drawing maps.

Jack Cade will have to know about this. "Listen here." Lindsey poked his finger at the little man's chest. "The moment, the very instant, you have a commencement date send me a signal. I'll make it worth your while. Is that clear?"

"Quite."

Lindsey fingered his derringer again.

Can't take chances with men who sell out their country's secrets.

He turned his back on the traitor and, braving the icy night, hurried out of the carriage house, cape flaring in a swirl of costly black wool.

Chapter 5

Near Manassas, Virginia
August 28, 1862

The rain pelted down, soaking the ground and making the roads near impassable. Jack Cade swore under his breath. He had to slow the wagon and pay close attention so he wouldn't damage a wheel in the muddy ruts. Water crept in around the collar and coat sleeves of his long, tan duster, drenching him to the bone. He ached from the jolting of the wagon, but refused to stop until he arrived at his destination. The thought that his quarry, Major Benjamin Bradley, would pay for this inconvenience brightened his dark mood.

He reached inside the pocket of his worn linen duster, now more brown than tan, and fingered a new handgun. A .40 caliber, nine-shot European LeMat, a revolver favored by the Confederate Cavalry for its tremendous fire-power. Hmmph. Can't trust Lindsey and the weapons Concord Armaments produces. No doubt I'd end up with a defective piece and get myself killed.

The relentless rain battered his wide-brimmed slouch hat, which offered little protection. As he wiped the water from his face, he envisioned the scenario he would soon dramatize. An ordinary sutler, Cade drove his wagon through the countryside, selling goods to the troops. With the help of friends he had obtained the necessary license to pass legally through Union camps. And he certainly had the goods soldiers craved--pastries, not exactly fresh, but better than the hardtack biscuits most troops were forced to eat--tobacco, canned meats, books, and toiletries like shaving brushes, razors and razor straps.

Although most soldier camps welcomed sutlers, Cade recognized they were often personally despised for their greed. Many took advantage of the men by charging exorbitant prices, sometimes up to three hundred percent more than going rates. But Jack Cade would not be greedy. He also wouldn't call attention to himself by charging much less than other sutlers. No, he would charge a fair price.

He squinted through the downpour and spied lights in the distance. As he approached the town, he noticed companies of Confederate troops guarding the supply depot at the Junction. The Union supply depot, or what used to be. He pulled the wagon to a halt in front of a livery stable, climbed down and turned the reins over to a lanky young Negro boy, barefoot and soaked.

"What happened at the depot, boy?"

"Genul Jackson done took it from da Yankees. Just today, yassuh." The whites of his eyes shone like he had a fever.

Cade smiled at the good news. "Two bits to feed and wipe down my horses, boy, and another to keep watch over my wagon tonight."

"Yassuh."

Cade stood in the stable doorway, out of the rain for a moment, and looked around. "Tell me, where's the nearest place to bed down in this town?"

The boy pointed. "Just 'cross the street."

"Mind you now, take good care of my horses and wagon." He grasped the boy's chin in his hand and squeezed hard. "Just so we understand each other--I know every item that's in that wagon, boy, so don't go thinking you can help yourself. Hear?"

"Nossuh, no. I never do enathin' like that."

Cade splashed his way across the street toward a dilapidated hotel, footsteps echoing on the deserted boardwalk.

The hotel sign hung crookedly and read Manassas Hotel in faded black letters. Proprietor: Jake Lemuelson. Cade tried the front door. It stuck and he had to push it, shaking the glass in its frame. A bell tinkled somewhere within. He eyed the lobby, garishly decorated in red, heavy tapestry drapes, discolored by a dark layer of dust. He sniffed and grimaced. The smell of urine permeated the atmosphere.

A young woman with frizzy blond hair slumped over the countertop yawning. She wore a flowered dress with dingy lace cuffs. When she spotted him, she straightened and smoothed the wrinkled muslin of her dress. She turned quickly to pinch her cheeks, then back again as Cade approached. When she smiled, Cade noticed her pretty face. She primped her hair and adjusted the low-cut neckline of her dress as he took off his hat.

“Ma’am.”

"My, ain't you the handsome gentleman? What can I do fer you?"

"I thank you for the compliment, but it's you who brighten this dismal room with that radiant smile. I’d like a room for the night if you have one." Cade spoke softly, leaning on the counter.

"Just one night?" She flipped the register around to face him and as she handed him a pen, brushed his fingers with her dainty hand.

The gesture started a fire in him. "Yes, just one night will be fine. How much will that be?"

"Fifty cents," she looked down at his signature, "Mister J. Cade."

He handed her a coin. As she placed the key in his palm, he closed his fingers around her hand. Soft and warm. "Much obliged." He held her hand. "What's your name, Miss?"

"Rosie, Sir."

"Rosie, perhaps you can help me."

"I'll try."

"I'm looking for a Federal Officer that might have come through here recently. He wore a uniform that had an insignia on his collar like this." Cade let go of her hand, picked up the pen and drew on the register page.

Rosie sighed and looked at the drawing. "Oh yah. He was here. Couldn't help but noticin' him--tall and good lookin, I mean, nothin' like yourself, but he would catch the eye of most ladies."

"When did you see him?"

Rosie furrowed her brow. "Just a day or two ago."

"Do you know which way he went?"

"I believe he was headin' to the Union encampment, down the South Road, 'bout a mile or so from here."

Cade beamed at her and she looked up at him, lips parted.

"Thank you, lovely lady. You've been most helpful. Now, would you be kind enough to bring some whiskey up to my room?" He started to turn away then looked back at Rosie. "Perhaps you could join me for a drink? If you're not too busy, I mean." He looked around the empty lobby.

The pink blush rose from her throat to her face slowly. "I'm not too busy, Sir, not at the moment."

He nodded, tipped his hat then climbed the stairs.

The room looked as grimy as he anticipated. An old rusted brass bed leaned against one wall, a deflated side chair, its stuffing long turned to dust, against the other.

He took off his hat, coat and boots and flopped down on the bed, fully clothed. It creaked and wobbled. He looked down at his wrinkled shirt and sighed.

I look like a ragamuffin these days.

Cade lit his pipe. As he smoked, he pulled out a piece of paper from his pants pocket, and impressed with Lindsey's sources, read:

I've interviewed and selected four eminently capable officers as agents for the government in a Special Services Task Force. Each is a graduate of West Point, currently assigned with Staff Headquarters at the rank of major here in Washington but have been on field duty with their respective units. Men are listed herewith for the record:

Major Benjamin Bradley, 13th Infantry Regiment, Massachusetts

Major Randall Sills, 67th Infantry Regiment, New York

Major Phillip Malone, 127th Infantry Regiment, Pennsylvania

Major Sean O'Connor, 5th Battery Regiment, Maine.

Other requisites: Each officer will carry White House credentials, wear dog tags, and will have authority to arrest and incarcerate any man who obstructs the investigation. Each officer will wear Federal staff uniform, bearing rank of major with special identifying insignia on collar: a cloverleaf design within a diamond shape, both of raised gold thread.

Cade scanned down the page to the signature: Colonel Sanford T. Baxter, Office of the Inspector General. His job was to oversee the agents listed above. From what Lindsey told him Baxter was a pompous ass.

Allan Pinkerton, however, was heading up the Secret Service. His job was to supervise the spies and photographers in the field. According to Lindsey, Pinkerton was a man to be reckoned with.

Cade folded the note and slid it back into his pocket. A few minutes later he heard a knock on the door and Rosie entered with a bottle of whiskey and two glasses on a tray. She cast her eyes down as she poured the drinks atop the dresser. Cade rose from the bed and slipped up behind her. He studied her for a moment: tall, slim, with a long, graceful neck. The smell of lilacs delighted him and he recalled the touch of her hand, the soft, warm skin. He eyed the buttons up the back of her dress to determine the best way to proceed. He ran his hands gently up and down her arms and kissed the back of her neck, her hair tickling his nose.

"You're very lovely, Rosie," he whispered in her ear. Then his arms slid around her and caressed small, soft breasts. She leaned back with a low moan and he spun her around, touching her face and neck gently with his lips, hands moving behind her to unbutton her dress.

"Sir, I don't even know your name," Rosie whispered. "I can't rightly call you J, now."

"J's all you need to know." He shoved her backward onto the bed.

Chapter 6

Manassas, Virginia
August 29, 1862

The day dawned warm and bright and muggy. Jack Cade vaguely recalled Rosie leaving early during the night, swearing at him for his savage lovemaking. He rose as the sun did, sluggish and heavy. He had slept poorly on the thin, lumpy mattress and his body felt bruised and sore from the jarring wagon ride the previous day. War's hell, he thought with a wry smile as he massaged his lower back to ease the gnawing pain.

Buttoning his last clean shirt, Cade walked over to his coat, which he had flung over the chair. He picked it up and fumbled in the inside pockets before he found what he was looking for. He held a well-crafted tool: an ice-pick, six-inches of finely-honed steel set in a rosewood handle. He shifted the weapon from one hand to the other, testing its balance.

He gazed out the window and watched the sun moving higher as the sky turned from black to blue on the horizon. He'd better get moving, especially if Jackson was nearby. Whole war might be over in a day if old Stonewall was leading the troops.

At the livery he paid the stable boy less than the two bits he'd promised, climbed aboard his wagon and took a quick inventory of his merchandise. All seemed in order, but he couldn't trust a darky.

Cade checked in his pocket for his sutler's license. It still astounded him that this little scrap of paper was his pass to follow the Union soldiers wherever they marched. His sutler's wagon, a large drummer's wagon with plenty of storage space, boasted decoratively on the sides a list of goods he carried: Tobacco, Spirits, Hardware, Necessaries. He drew in the reins and clip-clopped onto the South Road.

*

Cade arrived at the Federal encampment, which raged with turmoil and confusion. Soldiers charged back and forth, tore down tents, doused fires, wrestled with equipment. Officers shrieked orders and waved their arms frantically. Cavalrymen scrambled to pack and saddle their horses. Now that the rain had stopped, a choking dust clouded the air, already oppressive with the intense heat.

"Git this wagon outta the way," said a mere sprite of a soldier boy, pointing at him.

Damn. Cade pulled his wagon off to the side, barely in time to avoid soldiers hastening to block the road. He took a deep breath and held tightly onto the reins. Tension crackled in the air. He could see it in the men's posture and in the quickness of their movements. He could hear it in the sharp edge to their voices. The horses pranced skittishly, sensing the mood.

Cade jumped down from the wagon, tied his horses to a nearby tree. He headed toward the center of camp and came across a private guarding a small stockpile of supplies. The private hitched up his blue wool pants, two sizes too big, and eyed Cade as he approached.

"Private." Cade tipped his head.

"Howdy."

"What's the latest word? Looks like you're moving out."

"Not movin'. Gettin' ready for a fight's more like it."

"Rebs coming this way?"

"Guess so. Leastways Jackson."

"Any action yet?"

"I hear'd General Pope tried an assault on Jackson north of the turnpike but got turned back. Now there's talk that Longstreet's comin' to Stonewall's aid."

The odds had changed. Maybe if the Rebs beat back the Union army, the man he was stalking would already be dead. Save him the trouble. Cade suppressed a smile as he looked at the soldier. "I'm looking for Major Bradley. Know him?"

"No sir. Better check with the Quartermaster."

"That would be. . .?"

"Q-Sergeant Davis Cook. He's dolin' out supplies in there." He gave a chin nod to a small wooden hut.

Cade stepped into the rough-hewn log cabin, grateful to get out of the blistering sun. He glanced around at the shelves and counter tops, bare except for some cartridge boxes. It appeared that most of the equipment had been distributed to the Division.

"Somethin' you want, mister?" a voice called out from the back room.

"You Sergeant Cook?"

"That I am." The man came out to meet him.

"Pleased to meet you. Name's Cade. I'm looking for Major Benjamin Bradley. Do you know where I might find him?"

The sergeant came around the counter. He was a short man with a bristly, worn look, suspenders stretched over a round belly. "And what business might you have with a major?" Davis squinted up at Cade, half a foot taller than him and fifty pounds lighter.

"Well, Sir, I have a message to deliver to him. In my business as a sutler, I pick up messages regularly and deliver them when I can." Cade watched Davis's shoulders relax.

"Yeah, Bradley. Know him. Busy pokin' his nose in everybody's business."

"Oh?"

"Askin' questions about supplies and ordnance, checkin' to make sure goods were in order, or somethin' of the like."

"Did he inquire as to the suppliers?" Cade asked.

Cook popped a cigar butt, unlit, into his mouth. "Ask him yourself. He's around the camp somewhere."

"Thank you kindly, Sergeant." Cade stepped outside and pulled the hat brim down to shade his eyes. As he stared out across Chinn Ridge where he'd heard the Union troops had set about mounting a defensive in the hopes of delaying Longstreet, his eyes came to rest on a stone bridge. *The* stone bridge, where he'd read in *Harper's Weekly* that the opening shots of the first battle of Manassas were fired. A battle that the Confederates had won.

How the devil am I to spot one man, with a bloody insignia on his collar, among all these damn blue uniforms?

A bullet whizzed by his ear. Jesus God. He sank to his knees and crawled behind a large tree trunk. Then he scurried away at a crouch, edging closer to his wagon. The horses were dancing, eyes bulging, ready to bolt. "Whoa there." He tried to calm them.

He hopped up inside the wagon and dropped the tent flaps with a quick pull of the ties. Nervous sweat leaked from his body. He lay back for a moment and took a deep breath. He had a mission to accomplish and he couldn't do that if he was wounded.

A cacophony of noise filtered into the wagon. Drums sounded in the distance. Somewhere he remembered reading about a strange phenomenon in which loud noises could be heard from a great distance but not near, as if the sound waves skipped over the troops so as not to distract them. Acoustic shadows, the article had called it.

Suddenly, a barrage of artillery concussions rocked the wagon. Cade took the reins and trotted the goosey horses farther back from the battle line. He took his tobacco pouch and sat in the shade beneath the wagon. He rolled a cigarette. From this vantage point, he could watch the action but keep out of cannon range.

Cade wished the images he now gazed upon were out of range as well. Blue and gray uniformed men marched lockstep toward each other, then firing their muskets, they finally closed in on hand-to hand combat. The squeals of pain when a bayonet reached its mark, the howl of anger as a man charged. He turned his head. War was hell.

When the battle finally ended, it was late in the day. The sun sank low in the sky. Cade hunkered down near his wagon and watched the Union army withdraw across Bull Run Creek and with his eyes, followed the soldiers, the lucky ones, returning from the field.

Men limped, leaning on their weapons as canes, wrapped in makeshift bandages and blood-stained cloth, their faces colored with a thick layer of soot and dust so that only their teeth and eyeballs shone through.

Hoping the Confederates fared better than this, Cade winced and moved out of the way as the wounded advanced, sapped and squalid.

"How did we cope?" he asked a private limping slowly into the camp.

"Didn't gain the advantage. But then, neither did them Rebs. There's always tomorrow."

Fool. Why didn't you surrender?

Cade moved purposefully through the wounded troops. Army surgeons rushed about, bumping into him, trying to tend to the wounds, shouting demands, calling for orderlies.

"Get out of the way," a doctor yelled. "Better yet, why don't you help out?"

"I have a mission to accomplish, Sir." Cade pushed past the surgeon who just glared at him.

Passing one tent, a continuous stream of caterwauling caused him to cringe. He stopped a soldier. "What's going on in there?"

"That's the surgeon's tent. Amputations."

Cade's stomach lurched, and he hurried on, alert for that one blue uniform. He overheard reports regarding numbers of dead and wounded men, dead horses, status of supplies and ammunition. His ears perked up at the account of one soldier: the dead not buried today would be buried at first light or after the next day's engagement. He gazed out to the south across the Warenton Turnpike where Longstreet had arrived. Bodies lay strewn as far as the eye could see. A surreal landscape, Cade felt the soldiers would rise and walk away. He shook the thought out of his head.

So many blue uniforms out there. One more body wouldn't be noticed. Good. Now where in Hades was Bradley?

Daylight faded and stars began their shimmer in the navy blue sky. Cade traversed the encampment again, eyes peering through the dusk, now and then resting upon different uniforms. As the sites quieted down for the night the men either slept or sat around the fires to commiserate.

Through a smoky haze from a cook fire he saw the insignia that was etched in his mind. Gripping the ice pick in his trouser pocket, he stood perfectly still. His eyes followed Bradley as he joined a group of soldiers.

"At ease men." Bradley sat down on a camp stool.

"Some hardtack, Major?" a heavyset bald soldier asked.

"No, thanks. I just wanted to get your thoughts on something. Did any of you have trouble with your weapons today?"

"Yes, Sir, I did," said a skinny boy with pimples. "Had a problem with the sight. It was plumb out of line. Had to do without."

"Mind if I look at it?" Bradley held out his hand. The boy gave it to him and Bradley examined the wooden stock.

Cade saw him frown. Moving closer he saw the initials C.A. etched on the rifle. Concord Armaments.

"You suppose part of the problem could be the damn heat and humidity of this hellish place?" the skinny boy said.

"Or maybe these fat 'ole black flies are pluggin' the barrels up," snickered the heavyset bald soldier.

The men broke off their conversation at Cade's approach.

"Good evening, Sirs. Please, don't let me interrupt your repartee, but I just wanted to offer you some goods that might ease your troubles for a time." Cade took off his hat and bowed in false servitude.

Bradley looked up at him. "Say, are you that sutler been asking for me?"

Cade's mouth dropped open. "I, er, yes Sir. If you're Major Bradley, that is."

"I am. I understand you have a message for me."

"Not exactly a message, Sir," Cade drawled. "I have a letter, er, from your home, in Lexington, I believe?"

Bradley's face lit up. "A letter. Wonderful. Where?"

"In my wagon." Cade nodded toward his wagon standing in the distance, a glowing lantern perched on the seat. "Would you like to accompany me there now?"

"Indeed I would." Bradley stood. "I must say goodnight to you gentlemen. If this is a letter from my wife--well let's just say, I'd rather be with her, even in a letter, than with the tired lot of you."

They laughed.

"God speed tomorrow."

The men stood and saluted.

Cade escorted Bradley to his wagon. Each tread silently across the open meadow, littered with bodies.

“These men should be buried,” Bradley said. “It’s not right.”

Cade nodded. When they reached the wagon, he grabbed Bradley’s arm and motioned him to be silent.

"Ssshhh. I heard something. Might be a Rebel spy. Let's not chance it." Cade hurried to the backside of the wagon and pulled Bradley along with him.

"I didn’t hear anything." Bradley watched the sutler, a puzzled look on his face. Then he saw the ice pick gripped in Cade’s hand.

"What the hell do you think you're doing?" Bradley said, hand readied on his pistol.

"Nothing, Major. I realized I left this out and thought it would make an adequate weapon if some Reb crept out of the woods."

Bradley glowered at the man but dropped his hand to his side. "Where's my letter?"

Cade turned as if to reach into the wagon. Instead, with a flash of motion he whirled back around and thrust the ice pick deep into Bradley's chest. He held his breath as the major's eyes widened in astonishment, pupils dilated, mouth moving soundlessly. The officer's body sagged and he was dead before he hit the ground.

Cade reveled in his choice of weapon. Ice pick wounds bled little and closed up quickly. He knew that for a fact when he tested it on a farmer's pig. Good thing. He hated blood.

Cade reached for the lantern in his wagon. Bending over the body, he unbuttoned Bradley's uniform and dabbed at the tiny trickle of blood oozing from the chest puncture. The uniform, barely damaged, the wound closed up. He buttoned the jacket up, and tucked the ice pick in his trouser pocket. Cade stared down into Bradley's open eyes--a light brown flecked with green. He reached down and closed the lids. Breathing hard, his heart pounding, Cade wiped the sweat from his forehead with the back of his hand.

Then he searched Bradley's uniform and pulled out official looking papers, which he tucked in his pocket. He also tore off an identification tag and hastily stowed that away too. Next he lifted the body under both arms and dragged it away from the trees and out into the field where other corpses lay. He looked around with the meager light of a crescent moon, took a deep breath and dragged the body further onto the field. Propping it up into a grotesque pose, he rested briefly, Bradley's body leaning on him like lovers saying farewell. With a grunt, he rolled it into some shallow earthworks.

Chapter 7

Antietam Creek, Sharpsburg, Maryland
September 18, 1862

My Dear Sara,

I travel with the army in the blistering heat and damp toward the town of Sharpsburg Maryland, not far from you and yet millions of miles from you in Washington City, my love. Who could have dreamed the war would go on this long? And our marriage, our life together, waits on its end.

Passing mile upon mile of desolate road, I despair when I see fertile fields on either side–-fields which should be teeming with harvests of rich grain but which now lay fallow owing to thousands of feet tromping the soil. Fences are down, rails blackened and burnt; orphaned children wander hungry and homeless, begging for food from strangers.

From time to time we stop to rest and I seize these opportunities to photograph landscapes and pose the soldiers in groups, using the canvas tents or simply constructed earthworks as backdrops. In the distance are the splintered remains of battered caissons and massive cannon lying uselessly on their sides, ruined in battle.

Perhaps we will rest here for the night . . . and then my thoughts will turn to you, sweet Sara, and the evilness of war settles in the back corner of my mind for a brief while. I shall see your fair face before me and your smile will ease the loneliness. Ah, but the army moves on, and I must bid you farewell for now.

Yours ever truly,

Joseph

Joseph dropped the corpse he was dragging. It began toppling down a stony incline. He groaned and reached for the blue pant leg. Missed. The body landed near a large boulder, face up, eyes open. The soldier appeared to be staring at him. Thornhill shuddered and collapsed into a sitting position next to the boy. The heat was going to melt the skin right off his bones. And to think, he could be in a cool photographer's studio back in Washington, taking portraits of society matrons. Ha.

After a few shallow breaths, Joseph reached into his dead companion's pocket, pulled out a wallet and found identification of a sort. It was a scrawled note on a torn piece of paper that bore his name and address.

"Well, Private Stanley Brewster of Bangor, Maine, you're a long way from home. Sorry about this nasty turn of events." Joseph swallowed hard. "I'll make sure your family gets this back." He tucked the wallet into his own pocket. "God Almighty, Stanley, I'm about to make you immortal."

Joseph pushed himself to his feet and prepared for the loathsome part of his job. Rearranging the body and setting up the scene. *Maximum visual impact*, Pinkerton had explained, to elicit sympathy for the war.

Joseph gazed toward the horizon at the scores of bodies, blue and gray, littering the field. The thought of moving the soldier gave him the willies though he'd done it dozens of times. Sometimes, he recalled, in the early days of the war, the touch of cold skin stretched over broken bones would send him into shivers so violent, he feared others would think him ill or, worse, faint of heart. Today he no longer cared what others thought.

Movement across the meadow caught his eye. Straggling soldiers making their way to the encampment. Joseph took off in that direction to retrieve his camera and tripod, bypassing countless horse carcasses, which lay strewn across the landscape in bizarre, almost symmetrical patterns.

One horse lifted its head now and whinnied. Joseph bent over the heaving beast, torn and ravaged with sword slashes and bullet holes.

"Sorry, Boy." He picked up a musket from a dead soldier and riffled through his pockets for ammunition, a packet containing a lead ball, gunpowder and packing. He tore the packet open with his teeth, filled the barrel with the gunpowder, dropped in the ball and tamped it down with the rammer. He pulled back the hammer and inserted a percussion cap in the breach to ignite the powder. Damn, he wasn't experienced at being a soldier. He could load his camera much faster. Finally, tight-jawed, Joseph ended the Chestnut's misery. A new rent bruised his heart. Humans weren't the only casualty of war.

Joseph picked up his camera equipment and trekked back to the dead soldier. God, Brewster couldn't be more than sixteen. Just a boy. He grabbed him by his arms and angled the body up against the boulder. He placed other rocks, leaves and grass tufts around him. He took the boy's musket and laid it across the torso. He positioned Brewster's finger on the trigger.

The face. Eyes opened or closed?

He left them open, mostly because he couldn't bear to touch them. Still, he'd close them after he shot the photograph or the black flies would have a hearty feast.

The sweltering sun plus days of rotten corpses bleeding into the ground had effused the air with a suffocating miasma. Thornhill's stomach tilted and he swore at the futility of war.

Satisfied with the dead man's position, he went to retrieve his latest Lewis Daguerrotype. He positioned the box on a sturdy tripod and inserted a glass plate. Next, he leaned over the viewfinder, tossed the protective cloth over his head and observed the image. He prayed Brewster's family never saw this image of him.

He blinked in surprise. Out of nowhere, perhaps a dozen yards away, a man stepped into the background of the camera frame. He was dressed in a long tan duster and was most certainly a civilian.

How could he wear that coat in this heat?

The juxtaposition between the two subjects made for a compelling shot, so Joseph decided to take it. Pulling off the camera lens cap, Thornhill counted the seconds and exposed the image to a wet-plate negative.

The civilian turned suddenly and stared at Joseph. Joseph wiped his hands along the side of his baggy trousers and waved at the man.

"Good day," the civilian said, approaching.

"I wouldn't exactly call it good now," Joseph said, indicating the battlefield strewn with dead soldiers.

"Yes, I see what you mean." The man regarded the carnage, turned back to Joseph and studied him through narrowed eyes.

"Can I help you with something?" Joseph asked.

"I've come to deliver a message to Major Sills but fear I'm too late. He appears to be dead."

Joseph puzzled at the casual manner of the remark and studied the stranger's face. Long and dust-covered fair hair was tied back with rawhide. His fathomless dark eyes shot a chill up Thornhill's spine. In contrast, his countenance was almost feminine in its beauty, much like the man's voice.

Joseph followed the stranger's gaze to the dead major on the ground. "How do you know this is Major Sills?"

Without a reply, the civilian did an about-face and without a by-your-leave, retreated, navigating bodies and debris in his path.

"Hey, where're you going?" Joseph said. "Who are you?"

The stranger ducked behind a thicket of oleanders and vanished in a blink.

Joseph moved to the dead officer and peered down at the corpse. Wondering about the man's ID, he stooped and reached into his pockets. No identification. No dog tags. Perhaps the civilian took them?

The dark blue uniform with burnished gold buttons confirmed his rank of major in the Union army. A sword-belt remained cinched around the major's waist, and the sword, unsheathed from its scabbard, lay nearby, spotless. The body appeared to have no superficial wounds, no bullet holes, cuts or bruises. No fractured limbs. If, indeed, this major had engaged in battle, he exhibited no evidence of such. His uniform remained intact, relatively new and clean.

Joseph reexamined the body. Soft, pliable with still a touch of warmth. He had died within the last few hours and rigor had not yet set in.

Impossible. The battle took place yesterday.

He noticed an insignia stamped out in relief on the uniform collar:

a diamond shape enclosing a simple cloverleaf. It was the insignia of an investigative task force assigned by the President of the United States. This man was one of the investigative agents under Colonel Baxter and it was possible that he was not killed in battle.

Joseph switched his hat from photographer to Secret Service spy and figured what Pinkerton would have him do. Record the event, in detail, photograph it and courier it back to Washington. He lifted the flap of his satchel that he wore slung across his shoulders. Pinkerton had given it to him for his personal belongings, writing paper, writing utensils and other necessary items. It was stamped U.S. Government on one side and boasted his initials on the flap: J.A.T.

He raised his head at the sounds of a gravedigger detail in the distance beginning their grim task--mostly colored men exchanging one slave labor for another. He'd better photograph the dead officer quickly before they arrived.

An opalescent fog rose from the earth as the heat of the day dissipated. The sun was sinking behind the Dunker Church and myriad colors danced on the shadowy meadow. In a few moments the light would fade. As he hurried to focus his camera, Joseph observed something else irregular about the major's body.

He brooded on the civilian who, on a battlefield littered with hundreds of bodies, had somehow located Major Sills. Joseph rose from his knees and turned back to his camera. The image of the civilian stranger was not merely a picture in his own mind. It was a picture embedded on a photographic plate forever.

September 18, 1862
Journal Entry

A day of unbearable temperatures, I rest for a few moments under a large elm and like my comrades, pray for a breeze to dry my sweat.

Is it not enough to face your enemy and hope to escape with your life and your limbs? Must you also face the heat of nature's whims? I ponder such things on occasions as this, as I gaze across the landscape at the bloating bodies, swatting the flies big as dogs.

Despite the fact that Southern forces were outnumbered by General McClellan's Army of the Potomac, General Lee still positioned his troops for attack. The man is fearless. The Northern assault was unorganized, perhaps Lee expected this, and this allowed the Confederates to rally. Both sides suffered heavy losses, but in terms of strategy, Lee's troops held their ground.

In this brutal of all days, more men have been killed than I wish to give voice to. I've heard told that it numbers in the thousands. A colonel confided in me that over 2,000 were killed and close to 10,000 wounded on the Union side. Numbers, no doubt similar if not worse, for Confederates. Over 23,000 casualties in all.

And on this bloodiest day of the War, I had the opportunity to enlist my skills in the service of our government.

Joseph described the strange circumstances surrounding the civilian and the dead Major Sills.

On the morrow, I will send a dispatch, along with photographs, to Colonel Baxter, who in turn, will consult with Mister Pinkerton about the coincidence. For now, I am grateful that night falls, and the survivors of the day return.

Chapter 8

Fredericksburg, Virginia
December 12, 1862

Journal Entry

Word has it that Lee has his two fierce generals, Longstreet and Jackson, fortifying the hills across the river from Fredericksburg. As the Federal pontoniers begin their work down by the muddy shores, sniper bullets and Minié balls fly, halting the pontoon laying time and again. Finally, Federal soldiers ran a gauntlet of Confederate sharpshooters and set up a bridgehead in Fredericksburg. Now the pontoon bridge can be completed and Alex and I may be able to complete reconnaissance of the area. Colonel Baxter has been awaiting news but this is the first opportunity for covert operations. Alex received a letter from Allan Pinkerton, thanking us for our reports and photographs. I fear we have been of only small use to the detective to date, but anticipate the situation will change presently. . .

"Get yourselves ready now, men," a Union officer shouted and rushed by. "There's action across the River."

Joseph grabbed his satchel lying beside his camp stool and stuffed the journal and pen inside. He leaped up and seized the arm of a passing soldier. "What's going on?"

"Some nasty skirmishes since our men made it 'cross the river. Them Rebs won't quit. But leastways we'll see some combat, finally. We're all sick a waitin'."

Joseph shouted to Alex. “It’s starting, Alex, come here.” Alex rushed up to him and the two scurried to the edge of the river where weeks ago pontoon bridge construction had begun. They watched the pontoniers manhandle the last few boats into the water near the opposite shore, lined up parallel to each other and then lay down planking to complete the walkway.

Across the wide span of water, Joseph gazed at Fredericksburg and the enemy fortifications. An unusually cold winter for Virginia, despite the bright sunshine, he tucked his hands under his armpits for warmth. He made out puffs of white and gray smoke bursting over the opposite shoreline like iridescent bubbles, and heard the bridge builders hollering as they ducked sniper fire the closer they got to enemy lines.

Joseph turned back to the Union side at the sound of pounding hoofs beating a path close by; dust and dirt kicked up by the animals clouded his vision. He pulled Alex, slower to move, out of harm’s way.

"Holy Mother of God." Alex's breath vaporized in the frigid air. "I can’t believe it's finally begun. Maybe we'd best see to mixing our chemicals. Once that bridge is complete, we'll have our work cut out."

"Good idea." Joseph took off for the darkroom wagon. Alex hurried clumsily after him.

"Here, help me with these." Joseph stood in the wagon and handed down photographic equipment.

"An' what are you doing, might I ask? I thought we were going to mix chemicals. We don’t need our equipment yet."

"Of course we need our equipment. How else are we going to take pictures?"

"There's nothing here to take pictures of. The fighting's on the other side of the river."

"Exactly."

"What? Ye're joking." Alex's laugh caught in his throat.

Joseph stopped unloading his gear, pulled his collar up around him for warmth and stepped down off the wagon. He looked up at Alex, several inches taller and many wider than him. "This is the chance we've been waiting for. The enemy is right there." Joseph pointed across the river.

Alex simply stared at him. "Joseph. We are photographers."

"Alex, we are spies."

"This is not what Pinkerton had in mind. He didn't expect us to march across directly into enemy camps and set up shop, lad."

"I have my own expectations. Come on, help me with this and then I'll help you." Joseph hoisted a pack on his back.

Alex screwed his eyes up. "Ho, wait now. You think I'm going? You're daft. Across the river? To get myself killed or worse?"

"Worse?"

"Aye, losin' an arm would be worse."

"Spoken like a true artist. Alex, where's your sense of adventure?"

"I left it in Washington—-but not with me common sense. Tell me how in the hell we'll keep from being picked off by Rebel sharpshooters?" Alex said. "Do you expect to just stroll casually across the pontoon bridge and set up your cameras? Just bow to the Rebs nice and sweet-like and say, here we are, come to take your pictures?"

"The captain said our men ran a gauntlet and established a bridgehead in town. So we should be able to cross in relative safety." Joseph raised his eyebrows at Alex. "Are you coming with me?"

Alex stood there, arms at his side. "I can't let you go by yourself, now can I?"

"I won't be by myself. The whole of the Union army is on that side."

"So's the whole of Lee's army."

Joseph helped him with the equipment.

"Jaysus, and what if we do make it across? They'll know in an instant we're with the Union Army. Do you expect to fool them into thinking we're Southerners?"

Joseph laughed. "With your Scottish burr, Alex, I dinna think so. Look, we're civilian photographers. They'll want their pictures taken."

"Very funny. Och, what's the use in arguing? You've made up your mind."

Thornhill stopped what he was doing and looked at his friend. "I can go myself, Alex. It's important to take photographs there, maybe catch some spies in action for Pinkerton. I'm not afraid."

Was that true?

Alex stared at Joseph for a moment, then sighed and returned to his packing. "Oh, for the love of me dear, departed Mother. I'll go with you. After all, Pinkerton is my friend and he got us into this bloody mess. Spies. What was I thinking?"

Joseph hopped back up into the *whatizzit* wagon and quickly unloaded the rest of their equipment. Then he and Alex began piling the gear on their backs, securing it with sturdy leather straps. They gathered up the remainder under their arms. Joseph slung his satchel over his shoulders. Satisfied he had all he needed, he trekked down to the shores of the Rappahannock, carrying the cumbersome tools of the trade. Alex followed close behind as if using him for a shield.

Contemplating his destiny, Joseph stood on the water's edge gazing out across the river where icy patches floated like tiny barges. Something great was about to happen to him. He felt it in his bones.

This could make me immortal. Or just plain dead.

He looked back at his friend and partner then thought of Sara and wondered if he wasn't doing a foolish thing. Her last letter was filled with endearments and right now all he wanted to do was take her in his arms and hold her close, kiss her lips, feel her love. He shook away the thoughts and stepped out onto the pontoon bridge.

It was cold on the river and a strong wind whipped at him from the east, stinging his eyes to tears. He shivered despite the heavy winter coat and woolen trousers.

"If only these damnable gloves and socks weren't so thin," Alex said.

Joseph turned to his friend, tramping slowly behind him and again began to have second thoughts.

He kept to the right of the bridge. It was narrow, about eleven feet wide, and wobbly: a series of wooden boards anchored on pontoon boats, spanning over four hundred feet of Rappahannock. Soldiers hurried across, bumping into him.

"Move out of the way," one shouted.

Joseph held onto Alex's arm as they lurched and tilted. He felt slightly seasick on the swaying planks and it took all his energy to avoid falling into the river, particularly when the soldiers walked some skittish horses across and the clip-clopping reverberated through the bridge.

"Christ almighty, it's damned slippery." Joseph heard Alex mutter under his breath.

An ear-piercing crack of gunfire suddenly reached him as he approached the halfway point. As if he passed some sort of sound barrier, the noise level increased tenfold.

“Holy Mother of God,” Alex said for the tenth time.

Massive billows of white and gray smoke rose above the landscape and obscured everything around. A Minié ball landed a few feet in front of him. He hopped sideways and dropped to his knees, the heavy load on his back tugging at his strength.

Damn, that was close.

He glanced again at Gardner, face gray and covered with perspiration despite the cold temperature.

Joseph rose heavily to his feet and trudged on. He estimated another three hundred steps would get them across. If they weren’t thrown into the river first. Soldiers ran past him continuously in a blur of movement. Gunfire and artillery exploded, men shouted and screamed, horses thundered by. Joseph yelled at Alex to be heard above the din, but without success. Instead he pointed to a cluster of trees near the riverbank, where they removed the weight from their backs and set the equipment down.

Joseph's breath came in fits and gasps. He set his satchel down and helped Alex unload his pack. He noticed with relief that his friend’s color had returned. In a few minutes, Joseph trembled with chill, perspiration dry and cold on his body. He rubbed his arms and did a jig to stay warm.

Alex looked at him frowning, "Are you all right, my friend?"

"Yes, fine. Just a little chilly."

"Well, you don’t have as much body fat to warm you. What does the situation look like, do you think?"

Joseph sprinted up the bank of the hill and stopped some soldiers. He spent a few minutes discussing the situation then reported back.

"It appears our men have moved the enemy lines back up the hill a bit--maybe all the way to Marye's Heights, with any luck. I'm going to have a look-see before we drag the cameras any further. I'll keep close to the soldiers. Wait here for now, take a nap or something." Joseph's good humor was returning.

Alex rolled his eyes. "How nice, a nap."

"Watch my satchel, Alex. I'm counting on you."

"And I'm counting on you not to get yourself killed. Stick with the Union men. Don't stray too--"

"Yes, yes." Joseph thumbed his nose at him and headed off toward the town, following close to the blue uniforms for a while. He breathed heavily as he tromped up a steep hill. When he neared the top, he recognized the sharp pops of gunfire. The two Union soldiers ahead of him collapsed to the ground.

"Shit," Joseph cried. He darted off to the right, hoping to circle around and head back down. He'd advanced only a few yards when he heard the crunching of feet on dead leaves and twigs snapping nearby. He stopped suddenly. Tightness gripped his stomach. Three ragtag Confederates moved out from the trees. They quickly surrounded him, muskets pointed, faces grim. The soldiers wore only remnants of their uniforms, some butternut jackets, some gray trousers, the rest homemade apparel. Filthy, covered with dust and grime, the whites of their eyes shone in their sooty faces. Each wore a kepi, however, the traditional soldier's hat, battered and crushed with mud, but still sporting CSA insignia.

God almighty. Joseph abruptly raised his arms in the air. "W--w--wait gentlemen, don't shoot. I'm not a soldier. I'm unarmed."

"I see, yessuh. So what are you doin' here? Gonna have yourself a picnic?"

The other two snickered.

"Uh, no, a picnic? Of course not. I'm a photographer. If you'll allow me to show you my credentials." He looked at the leader and pointed cautiously to his pocket.

"G'wan, get it out, easy like."

Joseph gently pulled out his army pass and waved it in front of him, wondering if any of them could read. His heart was about to jump from his chest.

"So, if this here's a real pass and you be a real pitcher taker, where's your camera 'n all?" The leader grinned.

"Oh, it's here, Sirs, just down by the river. If you'll just follow me, I can show you." Joseph turned back toward the river.

"Whoa there, pal. Just you hold on now. Ya'all ain't goin' nowhere."

"I was just going to show you my camera equipment." Joseph slowly lowered his arms, half-expecting to get shot in the back.

The three Confederates looked at each other. One grinned a yellowed-tooth smile. "I think we should hang 'em."

"I say just shoot 'em."

"Don't wanna waste bullets. Besides, hangin's more fun. We can watch his tongue stick out, all puffy like and--."

"Yeah, but the smell, pee-ew, when he shits his pants."

Joseph gawked from one man to the other, trying to swallow but finding his mouth dry as the dust on the ground. God, would they really hang him?

The third man spoke up. "I don't like it, Andy, no, I don't like it at all. Cain't just go round killin' civilians. I'm thinkin' maybe we should turn this here guy over to the General."

The men fell silent while the leader stood thinking. "Maybe we should get our pitchers taken first."

"Nah, I think it's too risky. What if someone catches us, and here we are, posin' for some silly pitchers?"

"I think Gordy's right. Let's turn 'em in. Prisoner. It'll look mighty good for us 'n all."

Joseph addressed the leader, "Gentlemen, if I may speak? What good would it do to turn me in? I'm a civilian. They'll just let me go with a warning. Then you'll have no pictures. All I wanted to do was take pictures of the battle."

The leader interrupted. "What if he's a spy for the Union?"

Joseph felt his blood turn icy and goose bumps prickle his skin.

"Yeah, if he is, it could be good for us to turn 'em in. Then we can hang him legal-like.

Chapter 9

Fredericksburg, Virginia
December 12, 1862

Ten minutes later, Joseph found himself in a small clapboard house. The inside smelled dank from the wet winter. A sergeant stood inside near the door watching him through narrowed eyes. Joseph wiped the sweat off his upper lip, careful not to make any sudden moves.

Destined for greatness, am I? More likely for the hangman's rope.

He rocked on his feet and shivered.

From where he stood, Confederate Headquarters appeared to consist of two small rooms. The room he was in had a large square hole in a wall where a window used to be. Furnishings were made up of a simple wooden table and two rickety chairs. On the table sat a half-eaten plate of something covered with congealed brown gravy, several utensils and a pewter mug.

God, I would love a drink right now.

Joseph licked his lips and peered out of the large hole in the wall where he saw a familiar face. His mouth dropped open and he almost raced to the door. A young man with fair hair and an aristocratic nose and chin gazed back at him, a faint smile on his lips. The civilian stranger from Antietam. Here, in the enemy camp?

"Stand where you are, Mister," ordered the sergeant, jabbing Joseph with his bayonet. Joseph groaned and turned back to the hole. The civilian was gone, leaving only trees and an occasional soldier passing by.

It was him. Same coat, same black eyes.

His thoughts were cut off when the door opened and a large bearded man in gray uniform entered. Although the uniform was dust-covered, Joseph recognized it as that of a Southern General's. Joseph's breakfast began to rise into his gullet as his gaze moved from the swirl of gold braids rising from dirty white cuffs up to the heavy bullion-braided shoulder epaulettes. The General moved behind the table and gazed with deep blue eyes into Thornhill's soul.

Swallowing to ease his constricted throat, Joseph recognized one of Robert E. Lee's most famous commanders, General James Longstreet.

I'm a dead man.

He blinked rapidly as Longstreet looked down at his photographer's license. Lee's "Old Workhorse" walked slowly toward him, smoothing his long beard. Unconsciously, Joseph stepped back.

"I believe I've heard your name, Sir," Longstreet addressed him politely. "You're with Mathew Brady's Gallery, is that correct?"

"Yes, Sir, that's correct." Joseph squeezed his hands into fists to keep them from trembling.

"I don't believe I've seen your work, only Brady's and someone, some other photographer, what's his name?" Longstreet furrowed his brow. "Garner, something like that?"

"Gardner, Sir, Alexander Gardner. He's my partner."

"Yes, Gardner." Longstreet turned away momentarily then abruptly fixed his stare on Joseph. "May I ask what you're doing on this side of the river? Surely you're not lost?" A shadow of a smile crossed Longstreet's features.

"No Sir. I'm not lost. You see, General, I've been experimenting with new methods to take pictures of action and I, well, I wanted to try them out." Joseph didn't believe for a moment that Longstreet would accept that ridiculous explanation.

"Ah, I see. You wanted to be where the action is taking place, is that it?"

"Yes. Sir." Joseph looked down at his boots, not sure whether the Southern General joked or not.

"Well, Mister Thornhill, what shall I do with you?"

Joseph fixed his eyes on Longstreet, at a loss for words.

Longstreet circled him. "Shall I hang you for a spy?"

Joseph squeezed his eyes closed then opened them to find Longstreet staring at him. "Spy? No, Sir. I, I'm not a spy, just a simple photographer."

"Hmmph. Well you may be a photographer, but I doubt you're simple." Longstreet sighed. "Perhaps I should imprison you for breaching the Confederate lines?"

Joseph clenched his jaw. His teeth would ache that night. Thoughts crept into his mind of the dreadful stories he'd heard about Libby Prison in Richmond. Tales that described prisoners weighing less than a hundred pounds, shivering half-frozen, half-starved, drinking foul water and dying of all manner of illness. Joseph looked up at the bulk of a man before him and held his breath. What did he know about Longstreet, the man? Intelligent, well-trained, career soldier. One of Lee's favorites. But was he a compassionate man or--?

Longstreet nodded to his sergeant.

"Sergeant, I think Mister Thornhill needs to think about his foolhardy actions. Lock him in the confinement shed."

Joseph blinked, stepped backwards and nearly tripped over his feet. "Sir, must you, I mean, do you--?"

"That's all." Longstreet nodded to his aide, who called commands out the window.

Within seconds, two privates rushed in. Two out of the three that captured him near the river.

Oh my God. I'm going to hang.

"Take him to solitary," the Sergeant ordered.

"Why, yessir, we'd be most happy to oblige."

Joseph turned a last time to Longstreet, who gave him a thoughtful gaze.

Was that a smile he saw on Longstreet's face? A tiny, barely imperceptible smile? And what did it mean? Was this the General's joke? Or was there something bad in store for him? Joseph felt like he was gut-punched. Still, he'd be damned if he would show weakness.

As he was pushed and prodded to a new location, Joseph took the opportunity to study his surroundings. He could see dozens of tents dotting the gray winterscape, almost the same color as the dirty snow. He could hear the fires crackling as men prepared to cook the midday meal, but the smell of food was absent. The fires were to keep them warm.

They don't have food, he realized. The Confederates are in dire straits. That gave him a modicum of satisfaction. Until he arrived at his destination. A broken-down, gritty looking hut, more like an outhouse and barely large enough for one man to sit on the dirt floor.

"In thar, now, git," the man named Gordy said, and poked him with his bayonet.

Joseph cried out and moved into the shed. Before he could turn, he heard a chain being drawn between two hasps and a lock clanking into place. He rushed to the door, peered between the opening of two boards, earning himself splinters on his cheek.

Sara, my love, keep faith. I'll come home to you.

*

Cold, shivering, hungry and despairing, Joseph spent all day and night in that pathetic shack. He guessed this was an outhouse at one time because the reek of body wastes kept his stomach roiling. When the first rays of light streaked through the open slats, he had only just fallen asleep. A bugle squawked out a few jarring notes as the camp awakened for the day. He struggled to rise, but was so stiff from the uncomfortable squatting position all night.

Poor Alex. What must he be thinking? That I'm dead, no doubt. Jeez, God, he may be right. Joseph staggered backward. The day had barely dawned into a dismal gray with the threat of snow. In the pale light, General James Longstreet stood, hands clasped behind his back, staring at him.

"Come out here, Mister Thornhill."

Joseph moved forward, knees aching like his heart.

"I certainly hope you enjoyed our hospitality. I truly wish I could offer you a hearty, hot Southern breakfast, but, unfortunately, that's not to be."

Joseph held his breath.

Longstreet made a barely discernible gesture with his right hand and the sergeant sprang to his side.

"Provide this gentleman with safe conduct to the Heights. He can make his own way from there."

Joseph hiccupped out the breath.

Thank you, dear Lord.

He started to follow the sergeant then turned back slowly, warily, to meet the General's gaze. "Excuse me, Sir, General?" his voice hoarse and unsteady.

Longstreet frowned at him, hands behind his back.

"Alexander Gardner. He's here with me, Sir, waiting down by the river. I, um, I just don't want him shot by mistake."

Longstreet nodded to his sergeant again. "Safe conduct for Gardner too." The General sat down and studied Joseph. "You have courage, Sir, that I must admit." He turned away. "Action pictures, indeed."

Joseph took a deep breath and smiled tightly. "If the General would like, I can take your picture before I leave."

Longstreet fixed an unnerving gaze on Joseph. "Thank you for the offer, but unlike you, I am much too busy for such luxuries. You'd best be gone."

Chapter 10

Fredericksburg, Virginia
December 13, 1862

The next morning, Joseph hunkered down on a gnarled tree stump next to Alex before the breakfast campfire. Pulling his woolen jacket high around his neck, he quivered with cold and though he moved his feet dangerously close to the flames, he couldn't warm himself.

He looked up from the blaze as his friend patted him on the knee.

"That was indeed a brave thing you did. I went nearly out of my mind with worry when ye didn't come back last night. Thought for sure you got captured, or. . . or worse."

"Well, I did get captured. . . but no worse." Joseph took a deep breath. "You know, Alex, even though it was a foolish thing to do, I mean, I could've gotten killed, gotten us *both* killed or sent to prison, even with that, I'm not sorry I did it. Can you understand?"

Alex looked at him with a rueful smile.

"You think I'm crazy, don't you?" Joseph turned back to the fire.

"Nay. Jest a wee bit ambitious." Alex stirred some molasses into his mug of black, bitter coffee. He lowered his voice. "Did you learn anything useful to report back to Pinkerton? Anything about the camp, or the number of soldiers, did you see the quartermaster's stock?"

"I'll jot notes and courier them off this morning," Joseph said. "I didn't get to see much of the camp. I will say that the Rebs are in trouble, though. Hardly any food and their clothing and boots are pathetically thin and worn. They can't last long."

"Troops?"

"Counted maybe forty tents nearby. Didn't have much time before--."

"Before what?" Alex said.

"I did see something." Joseph crossed his legs and sat up straight. "That civilian. Remember the one I saw at Antietam? Said he was looking for Major Sills, but Sills was dead."

"Sills. One of the investigators, right. Aye, I recall."

"The civilian was on the other side of the river." Joseph turned to look at Alex. "How can that be?"

"Maybe he's a spy too?"

"And Sills had no obvious battle wounds," Joseph said more to himself. He hopped to his knees and started scrambling through his satchel. He pulled out a sheath of papers, the worse for wear.

"What now?" Alex said, with a slight smile.

"I thought I remembered," Joseph said. "A report from Colonel Baxter. Yes, here it is." Joseph read to himself.

"Well, are you going to tell me?"

"Baxter had a report of another agent, a Major Benjamin Bradley. Also died of unknown causes. Back in August, Manassas." Joseph fell silent.

"What are ye thinking, then? Someone is murdering the government investigators?"

"I think that's pretty obvious. The question is--"

"Is it that civilian?" Alex finished for him.

Joseph nodded.

"Well, there's not much proof, is there? One photo at Antietam and your witness to his appearance in the enemy camp. We have no way of knowing he was around when Major Bradley died."

Joseph didn't speak. But his stomach ached in that peculiar way it did whenever he felt a strange foreboding.

"Sorry," he said, realizing Alex was staring at him. "Not much of a spy, am I?"

Alex ignored him. "Nonsense. You're a good man, Joseph. It takes a special kind to brave the enemy camp." He sighed. "Too bad Longstreet would'na allow a photograph. Now that would have been something. A picture of General James Longstreet."

Joseph tipped his head in a nod. If he had had a chance to take a picture, it would have been of the civilian, not Longstreet.

"The General is an interesting man, I hear tell," Alex went on. "I read somewhere he said, 'Why do men fight who were born to be brothers?'"

Joseph smiled inwardly. That *was* a smile he saw on Longstreet's face. The General never meant to kill him, after all, just scare the bejeezus out of him.

He stretched his aching limbs and listened to the sounds of dawn--men softly moaning, awakening in their tents, battle-weary, bruised, and injured after yesterday's defeat, a few early risers crooning *Aura Lee* to the strums of a three-stringed guitar. The rustling of withered leaves blowing in the chilly wind reminded him of home and the maple tree in front of Sara's house on Dumbarton Street in Georgetown. God, how he missed Sara. Her lopsided smile, her sweet laugh, the way she flicked his hair back off his brow.

He heard in the distance the baleful howl of a wild dog foraging for food this long, desolate winter. Like us, Joseph reflected. Trying to survive.

He stared quietly at the wispy tentacles of smoke drifting up from the fire. After a time he said, "You know, Alex? Men get to know each other pretty well in this sort of experience, being confined so closely together. Living together, working together, *freezing* together for more than a year. Some form bonds that will last a lifetime. But, even though I've come to know some of these soldiers pretty well, I still feel like an outsider." He gazed at Gardner in the firelight. "Maybe it's not the working or the living together, or the freezing. Maybe it's the fighting and the dying. I don't stand with them and fight side by side. They don't depend on me to save their lives. I'm not there when they get hit and need someone to lean on." Joseph turned back to the fire. "They respect me, perhaps, but that same bond isn't there."

"Aye, I ken what you mean. Even yesterday when we crossed that bridge and the men rushed by us, like we were in the way, or worse, like we were not even there." Alex frowned. "But, Joseph, maybe it's just as well that this is the way things are . . . for the very day after battle we might just be photographing their remains."

Joseph sat silent for a time, sipping bitter chicory when, through the flicker of the flames, he caught sight of a pale-colored duster. That civilian again, this time walking freely in the Union camp.

Joseph jumped up. "Alex, there, that man. That's the civilian, there--standing by the quartermaster's station. Same coat, same hair, I swear it. It's the same man."

Alex didn't have a chance to answer before Joseph threw down his tin mug and took off in pursuit. He went crashing over rocks and horse tack, tripping a few times but not slowing down. As he reached the door of the quartermaster's hut, the man was no longer there. For a moment he walked back and forth in front of the cabin, searching the area. Staring off into the encampment, Joseph watched the few remaining fires, most dying now, as the men readied for the day.

Just at that moment the Quartermaster Sergeant opened the door of the supply cabin.

Joseph turned to him. "Sergeant, where did that man go?"

"Who, Mister Thornhill, what man?" The sergeant tied a moth-eaten scarf around his neck with stiff, gloved fingers. He stepped outside into the cold air, and his breath rose in white billows before him.

"That man, a civilian, just here just a moment ago."

"Sorry, Sir, I didn't see him." The sergeant wrinkled his brow. "You sure you're not conjurin' up some photograph. . . in your mind, like?"

Thornhill smiled faintly then walked away. Conjuring, hmmph. He returned to the fire, kept watch until late, hoping to catch a glimpse of the stranger. Finally, cold and tired, he put out the remains of the fire, took off his jacket and shirt, rolling them up together. Then he pulled off his boots and quickly slid shivering into the cocoon of his bedroll. Even though it would be warmer in the tent, Joseph wanted to sleep outdoors tonight. The sky was clear and without the moon, he could reflect on the beauty of the pinprick light of the stars and the patterns they formed. Patterns that had led great men to their destiny. He lay there awhile, trembling, thinking of the stranger, and feeling vaguely disappointed and uneasy.

Chapter 11

Fredericksburg, Virginia
December 14, 1862

Journal Entry

Sad defeat for the Union army this day. Burnside's attempts to dislodge the Rebels from their positions at Fredericksburg were met with failure. After heavy fighting the Federals were unsuccessful in breaking through Stonewall Jackson's line. Later they attempted an assault at Marye's Heights, but the Rebels had a formidable defense mounted, and we were repulsed. Still Burnside ordered another attack and still we failed. . .

Joseph did not even attempt sleep that night. It was two days since his imprisonment in the Rebel camp and his nerves were still tense. Instead of sleep, he spent the time in the darkroom wagon. In the dim yellow lamp light, he varnished the processed plates to protect their thin, fragile emulsions from damage. And, as he began to write the captions for the photographs of that day's carnage, the images returned in full force--graven images of frozen corpses used as shields and shelter by the living, heroic images of the wounded and maimed. When the counts had come in, he'd shuddered. Seven thousand men, all bitter casualties of Burnside's ineffectual leadership.

His body felt numb from cold and despair. Many men he had shared supper with these last few months were dead. As he developed the post-battle images, he looked upon these men again. This time they were not smiling bravely, but lying mangled and lifeless, crumpled in ditches or twisted grotesquely on the field.

One in particular caught his eye.

Joseph gazed at the young boy in the photograph, bucktoothed, cowlick atop his head, grimacing in his death pose.

Probably wasn't even seventeen. Will it never end?

Joseph stood up, stretched his limbs, and blew on his fingers for warmth. The camp was eerily silent; even the horses were asleep.

He shook his hands and tucked them under his armpits for a minute. The cold was making the emulsion sluggish. The process of developing the pictures took forever in winter. He wished to hell someone would invent thin gloves that would allow his fingers range of movement and still keep them warm.

Joseph sagged, bone tired, but it was already dawn. Pouring water that he wished had been heated into a basin, he half-heartedly washed his face and hands.

Ahh, what I wouldn't give for a long, hot soak in a tub.

Then he opened a little wooden chest and pulled out a sliver of broken mirror that he had saved. Sitting on a trunk, he studied his face in the scratched silver and grimaced. He was glad Sara couldn't see him now, or worse, smell him.

She would run as fast as she could.

Joseph lightly fingered the hairs that had turned gray in the last year and wondered how many more there would be before the war ended.

Sara. He pulled out a rumpled envelope and unfolded her last letter, reading it for the fourth time.

My Dearest Joseph,

I hope this letter finds you safe and well. We are all fine here in Washington, although some goods and services are getting harder to come by. Fresh vegetables, beef, and flour are scarce. But here I am talking about minor problems when your situations are so much greater. I have heard so much talk of illness in the ranks, that I pray you have not contracted any unseemly fever. Father says that for every soldier who dies in battle, three to five die of disease . . .

Joseph smiled, remembering Mister Kelly's apothecary advice on keeping healthy. No ardent spirits, no bathing in cold water, no sleeping on hard ground. He read Sara's final remarks:

I long for the day when you shall be forever by my side. Write soon and take extra care of yourself.

Love always, Sara.

He slid the letter back into his pocket, got up stiffly and rubbed the back of his neck. Hmph. No sleeping on hard ground. Donning his heavy woolen jacket, brittle with fetid-smelling mud, he left the darkroom wagon to join the men for breakfast. The remainder of the army began to awaken now. As Joseph moved toward the center of activity, he frowned at the dead bodies that had been dragged back from enemy territory. Awaiting burial they looked like so many bundles of rags.

He tried not to look but his eyes were reluctantly drawn to the loathsome sights. He recognized one soldier, the crooner, who just last night had entertained with his guitar. A mere boy. But then, it was called the "boys' war".

"Joseph, Joseph." Joseph looked up to see Alex waving frantically at him. He hurried over.

"Look at this," Alex said. "There's that insignia, look, see his collar?"

Joseph knelt down. Alex was right. A dead Federal soldier in major's uniform brandished that familiar insignia design on his collar. He examined the corpse more closely and found no identification.

"Jesus, Alex, this is just like Antietam, this is a staff officer on the front line, and he's dead with no obvious wounds."

Alex did his own examination. "How in hell did he die? Heart attack?"

Joseph stood, spun in a circle, on the lookout for that civilian he knew was somewhere nearby. His skin prickled with angst.

Troops rushed by, shouting orders, saddling horses. He grabbed an officer in mid-stride by the arm. "Lieutenant, do you know this man?"

The lieutenant looked down at the dead officer, shook his head and moved on. Joseph wasted no time.

"Where are you going?" Alex called out.

Joseph didn't take the time to answer. Pushing his way past the confusion of battle preparations, he fled back to the wagon for his camera equipment.

*

Jack Cade strode into a two-story building on the main street of Fredericksburg, peeling off his calf-skin gloves and slouch hat. The boarding house was a dilapidated structure, its boards lopsided, the paint sloughing off. He recalled in the past how it had once been a beautiful hotel, celebrated in all the South, boasting rich and famous guests. Now, a pathetic hovel. Cade felt a renewed loathing for the Union army.

Inside, the proprietor, a sleazy man with hair greased back and fingernails long enough to pluck one's eye out, handed him a key.

In his room, he tossed the key, gloves and hat on the unmade bed. He headed for the curtain-less window and looked out on the street. This had been a brutal winter for the South. Eight-foot piles of snow lined the street, which was a hazard of icy rivulets carving nasty gullies down the path. Wagons could barely get through and one remained stranded, a wheel broken from tilting into a ditch.

Now a unit of bedraggled Confederate soldiers marched through, tripping in their pathetically worn boots, looking bone-weary but not downtrodden. In fact, there were hints of grins on their faces. Fredericksburg was, astoundingly, considered a victory.

Cade smiled.

Good ole Pete. Cade wondered how James Longstreet got the nickname *ole Pete*. He shrugged.

No matter. Burnside can't hold a candle to the Southern General.

He reached into his pocket and drew out his latest prize. A dog tag with the name Philip Malone. Polished steel, still shiny. No soldier would wear such a tag. But as Cade well knew, Malone was not just a soldier.

He slid the tag from right hand to left hand and back again. Three down. One to go. Abruptly he threw the identification piece on the rickety chest of drawers. Above it hung the room's only mirror. He glanced up at it. The mirror suffered a jagged crack running through its length from upper left to lower right.

How fitting, he thought. After all, I *am* two men.

He lifted the blond wig off his head with relief and shook out his shorter, curly brown hair with a deep sigh. As he met his dark eyes in the mirror, he couldn't avoid thinking of the future and the big plans he had in store for himself. Thanks to Samuel Lindsey, he had the opportunity to save the Confederate States of America. To break the Union. Overthrow the tyrant, Lincoln. Cade could feel the power surge through his limbs.

He stared in the mirror, envisioning his face as an elegant woodcut, printed on the cover of every magazine, every tabloid in the country. His name would be on everyone's lips, he would be talked about in bars and saloons, salons and parlors. Women would covet him, would vie for the chance to touch him, to make love to him.

Oh yes. He would not only be the handsomest man, but the most sought after man. Indeed, the most famous man in America.

Chapter 12

Washington City
April 30, 1863

Joseph and Alex arrived in Washington City on a sunny morning at the end of April. They strolled along Pennsylvania Avenue, happy to be home if only for a few short weeks.

Alex moaned and ran his fingers through his matted beard. "Would ye tell me why, now, after months on the field, with little or nothing to eat 'ceptin' miserable hardtack, do we arrive home to find the whole city fasting?"

Joseph grinned at his friend. "You'd have to take that up with Mister Lincoln. He proclaimed a day of fasting and praying all over the Union."

"Bah," Alex said.

"Well, in lieu of food, what say we head over to the barbershop for a shave, cut and bath?"

"Cut did ye say? I'll not cut this glorious mane."

"A de-tangle, then," Joseph said. "And a de-lousing of this loathsome, grimy body before I see my dear Sara."

The two men continued down Pennsylvania, their worn boots clomping on the boardwalk as they passed the elegant Willard Hotel, the most prestigious boarding house in the city. They next came upon the National Theatre, where they stopped to peruse the posters outside.

"Ah, Julius Caesar," Alex said. "My favorite of Willie's."

"Willie?"

"William Shakespeare, man, aren't ye civilized? Have you been out in the wilderness too long?"

Joseph laughed. "I'm familiar with Shakespeare, just not referred to as Willie. In fact, Sara and I attended MacBeth a year ago. With the same acting company."

"Indeed," Alex said. "Famous thespians, the Booths."

"Let's go. The barber awaits to perform his surgery on me, if not you."

*

Joseph lifted the brass knocker on the Dumbarton Street Brownstone and felt his heart rapping in his chest. It had been nearly a year since he'd seen Sara, and although they'd written each other often, he feared she'd suddenly find him a poor match. The gray in his hair, the lines around his mouth, the eyes that had lost their fire, seen more than any human being had a right to see. He had changed. Would she notice? Would she still care about him? And how would he feel about her? Would she look the way he remembered? Would he still have the same sweet tingling when he saw her? Dear Lord, time. . . and war. . . could turn your life upside down.

He licked his lips and knocked.

The door opened and all his reservations melted away in one tick of a clock. There she was. Sara. He looked down from his six feet to her five foot four and the tension eased. She was still his Sara. She wore a flat gray muslin dress because fabrics were hard to find but he didn't care a whit about her wardrobe. Her green eyes sparkled with joy, her cheeks flushed with pleasure and her lips smiled that same crooked smile.

He was home.

*

The next day, just as Joseph had asked, Sara arrived at Gardner's Gallery by noon, but was not alone as he had expected. When he opened the door at the Gallery, he found himself facing his fiancé and, at her side, another young woman, pale and small in comparison. She had drab chestnut hair tied back in a bun and wore a dress of tawny wool that blended with her complexion and which did not display an inch of lace on the cuffs or collar. In fact, all of her seemed dull brown and he suspected she might be weak of constitution. Yet this woman was not weak of temperament. Like Sara, she had a sparkle in her eye and an impish smile on her lips. He ushered them into the hallway.

"Joseph, oh Joseph, every time I see you my heart gladdens." Sara reached out and their hands touched.

A tiny cough came from her friend.

"I'm so sorry. This is my dearest friend, Louisa May. I've told you all about her in my letters and--"

"Yes, of course," he said. "Miss Alcott, I am most pleased to meet you. Sara's written me about your tireless work at the hospital."

"It is wonderful to finally meet you, Joseph. May I call you that? Please call me Louisa."

He smiled, about to say more, but couldn't get a word in with both women chattering.

"Joseph, this is a lovely space." Sara looked around the entry room. "It's just as impressive as Brady's Gallery and yet it's Alex's. How wonderful."

"Alex?" Louisa said. "That would be Alexander Gardner?"

"Yes," Joseph said. "He left Brady to start his own Gallery. And I went with him."

"But you are still out in the field?" Louisa said.

"Yes. Other photographers mind the Gallery while we're gone. It gives us a new home base."

"Sara has told me oodles about you and your photography," Louisa said. "You are very brave, taking pictures of our men on the field."

"Most of the fighting is done before I go out there," he said.

"You must see the worst of it," Louisa said. "The dead, the maimed, the fields of. . . of blood. It must take a terrible toll on your emotions."

Sara reached out and touched Joseph's arm, as if she felt the emotional toll herself.

Louisa's words struck Joseph hard and he burned inwardly with reproach. If Sara knew about his covert work for the government, she might not be as supportive. He'd wrestled often with confiding in her, but Alex spoke the truth when he said, "*She will be nought but worried every minute you are gone. Do ye want that burden on her, then?*"

Joseph brought his thoughts around to present conversation. Both women were staring at him, waiting.

"Sorry, I was in my own little world." He smiled. "Thank you for the compliment, Louisa. Indeed, I have heard much about your work as well. Your writing, that is. Sara tells me your stories about the hospital are very moving."

"My hospital sketches?" Louisa said. "I hope to have them published someday."

Joseph said, "I'm sure you will. Perhaps you'll allow me to read them?"

With a mischievous grin, Sara pulled out a sheaf of papers.

"Sara," Louisa said. "No, you mustn't, they're not for--."

"Louisa, you must let me share them with Joseph."

"Are those your writings, then?" he asked.

"Please, Louisa, just a few words." Sara turned to Thornhill, whose brows were arched. "This part so aptly describes our house on Dumbarton Street, I thought you should hear it."

"If it's all right with Louisa," he said.

Louisa nodded, pink rising into her cheeks and transforming her pallor to a healthier looking glow.

Sara shuffled through several pages then began, "*One trip to Georgetown Heights, where cedars sighed overhead, dead leaves rustled underfoot, pleasant paths led up and down, and a brook wound like a silver snake by the blackened ruins of some French Minister's house. . .*"

"Ah, I know that Minister's house." Joseph smiled. "It does, indeed, sound like your house in Georgetown, Sara."

"*Our* house someday." Sara cleared her throat and brushed some invisible wisps of hair from her face. "Now I promised Louisa that you will show her your studio, even the darkroom."

"Yes," Louisa said, tucking the pages of her writings in a small purse. "I've seen your photographs. They are truly remarkable. I would love to see the process."

Joseph beamed. "Then let me lead the way."

He started up the stairs with Sara on his arm, Louisa right behind.

In the darkroom, Joseph demonstrated the process of developing a photograph from a plate negative. He took them through each step, developing one photo from beginning to end.

"Who is that?" Louisa asked of the man in the image.

"I wish I knew."

"I imagine you don't know the names of your subjects very often, do you?" Sara said.

"He doesn't look like a soldier," Louisa said.

"He's a civilian," Joseph said.

"Are there many civilians on the battlefield?" Louisa asked.

"Occasionally. They are couriers or sutlers, delivering goods, letters or supplies. Mostly you see soldiers."

Joseph gazed at the image for a full minute as the women conversed in the background. Then he rolled his sleeves down a second time that day and grabbed his coat. An idea was taking shape in his mind.

*

After Louisa returned to her quarters Joseph escorted Sara home. She held his hand as he opened the front door. Then he backed up.

"Aren't you coming in?" she said.

"It's late and your parents--"

"They're asleep and even a cannon explosion in the living room couldn't wake them." She smiled. "Please come in. I want to talk to you."

Joseph followed her into the parlor.

And I want to talk to you.

He sat on the velveteen divan, now threadbare and faded. Sara sat next to him, hands in her lap.

"Is something wrong?" Joseph said, his heart clamoring so hard in his chest he didn't know if he'd hear her answer.

"I think there is," Sara said. "I think you're acting strangely. With me." Her face suddenly flushed. "What is it, Joseph? Please, tell me."

A huge relief lifted off his shoulders. It wasn't a change of feelings on her part. Thank God.

"There is something, my dear, I'm rather contrite about. About not telling you sooner, that is."

Her green eyes bore into his.

"When I first signed up as a photographer for the Union, I was, Alex and I were, presented with an opportunity to do more."

"More?"

"More than just take pictures." Joseph rested back on the couch and drew a deep breath. "Alex's good friend from Scotland is Allan Pinkerton. You know who he is?"

"He's a detective, working for the government. Everyone knows of him."

Joseph nodded. "Pinkerton asked us to work for him in the field. . . as spies."

Sara opened her mouth, closed it and waited.

For the next twenty minutes, Joseph explained his role to Sara.

"I'm still mainly a photographer, Sara, but there are those times when I'm on the lookout for enemy activity."

God, he shouldn't have told her. Sweat broke out on his lip.

Sara searched his eyes, took one of his hands.

"My darling, I, I can't tell you how pleased I am that you've seen fit to tell me, confide in me. That means a lot."

"But are--?"

"I am very proud of you, Joseph. Very proud, indeed. I am not surprised, of course, that you are so brave. And I can better understand that, er, escapade at the Rappahannock with General Longstreet, getting captured by the Rebels, nearly getting yourself hung. Why, you could've been sent to Libby and I would have never seen--" She ran out of breath.

Joseph brought her hand to his lips. “You are a special woman, Sara Kelly. Very special to me.”

She ran her fingers over his hair and down the side of his face in an endearing gesture which sent a shiver of pleasure down his back.

“I love you, Joseph. Now and forever. You must promise to take special care of yourself. I do want you to come back to me.”

“I will take care and I will come back to you.”

Sara chewed her lower lip.

“What are you thinking?”

“I’m just wondering if there’s some way I can be of assistance. To you, I mean. Oh, I have my hospital work and that is important, of course. But if there’s anything I can do to help you, to help my country, then please--”

“You are an amazing woman and I thank you from the bottom of my heart. But there is nothing, my dear, that you can do.” He took her hand. “Simply to know that I can confide in you will be enough.”

Joseph took his leave and began his walk to the Gallery, where he and Alex had made up cots in small upstairs room for their short stay in the City. His mind spun around his conversation with Sara. He would cut out his heart before he’d put her in danger, but she was his life and she needed to know the truth.

Chapter 13

Emmitsburg, Maryland
June 27, 1863

Major Sean O'Connor yawned and stretched. His body ached from sleeping on a lumpy cot in his tent. He swore he'd use a bedroll next time. Fine place to be spending his twenty-fifth birthday. He rubbed a square chin and ran his fingers through fine blond hair. The day dawned clear and cloudless in a soft blue sky and the early sunshine promised a very warm day.

As he poured a cup of scalding brew from a nearby cook fire, Sean geared himself for the coming unpleasant encounter he anticipated with the Quartermaster Sergeant. According to Colonel Chamberlain, most of the weapons came from Concord Armaments. And many of them were defective. It was well-known that the Colonel was meticulous about his men's equipment and often conducted inventory of the arms and ammunition in his division.

Not a hell of a lot of good fighting a battle with faulty weapons. But that was his job, not Chamberlain's. To find out the extent of the ordnance problem and who was responsible.

For a moment, Sean mused on Joshua Chamberlain, a college professor from near his own hometown in Maine. A college professor turned officer. Hmph. He liked and respected the man.

A group of soldiers caught his eye and he stopped, watched as they stood posing for a photograph. Two photographers scurried back and forth between their camera and an old battered wagon, presumably their darkroom. Dust kicked up around them in whirlwinds. The lead photographer was about thirty or so, clean-shaven, thick brown hair and dark eyes. The other man seemed older, craggy, gray stubble on his chin and he coughed and spit frequently.

Well now, I wonder if I could get a photograph of myself to send home.

Sean approached the younger photographer, the one giving orders. "Excuse me, but might it be possible to have a picture taken this morning?"

The photographer turned. "Why yes, Major, if you don’t mind waiting a bit ‘til we’re through. We're just wrapping up the last shot, and I'm going to develop these plates."

"Sure enough. I’ll be in the quartermaster’s cabin meantime." Sean smiled and his face lit up. "Don’t go off now and forget."

"I won’t forget."

Sean stepped into the dusty cabin and peered around. He moved out of the way as several privates brushed past him, arms loaded with boxes. None were dressed in full uniform, just ragged shirts and ill-fitting trousers. He wondered how the supplies were holding up.

The air felt cooler inside and Sean breathed a sigh of relief, wiping sweat off his brow with a forearm. At the counter, the Quartermaster Sergeant waited on two soldiers. So, that must be the infamous Scofield, Sean assumed. Chamberlain had given him fair warning last night about the quartermaster, and now he studied a hefty, gorilla-like man. Scofield's face sported a dark growth of beard. His hair stuck out around his head, as if a comb couldn’t get through, and his large hands were scarred, fingernails black with dirt. A cigar dangled from his lower lip, which was twisted in a snarl.

The privates left. Sean approached the counter. Scofield began tidying the shelves, moving dust around with a filthy rag.

"Excuse me," Sean said, trying not to grin at the absurdity of the man cleaning in this hovel. "Are you Sergeant Scofield?"

"Yep."

"You mean yes, Sir, *Major,* don't you?"

"Yep. That's what I mean." Scofield gave him a weak salute.

"You know who I am?"

"I heard that some officer be comin' by to check on supplies and the like." The Sergeant's voice was a low growl.

"I want to know if you've had any complaints about substandard equipment, guns, cartridges, other supplies."

"Aaach. Complaints. Ha. The men are always complainin' . . .'bout the cold, the heat, 'bout the bugs or the lousy food. But I can't rightly say as there's a noticeable problem with guns." Scofield squinted at the major, arms folded, cigar dead in his mouth.

"Tell me, Sergeant, who are the suppliers to this regiment?"

"Well, I don't know if I can recollect their names right off the top."

"Then perhaps you'd better get the log books out here so we can check them together." Sean, not much taller, managed to stare down at the Quartermaster.

Scofield eyed him unpleasantly, clearly trying to decide what to do. In the end, he shrugged and went into the back room. He returned carrying a large record book and slammed it down on the counter.

Sean scowled. "Looks like your dust rag missed this logbook." He blew off a layer of surface dust and opened it, flipping silently through the pages. One name stood out as the primary supplier, Concord Armaments. He read further. A substantial number of weapons and artillery supplies had been returned as defective, most complaints directed toward Concord Armaments. Sean jotted down notes then closed the book. When he looked up he came nose to nose with Scofield who sneered, caught himself and backed away.

“Them guns’re junk,” Scofield muttered.

Sean stared at him. "Thanks, Sergeant. You’ve been most helpful."

Scofield grunted.

Sean let out a long low whistle as he stepped back out into the sunshine and headed toward the photographers. Just finished with the group portrait, their camera and equipment remained in place.

"All right, Major, er. . .?" The photographer stuck out his hand.

Sean shook it. "Sean O’Connor."

"I'm Joseph Thornhill, and may I introduce Jeb Reilly. We're from Alexander Gardner’s Gallery in Washington."

Jeb said, "Howdy do, Major. Right this way."

Sean brushed his uniform off and straightened his jacket. As he followed Joseph he combed his long blond hair back with his fingers. He allowed Joseph to pose him before a tent cabin, with his foot propped up on a stool and his right hand on his sword. Jeb slid a new glass plate into the camera.

Several minutes later, three pictures were taken and catalogued: *Plate numbers 115A, 116A, 117A, Major Sean O’Connor, Emmitsburg, Maryland, June 27, 1863.*

"Come back later, Major, and we’ll have some photos ready for you," Joseph said then suddenly frowned.

"Something wrong?"

"That insignia. On your collar." Joseph pointed to the cloverleaf and diamond braided design. "You're with the special unit dispatched from the Inspector General's Department. Under Colonel Baxter."

"You recognize this?" Sean pointed to the symbol on his collar.

Joseph led O'Connor by the arm and walked him away from the encampment. When he lowered his voice, Sean leaned over to catch the words.

"Yes, I recognize it," Joseph said. "I'm working under Mister Pinkerton. He and Colonel Baxter both report to the President. Thing is, I've taken pictures of that emblem before. At Antietam and Fredericksburg. Same design on the collar."

Sean rubbed his chin. "Interesting, although I'm not surprised. If you've been photographing the front, you probably did run into one or two of our officers."

"Both of them were dead."

Sean steadied his gaze at Joseph. "Do you know their names?"

"No, that was also strange. Neither had tags, no identification of any kind on them." He frowned. "And then there was the civilian."

"What civilian?"

Joseph relayed his suspicions to Sean. "I think he might have killed them."

"A civilian. What makes you say that?" Sean asked.

"At Antietam, the civilian told me he had a message for Major Sills. Sills was dead. If the man was Sills." Joseph shrugged. "I sent the information to Pinkerton. Haven't heard back yet."

"I'd be curious to see those photos."

"Well. I'm afraid you'll have to go to Washington. That's where they are now. At Gardner's Gallery."

Before Sean could respond, the sound of shouting and a sudden blur of activity caused him to turn. Soldiers circled a scout that had just ridden into camp, his horse in a lather, eyes blazing. Sean rushed toward the melee, Joseph a step behind. The only words he could make out in all the commotion were "the whole of the damned Reb army" and the name of a town. *Gettysburg*.

*

Gettysburg, Pennsylvania, June 29, 1863

Two days later, after a short but very hot march to a small and charming village amidst verdant rolling hills, Joseph arrived at the Union encampment. Tired now, he ambled over to a copse of trees on a steep rise. It was early evening but the moon had settled high and bright in the sky-- enough to illuminate the meadows that stretched out before him, dusted with a silvery hue.

He shuddered at what he knew tomorrow would bring to this pristine landscape. He reached into his pocket and brought out his pipe and tobacco pouch. Smoking relaxed him. He gazed out over a split-rail fence.

Startled by footsteps, Joseph spun around. Sean O'Connor came up beside him and leaned over the fence.

"Indeed fine country," Sean said. "Reminds me a bit of my home in Maine. Woods and meadows, changing colors."

Joseph breathed out a sigh, turned back to the landscape. "Maine? Isn't that where Colonel Chamberlain's from?"

"That's what I hear."

"I thought you'd be heading back to Washington to report to Baxter, and see those pictures," Joseph said.

"From the looks of the Rebel Army's position, I might be here a few days. As for those pictures, I've been thinking about this man you saw both times near the dead investigators. Can you tell me anymore?"

Joseph puffed on his pipe, a cloud of sweet smelling smoke billowed up between them. "There is something I remembered. At Fredericksburg, I saw him twice. In both camps."

Sean squinted at Thornhill. "Both camps? How do you know about the Southern camp?"

"I decided I needed to photograph the action across the Rappahannock."

Sean's mouth fell open.

"Yes, well, one of my more foolish moments. Anyway, I did get across but got captured and brought to General Longstreet's headquarters where--"

"Holy Mother of God." Sean spun around in a circle. "Captured by Ole Pete. And he let you go?"

"Decent of him, don't you think?"

Sean gaped at Joseph.

"Well, the point here, Sean, is that in Longstreet's camp I saw that civilian again. Then that same night, I saw him again back on the other side of the river."

"Damn. How can he travel so freely to both camps?"

"I wondered at first if he'd been captured by the Confederates. But then I saw him back in the Union camp." Joseph stuck one hand in his trouser pockets, still puffing on his pipe.

Sean worked his jaw. "You only took the one picture of him--at Antietam?"

"Right. And that's back in Washington." Damn but he should have made more prints.

Sean said, "Anything else to make you suspicious of this stranger?"

Joseph stared across the moonlit fields. "Not really. Just a feeling. I thought he was watching me but, I don't know." He shook his head. "Photographing dead bodies hour after hour can make you a little spooky, if you know what I mean."

"Joseph, if this stranger had anything to do with the deaths of the investigators, you'd better keep a close watch for him."

Joseph turned, intent on Sean's expression of concern.

"Yeah," the young Major said. "The next time he turns up, he'll surely be looking for Baxter's other agent . . . for me, and, Joseph, for you."

Chapter 14

Gettysburg, Pennsylvania
June 30, 1863

Jack Cade skirted the edge of Cemetery Ridge as he led his horses and sutler's wagon through the bivouacs of the Federal regiments. His head swiveled back and forth, body in a constant state of tension, as the night held unseen dangers. He knew that photographer was somewhere nearby--the same photographer he'd seen at Antietam, and then again at Fredericksburg. Tonight, he didn't want to be recognized by someone trained to be observant. As an added precaution, Cade had trimmed his hair and shaved his mustache. It was far too hot to wear his duster, so he'd donned a tan shirt and dark trousers, much worn for wear, with suspenders to hold them up. A pair of beat-up shoes, holes in the soles, and he fit right in.

As he ambled by the campfires, soldiers ignored him. The tempo in camp tonight was slow, the mood subdued. He knew most of the troops were too nervous to be bothered with him, their minds on the next day's battle, wondering if they'd live or die, be captured or turn tail and run.

Cade's mood turned black. Hellish heat. Being covered head to toe with dust and dirt didn't help either.

A hot bath would do nicely. Ease these sore muscles. A body oughtn't be sleeping on the rock-hard ground night after night.

He felt a sudden sharp pain in his neck. *Damn mosquitoes.* He slapped at the insect, leaving a bloody welt behind. *Big as elephants around here.* He snorted, coughed and moved on, leading his horses through the camp.

Where was that uniform, that bloody insignia? He pulled out Lindsey's note with the list of agents he was to dispatch. Four, now only one left. Major Sean O'Connor.

He reached into his pocket and pulled out that polished steel dog tag again. It glinted in the firelight. *Major Phillip Malone.* Cade reflected back on that kill. It had been so easy. He'd befriended Malone on the march to Fredericksburg. Nice fellow, if not for the side he'd chosen. Nice family too. Cade brought out the photograph of Malone, his wife and two children he'd stolen from Malone's corpse. Ah well, many women were widows these days, many children orphans. That was the way of war, he mused.

This might be his last mission. Then he could go home, resume his former life. See his mother, brothers again. It had been a long time. Cade let out a deep sigh. Soon.

But for now, there was O'Connor. He'd done some checking around earlier and learned that the man was here at Gettysburg.

Cade smiled. He was getting good at this business.

Close to midnight, men began dousing fires and bedding down. Only a handful of guards remained on watch. He reached into his wagon and pulled down his bedroll. Then he took one last look around. An owl hooted in the distance. Crickets chirped. The only other sounds that broke the night were those of men coughing, snoring, or moaning in their sleep. A three-quarter moon hung low in the blue-black sky. Cade lay atop his bedroll, the night air still and warm. For now, he'd count the stars and wait.

That night Joseph penned a letter to the woman he would marry:

Dear Sara,

I hope this letter finds you and your family well and in good spirits. It was splendid seeing you in May and meeting your friend, Louisa. She's quite lovely and a very talented writer.

In your last letter you asked many questions about the state of the army and the fighting men and I take pleasure in writing you the answers. But describing the men is not a simple task.

If you can imagine, an army encampment is like a moving city with many different personalities living together, sharing, for better or for worse. Some men are quiet and keep to themselves--they do well on picket duty. Then there are the braggarts, always talking about themselves and their accomplishments, but who don't manage to distinguish themselves in battle as you might expect. There are 'snobs' or 'puff-ups' who look down on other men, unwilling to perform menial tasks as if beneath them.

The 'rogues' are usually drunk and starting trouble, while the 'jonahs' are the clods that seem to disrupt everything they touch. These two get along well, the rogues taking advantage of the jonahs for the most part. The worst personality in my opinion, is the 'beat' who always finds a way to shirk his duty out of sheer laziness. But, in general, men are men, either here in the army or at home on farms or in businesses.

While Alex remains in Washington at his new and prosperous Gallery, Jeb and I enjoy taking photographs of the men in their more relaxed state. I say relaxed, although fighting is never far from their minds. All the men are afraid of battle, not just of being killed or wounded, but fearful of losing their nerve and running away. Despite this fear, during battle most men hold their lines and fight courageously.

As we follow the army north, there is something in the air. I can smell it. I can feel it. So can the men. There is a jittery intoxication as if we are all rehearsing for some grand drama to be played out soon. Very soon. Perhaps you'll think me foolish, but I intuit that death on a monstrous scale is near.

We are closing in on a little town in Pennsylvania called Gettysburg. Only a few days ago President Lincoln accepted the resignation of the Commander in Chief, Joseph Hooker, from the Army of the Potomac and in his stead placed George Mead, a General from Pennsylvania. We hear tell that Mead has a volatile temper and is called 'the old snapping turtle' behind his back.

Now, with the Federal blockade causing such desperate hardship for the Confederacy, General Lee is gambling on a second invasion of the North and is marching his army to Pennsylvania. It is inevitable that North and South will clash brutally and bitterly to the end, and very soon. Let us hope it is a decisive end, and one in our favor.

I miss you terribly, my love. It is all the more apparent to me since we spent time together so recently. You are part of my days, my nights, and ever in my thoughts. I count the days until we are as one, man and wife.

Yours ever truly,

Joseph

Chapter 15

Gettysburg, Pennsylvania
July 3, 1863

Joseph Thornhill took a moment from setting up his equipment to study his surroundings. Here on Cemetery Ridge, emerald fields with their rich earth fragrance were broken by an occasional cluster of trees, otherwise they rolled for miles coming to rest at the foot of gentle hills. In places, the grass was burnt brown and gold from the parching heat and the land was rugged and fissured with rock. Once again, his thoughts turned to Sara, her red hair contrasting with the colors of the landscape.

He stretched his fatigued and aching muscles then removed his jacket and tossed it on the ground as the heat of the day began to sink in. Pulling down the brim of his hat, he watched the troops going about their daily routines. He reflected on his conversation with Sean O'Connor the previous night, where the major reveled in the success of the siege at Little Round Top. Colonel Chamberlain had pulled off the most amazing ruse of the War. On a more disturbing note, however, was what Sean had told him regarding the soldier's guns. One out of three weapons produced by Concords Armaments were defective. He shook his head and wondered at human nature and man's insatiable greed. How could men deliberately put other men's lives in jeopardy for a profit? How many men had died so far because of faulty arms?

Joseph's eyes gazed out again on the stunning landscape. Peace and stillness reigned so far today and it was already one o'clock. Perhaps General Lee's given up, issued the order to march back to Virginia. Maybe the Confederates are packing up even now. Not likely, he almost laughed at himself and resumed his task of setting up the camera.

Suddenly the quiet of the day shattered with the first booms of cannon fire and the peaceful landscape turned into a smoke and fire-filled arena. For miles across, the enemy lines blurred with huge billows of dense slate clouds erupting from their artillery assault. Robert E. Lee had not retreated.

By instinct, Joseph covered his ears and ducked behind a tree. He knew that the Parrotts had a range of nearly three miles, yet somehow he felt safe, invincible here across the huge open field. He stepped back up to his camera and began readying the plate holder. Above the terrible din he heard a voice scream.

"What in the Sam Hill are you doing? This is a dangerous spot to be, for God's sake, man." Joshua Chamberlain rushed up to him, a layer of reddish dirt covering his uniform.

Joseph turned and grinned. "That's the point, Colonel. Just think of the photographs I can get from this vantage. Look out there. You can actually see fire bursting from their cannons. What an image--I know I can capture that."

"If you don't get yourself killed." Chamberlain dodged a blast of case shot as it splintered a tree nearby. Along the ridge, a soldier howled, and his body fell and rolled down the hill.

Joseph took a step back, blinked. *Jesus God.* He turned to the Colonel. "I have to do this, Sir. This is much too great an opportunity to miss, and--"

A nearby concussion hung his words in the air amidst flying debris and shrapnel. A huge chunk of twisted, burning metal from a blasted shell punched into his shoulder and knocked him off his feet. He lay in the grass stunned, breathless. Daggers of pain bolted up his left arm.

Chamberlain rushed to his side, rolled him over. "Easy now. There's no artery hit." Chamberlain held a dazed Joseph in his arms and looked around for help, shouting to be heard above the head-splitting clamor. A private ran up, red-faced, breathing hard.

"Get a stretcher right away."

"Yes, Sir." The private rushed off.

Joseph rested against the Colonel, feeling woozy. "I guess I'm not as lucky as I thought."

"We need to get the surgeons to pry out that hunk of metal."

Without warning, Joseph struggled to sit up.

"What are you doing? Lie still."

Joseph looked at the Colonel in despair. "My camera. What happened to my camera?"

*

Several hundred yards away near Culp's Hill, Sean stalked away from Chamberlain's tent tightly gripping a defective Concord Armaments musket in his hand. One more piece of evidence. Anger boiled in him as he realized how many men might have died at Little Round Top because of weapons like these. As the first sounds of battle reached him, he threw the musket into his tent then fell back behind a supply wagon. As the artillery storm increased in intensity he watched soldiers scramble about, gathering up guns and ammunition, shouting orders and dodging the cannon brigades as they dragged heavy artillery to the front of the line.

Above the mayhem, Sean noticed the sutler, the one he had seen briefly in the camps before, ducking and darting to avoid getting shot.

What the devil is he doing wandering around in the middle of an attack?

Sean shouted and waved to catch his attention and warn him away, but the sutler appeared to be looking for something.

Just then a huge burst of canister exploded in front of the man. The sutler vanished in a cloud of smoke. Sean began creeping to the spot where the sutler had been standing. The blast left the ground ragged and burnt. Black powder and iron balls littered the field. The sutler lay wounded on the ground.

"My arm, my arm, Christ, help me. Look at all the blood, ooohh God."

"Take it easy, let me bind this up then I'll get you to the hospital." Sean grabbed the scarf from around his neck and tied the cloth around the injured arm. He fastened it with a stick he found on the ground to tighten or loosen like a tourniquet. Then he carefully lifted, half walked, half carried the sutler to the surgeon's tent. Laying him on the ground to wait his turn, he noticed the rank aroma of the area. The putrid smells of blood and death made him want to gag and he breathed through his mouth. "Stay here," he told the civilian. "The surgeons will get to you." He stood.

"Wait, please. There's some. . . medicine in my wagon. In a little chest. You can't--." The sutler had difficulty breathing. "You can't miss it."

"Sorry, wait for the surgeon." Man was crazy to think he'd do his errands.

“There’s morphine,” the sutler said. “Please. Not just for me. For the others . . . the wounded.”

Morphine? That was a different story. Sean surveyed the immediate vicinity, spotted the sutler’s wagon with its garish advertisements on the sides. Union soldiers busied themselves moving equipment behind a split-rail fence in an attempt to outdistance the artillery barrage.

How the hell will I get to that wagon in one piece?

Dodging and weaving from tree to tree, behind rocks and fallen soldiers, Sean finally reached the sutler's transport and stopped a minute to catch his breath. Smoke covered the entire field and smarted his eyes. He shot around to the back and ducked inside.

Instantly he felt relief from the haze and soot and could breathe easier. But the noise of gunfire seemed just as horrific, echoing in the little canvas-walled chamber. He tied open a flap to let some light in, then scrambled around trying to find the box. The wagon overflowed with trunks and crates: blankets, tools, foodstuffs, cooking utensils.

After a moment, he spied a little wooden chest with a bronze latch. It sat prominently atop two large leather-bound trunks. Sean lifted the lid and found a brown bottle of liquid. He held it up to examine it, but there were no labels. Assuming this was the morphine, he was about to close the chest when his eye caught something. He reached back in and withdrew an ice pick. . . long, clean and sharp with a rosewood handle. The long metal spike was coated with a rusty material. He’d seen that material on the blades of knifes and swords. Blood. Alarm bells went off in his mind but frantic shouting from outside forced his attention away. He replaced the ice pick in the box and cautiously stepped outside.

"What's going on?" He stopped a soldier running by.

"It's the Rebs, Sir, infantry. Artillery been blasting us for hours. Now, lookee, they're coming across the field."

Sean stared in disbelief across the wide spread of acreage. Lines of infantry, perhaps half a mile wide, more, advanced across the open space toward them. The sight mesmerized him. Row upon row of ragged Rebels, no longer in proper uniform, marched like wooden soldiers across the space. Most wore the traditional kepi on their heads and carried muskets at their side. The Stars and Bars waved at both ends of the line. O'Connor could swear their eyes were glassy and fixed. Fixed on a sole purpose. Destruction of the Union Army.

My God. Bobbie Lee must be crazy.

He remembered his own purpose, looked down at the bottle he held in his hand and raced off to the surgeon's tent and the sutler who still lay on the ground.

"Is this it?"

The sutler opened his dark eyes that dominated his face, looked at the bottle and merely nodded. Sean leaned the man backward, gave him a sip. Then he checked his damaged arm. The debris appeared to have torn deeply into the outer tissues, no doubt destroying muscles and tendons. But the bone seemed not to be broken.

"I can't move my arm, it's dead," the sutler said. "You, you don't suppose they'll have to . . . take it off?"

Sean blanched, recalling the gruesome scene he'd happened upon yesterday. He'd entered the surgeon's tent to search for a doctor and in the confusion tripped over a bucket. He went down on his knees and found himself eye level with a tangle of amputated limbs that had toppled out of the pail. He barely avoided vomiting.

"Don't let them, whatever happens, don't let them--"

"It's not up to me." Sean's jaw muscles twitched. As the orderlies brought the stretcher to carry the man into the hospital tent, Sean stood, breathing heavily. He watched them lift and carry the sutler away and was surprised to notice Joseph Thornhill exiting the tent, intent on the bandage around his arm. The photographer, not looking up, stood aside to let them pass.

*

Jack Cade cursed under his breath. What twist of fate had disabled him only to be saved by his enemy--the man he stalked? Hot anger surged through his veins as O'Connor's face, the insignia on his collar, burned a hole in his gut. He had failed his mission. Anger settled into despair and combined with the drowsing effects of the medicine, his body fell into a limp, fatigued state.

*

That night, Joseph couldn't sleep. Instead, he removed the journal from his satchel and wrote an entry, and after much soul-searching decided to write a letter.

July 3, 1863

My Dearest Sara,

I felt I had to write you today, after three of the bloodiest days I have ever witnessed. I must get it off my mind, and I might not even post this letter, lest you be terribly offended. But I feel I must unburden myself somehow.

Rumors have it that General Robert E. Lee and the Army of Northern Virginia suffered great losses, maybe one third of their forces dead, wounded or captured. The Union Army is said to have lost a good deal, maybe one quarter of their troops, but it is safe to say we won the battle of Gettysburg. Lee's army is retreating back to the South and Mead's men are elated. Finally, victory, and an important one.

It is sad to think that this particular battle may have been fought over something as simple as shoes. There was rumored to be a large supply of shoes in the town of Gettysburg and on July 1 an officer under Ewell's command led his men there to confiscate these shoes. Unfortunately for them, they ran into the Union Army.

I was slightly wounded today, some shrapnel lacerating my arm. But don't worry. The doctors have bandaged me up and say I will be fine, no permanent damage, and I take a bit of laudanum for the pain. Luckily my camera, which was caught in the crossfire suffered no harm.

I must admit that until now I had no real concept of the power our modern weaponry wields. The force of the injury knocked me clean off my feet. I think this experience will prove useful to me in my work.

The wound has not stopped me from working, however, although it is a bit difficult with one arm in a brace. I rely on my apprentice more. I've been busy photographing the town and its people. Now I'll begin, once again, to shoot the battlefield remains. I am steeling myself to this task slowly, but have not made much progress.

Both Alex and Tim O'Sullivan--you remember, I mentioned this fine young man and competent photographer to you--will arrive in the next few days. I look forward to working with them.

Now, other gruesome scenes await my camera. Embalming surgeons, as they call themselves, have arrived. Although many of the dead soldiers are hastily buried where they fall, many end up in mass graves. Some are later exhumed and buried in military cemeteries, whether they've been identified or not-- often with the headstone reading only: "A Union Soldier" or "A Confederate Soldier." It is hard to imagine--dying in the name of one's country but that country not even knowing your name.

On a lighter note, I have also photographed some of the Union soldiers and officers after the final skirmish, and they were truly in high spirits--dirty, sweaty, exhausted, some wounded, but all euphoric. There was optimism in the air and hope, hope that this war would soon end. But for now we must deal with the brutal aftermath of this battle. Hospital tents crowd the countryside and the small population of Gettysburg is inundated with the sick and wounded. I doubt this town will ever be the same.

Tomorrow is July 4. I wonder if anyone, in the midst of all this furor, will appreciate the irony that this day marks the eighty-seventh year of our nation's birth.

I miss you, my dearest, and long to see you this Christmas. You are always in my thoughts as I pray I am in yours.

Yours ever truly,

Joseph

Chapter 16

Union Hotel Hospital, Washington City

December 28, 1863

Joseph Thornhill hurried his step to keep up with Sara. He clutched his camera and tripod in his hands, while a young apprentice followed behind with a boxful of accessories. Formerly an elegant boarding house, the Union Hotel was now a hospital, filled to overflowing with wounded soldiers. Joseph moved down one crowded, frenetic corridor after another, bumped into small boys carrying water pails and several frenzied surgeons, and hustled up one flight of stairs to the rear of the building. Abruptly, Sara stopped short, and Joseph nearly crashed into her.

She whirled around and spoke in a hushed voice. "Now, Joseph, let me talk to her. I'll explain about the photographs, that it would be good for the soldiers' morale and that the pictures will be hung in the Gallery and also lithographed for the Weeklies." She gave him a smile and his heart swelled with love. He was glad he had confided in her about his role with the Secret Service.

"Joseph?"

"I'm ready, dear," he said.

Sara smoothed the skirts of her plain woolen dress. Then she turned back to the door of the hospital nurse administrator and knocked with purpose.

Joseph propped his heavy equipment against the wall and winked at his apprentice, who stood wide-eyed, staring at the sign on the door: *Miss Dorothea Dix, Nurse Administrator*.

Within a few minutes, the door swung open and a woman of about sixty years of age burst through. Medium stature, gray hair parted severely in the middle and tied back, every strand in place, Miss Dorothea Dix looked like a dragon about to breathe fire.

"What is the meaning of this? I have not given permission for photographs to be taken. Miss Kelly," she turned Sara, "you should have informed me that these gentlemen were to be here."

"Now just a minute, Miss Dix, I did--" Sara began, straightening her back when a loud, jovial voice from the far end of the hallway caught her attention. Alexander Gardner ambled over to meet the group, wide smile beaming through his bushy beard. "Och, what's this now? Is that Miss Dix? The matron saint of all wounded soldiers?"

Atypical of the woman, Miss Dix blushed and brought her hands up to her mouth, hiding a slight smile. Joseph bit his lower lip to keep from chuckling. Alex was a charmer, no doubt about that.

"Mister Gardner, you know very well it is me. No one mentioned that you would be here."

"Aye, not to worry, Madam. This is Joseph Thornhill, my associate. Not quite the photographer as myself, but adequate." He grinned at Joseph who started to open his mouth then thought better of it. Instead he rolled his eyes at Sara.

"Well then, Miss Kelly, you should have told me." The dragon said. "Never mind, never mind. Now how can I help you, Mister Gardner?"

Alex winked at his friend and took Miss Dix by the elbow, leading her down the congested hall. He waved at the group to follow, and once more they wound their way around nurses and orderlies rushing to and fro. Joseph, Sara and the apprentice accompanied Alex and Miss Dix back downstairs into a vast space that had originally served as the hotel's main dining room. Dozens of beds lined up facing each other on both sides. The beds, more like crude cots, consisted of thin mattresses atop spindly metal frames, now rusted and peeling. Above each row of cots, two well-worn American flags hung limply from wooden poles. The ward overflowed with patients, all eighty sleeping places occupied.

Joseph asked Sara, "How is Miss Alcott? I haven't seen Louisa lately."

"Oh dear, I didn't tell you. Poor Louisa. She contracted typhoid pneumonia this fall and was forced to go home."

Joseph said, "I'm sorry to hear that. Is she recovering?"

"Yes, but not as quickly as she'd like. Louisa's most impatient."

"Hmm," he said. "Like someone else I know."

"She's a long way from here. Her home is in Concord, Massachusetts."

Concord. Like the armaments company.

"Thank goodness she's on the mend," Sara went on. "I can tell you, she's sorely missed around here. She always remembered to bring her perfume and sprinkle it around the ward to make the terrible stench more bearable."

Joseph had noted the stench was not so different from the battlefield. Instinctively he breathed through his mouth. As they passed through the wards, he noticed his young apprentice, face tinged green, covered his mouth with his hands as if to keep his breakfast in.

Before he could suggest to the boy that he find a bucket, a tall, stately man caught his eye moving toward them from the opposite end of the hall. The man approached, undoing the top buttons of his rich lambs' wool coat crowned with beaver fur then slowly removed expensive leather gloves, one finger at a time.

The dragon rushed back to Sara's side.

"Ah, Miss Dix." Samuel Lindsey smiled and gave each of the visitors a cool gaze. "Giving a tour?"

"Mister Lindsey. This is an honor." Miss Dix rubbed her hands together. She turned to the group and addressed them like a schoolmistress. "This is Mister Samuel Lindsey, the hospital's most generous benefactor." She introduced the rest of the party.

Lindsey spoke to the group. "Photographers, how interesting. I presume you're taking pictures of Miss Dix's spotless wards? She is a marvel, don't you think?"

"Mister Lindsey, you are too kind." Miss Dix waved her hands.

Turning frosty gray eyes on Joseph, Lindsey said, "Have you been out in the field recently?"

"Just returned from Chickamauga in October," Joseph said.

"Ah, Georgia, the heart of the South." Lindsey kept his eyes pinned on Joseph. "Difficult job I imagine, being a field photographer. And dangerous."

"At times," Joseph said.

"Och, now, Mister Thornhill's being modest," Alex burst in. "You've no doubt heard of his capture at Fredericksburg, when he walked into the enemy camp to take pictures?"

Lindsey narrowed his eyes. "Enemy camp? Did you get the photographs you wanted?"

"Nay," Alex went on. "General Longstreet wouldna allow it."

Lindsey smiled and reminded Joseph of a fox in a coop of chicks. His eyes remained fixed on Joseph. "Are your field photographs on exhibition at Brady's Gallery?"

"That's Gardner's Gallery," Alex said.

"Ahh, on your own, then?" Lindsey said. "It's time Brady had some competition."

"I heartily agree," Alex said.

"I'm afraid, I must take my leave," Lindsey said. "Business, you know. But I would like to extend an invitation to you all to my New Year's Eve gathering. I do hope you will be able to attend." He tipped his hat. "Gentlemen, Ladies."

"How wonderful," Miss Dix said. "An invitation to the most magnificent event of the season."

Joseph faced Miss Dix. "Might I ask what business Mister Lindsey is in?"

Dorothea Dix nodded. "He is the principal at Concord Armaments. They provide arms to our men in the field, as you know."

Samuel Lindsey was a name he was not familiar with. Concord Armaments was a name he was. Joseph felt his pulse quicken.

*

The next morning, Joseph escorted Sara to Alexander Gardner's gallery at 7th and D Streets. They looked up at the building, which occupied the corner lot and stood like a massive barn three stories tall. It might have been impressive except for the myriad signs which marred both sides of the building: *Photographs* stood in bold letters on the roof, *Books and Stationery* plastered across the side, above which a list options: *Carte de Visites, Stereographs, Album Cards, Ambrotypes.* A colossal banner proclaiming *Views of the War* whipped in the breeze.

Inside the gallery, the ambiance inspired a subdued museum-like feeling. Special lamps lit the halls, and only an odd table and chair here and there broke up the emptiness. An occasional window added light to the atmosphere of the gallery and Gardner took special pains to hang his best works there. Room after room filled with Civil War field photographs and portraitures drew hundreds of visitors daily. They gaped at the images so powerfully depicting the brutal nature of war. Ladies, dressed in their finest, with parasols folded at their sides gasped at the scenes, covered their eyes from one horror only to come face to face with another death scene. Joseph led Sara to the Main Gallery Hall.

"Joseph." His name echoed in the large, sparsely furnished room.

He and Sara spun around. A handsome fair-haired young man in a dark blue uniform marched toward them, his boots resounding on the floor.

"Sean, nice to see you again. Major Sean O'Connor, Miss Sara Kelly."

"It's a pleasure, Miss Kelly. Joseph has told me a lot about you." Sean grinned and took off his hat.

"Oh? Has he now?"

They both looked at Joseph who cleared his throat and said, "Are you visiting the Gallery again? Surely you've been here many times."

"I have, but I'm drawn to it. The men, the places. All so familiar."

Sara said, "You two gentlemen can talk while I explore." She moved off.

Sean ushered Joseph to a corner. "That civilian, Joseph, the one you told me about? The more I think about him, the more I believe there's some connection between him and the dead operatives. It's just too coincidental that you saw him and the dead majors at the same time and place." He paused. "Another has gone missing. Philip Malone, last seen at Fredericksburg."

Joseph shook his head.

“Where would I find that photo of the civilian? I came the last time I was in town, but the other photographers here couldn’t locate it."

"It’s in the collection albums upstairs. Let me tell Sara we'll be a few minutes."

*

Joseph led the major to the end of the hall and into the studio located upstairs from the public Gallery. The room, warm and inviting, resembled a small library except instead of books, rows of photo albums lined the shelves. Joseph set several large albums down on an oversized table. He began turning pages of one album.

"They're painful, these photographs."

Sean looked down at the pages. "I cannot imagine how you can take pictures of these men--alive one minute . . ." His voice trailed off.

"You just steel yourself to do the job. It's a job, you know. These men aren't real, you see. They cannot be real to a photographer. Listen to me. I'm sorry. I guess it gets to you sometimes. Now, where were we? Look." Joseph pointed. A man in a long pale coat with shoulder cape stood in three-quarter view, contemplatively studying the battlefield.

Sean squinted at the photograph.

"Here, try this." Joseph handed him a magnifying glass.

Peering through it, Sean caught his breath. "I know this man. This was the sutler wounded at Gettysburg.”

“What? A sutler?”

“I dragged him to the hospital. His hair was shorter and he had no mustache like in this photograph, but it's the same man. I'd know those eyes anywhere.”

Joseph looked at Sean, brow creased.

"Those eyes, yes. I'd recognize them as well."

Chapter 17

Washington City

December 31, 1863

Joseph Thornhill unwound the wool scarf from his neck and added it to the coat, hat and gloves he had draped over the servant's arm. Then he smoothed his waistcoat jacket, reassuring himself that all buttons were fastened. He squared his shoulders and ran his hand through his hair. With a silent prayer, he urged his flip-flopping stomach to hold out.

"Joseph?" Sara said, removing her own hat and gloves. "Are you all right?"

"Yes, I, of course." He sucked in a breath.

The corner of her mouth tilted up in a wry smile. "You're not comfortable in formal wear, are you?"

"Is it that obvious?"

"Ahh, there you are. I was wondering when you two would arrive." Alex came up to them carrying a plate piled high with food of many colors.

Joseph didn't think he could pull this off alone. Thank God, Alex was here. And Sara. She was clever, diplomatic and had the social grace he wished he had. Besides, she was beautiful. They were to be married in the spring. It couldn't be too soon.

He took Sara's arm and followed Alex down the two steps from the foyer into the ballroom and moved toward the festivities. A waiter offered him a tray of champagne glasses and he took one without hesitation, handed it to Sara, and then took one for himself.

"Oh, there's Mrs. Stanford and her daughter. I must chat them up. Please, excuse me, Joseph." Sara was off across the room.

Stationing himself in a corner of the large room, he sipped his drink and gazed at the splendor before him: Samuel Lindsey's famous New Year's Eve gala, an event the elite of Washington looked forward to each year. The Georgetown home glittered with lights from hundreds of candles and numerous gas lamps. The silverware, polished to a high sheen, shimmered on the long banquet table; the quantity and quality of the food befitted a royal family and smelled heavenly. Stringed music wafted through from the great hall as couples danced to a waltz and reminded him how much Sara adored Johann Strauss.

You'd never guess we were in the midst of a war.

Alex nudged him with an elbow. "Mark me words, Joseph, see those men? They're reporters, invited solely to write stories for the society columns."

"Now how do you know that?"

"Look at their dismal attire. Surely they are not society. Hmm." He lifted his head and sniffed the air. "Delightful smells. I canna resist some of these delicious foodstuffs. Help yourself, man."

"Sorry, I'm too nervous."

"Then why are we here, for the love of Mary?"

"Shh. For heaven's sakes. We're here because Samuel Lindsey and his partners own Concord Armaments and Sean O'Connor--"

"Och, speaking of partners, there's one now."

Joseph turned his head slowly.

"Porter Hobbs, aye, pompous ass that he is, but a powerful one in this town. Perhaps we'd better split up and see what we can see."

With that Alex strode toward Hobbs and took up a position behind the man as he conversed with guests.

Joseph set his empty glass on a tray and picked up a new one as he strolled through the smoke-filled room. Men had gathered in small groups, drinking, laughing, and smoking. Women lifted their skirts as they flitted around the room, gloved-hands covering their mouths as they giggled. He nodded to them as he passed, inhaling their sweet perfume.

Where was Lindsey? Suddenly he stopped short as he heard the name.

"I say, Lindsey, splendid party, splendid." A slightly inebriated guest slapped Samuel Lindsey on the back, causing him to spill his drink. "Sorry, old man. Now, tell me, what do you think of the war these days? Will those damned Rebs ever quit, I say?" the man blustered, spittle flying from his mouth.

Lindsey, apparently not in the mood to discuss theories on the war, signaled his wife with a crook of his finger. She scurried over and hustled the guest away. Amused, Joseph noticed Lindsey's eyes widen in surprised recognition. Joseph collected himself for the offensive.

Samuel Lindsey replaced the surprised look with a tight smile.

"Ah, Mister Thornhill, we meet again. So glad you could come."

Sara was suddenly at his side. "Thank you, Mister Lindsey for the invitation."

"Miss Kelly. You look lovely this evening. I'm pleased to have you here."

"Aye," Alex said, arriving then. "Food is magnificent."

Lindsey smiled, but it never reached his eyes. He swiveled his head back to Joseph. "It's too bad you cannot take pictures here. It would be splendid to have photographs of the ball, don't you think?"

"I do," Joseph said. "Perhaps someday in the future, when we can take pictures without natural light--" He stopped as a red-haired, red-faced man joined them.

"Do you know Harlow Knox?" Lindsey introduced everyone. "Harlow is my, er, brother-in-law and one of my business associates."

"And what sort of business are you in?" Sara asked.

Knox snickered. "The gun business, Miss. We produce guns for the army."

"Artillery?" Alex asked.

"That too," Lindsey said. "Do you know much about guns, Mister Thornhill?"

"Not much, no."

"He just knows how to shoot." Knox laughed at his own witticism.

"Perhaps sometime I can give you a tour of Concord Armaments?" Lindsey said directly to Joseph. "Maybe you can take some photographs."

"I would like that," Joseph said. "Where is the factory?"

"Concord, Massachusetts. Hence the name."

"How extraordinary," Sara said. "That's where Louisa May lives."

Lindsey focused on Sara a moment then said, "Now, if you'll please excuse me? I must see to other guests. Do enjoy the party." The older man bowed his head and left. Knox had already joined another group of men and Alex went off in search of more to eat.

Joseph stood with Sara. *Concord, Massachusetts. Well, Miss Louisa May Alcott, perhaps you and I are destined to meet again. He'd broach the subject with Sara. She'd know more about Louisa's sensitivities and her willingness to help his mission.*

Friends of Sara's family rushed her away to meet their cousins from New York. Joseph was alone again. He wandered around the ballroom, wishing he could leave, when his eyes spied a set of large double doors across the room leading to a library. Slowly, he strolled in that direction, picking up a new glass of champagne. As he moved toward the library, he saw Alex heading in the same direction. They met in front of the doors.

"Do ye suppose anything of value might be found in that desk over there?" Alex's eyes surveyed the crowd.

"I'd like to find out. But it's too dangerous to close the doors. Someone would notice."

"Aye. Why don't you just sneak a peek at the desk? I'll stand here and create a distraction, warn you if anyone comes near."

Joseph gulped. "Er, right. Keep your eyes open for Sara too." His eyes darted around then he slipped into the room. Quickly he walked to the desk, his mind furiously trying to come up with an excuse if he got caught. No time. He pulled open the drawers one by one until he came across a log book. He yanked it out, opened it and ran his fingers down a page, then another.

Jesus. Look at these profits.

He flipped through the pages. Ordnance orders from the Quartermasters' Department, production inventories from the plant. His eyes popped at the huge quantities of guns and ammunition. He flipped back to the ordnance orders. The numbers didn't match. Concord Armaments was producing almost three times the number of guns that were ordered from the Union Army. He kept skimming. A name kept reappearing. A cargo ship called the Blackhawk and the Captain's name, Geoffrey Farrell. Perhaps the Blackhawk was used to ship the goods down from Concord to Washington. He turned the page and heard Alex's braying laughter. Joseph thrust the book back in the drawer, pulled out his pipe and revolved around to find Lindsey entering the library, Alex trailing behind.

"Oh, good, Mister Lindsey," Joseph said, "I was hoping to find a light for my pipe. I seemed to have forgotten matches."

Lindsey clenched his jaw. "Certainly, right here." He opened a desk drawer and pulled out some matches.

"Thank you. Sorry to be a bother," Joseph made a show of lighting his pipe. He could see Sara moving toward them, her face scrunched in a puzzled expression.

The evening's host ushered them out of the library and closed the double doors behind them with a sharp click. Joseph could feel the heat of his glare on his back.

Chapter 18

Spotsylvania Court House, Virginia

May 19, 1864

Joseph and Jeb perched on rickety camp chairs on a patch of smooth, flat ground near a tiny village called Spotsylvania Court House, fifteen miles southwest of Fredericksburg. Fat black flies buzzed thickly around them, viciously attacking their sweat-streaked faces.

Joseph fanned himself with Sara's latest letter. May in Virginia. The March 11th Harper's newspaper lay across his lap.

"This dried beef is wreaking havoc on my stomach," Jeb said and spat on the grass.

"Listen to this article, Jeb. 'Lieutenant General Ulysses S. Grant made a surprise appearance at the White House reception on March 8. Grant had just arrived in Washington and made his entrance into the crowded East Room late in the evening. This was the first meeting between President Lincoln and his new U*nion* Forces Commander.'"

"Hmmph," Jeb grunted. "Never mind Harper's. What does Sara say?"

"That she misses me, that she loves being called Mrs. Thornhill now that we're husband and wife, that she's tired of the war--"

“And you having to go rushing off again. Not a fit honeymoon, I say.”

"Amen." Joseph sighed and took a bite of the tough beef. Ugh. His jaw ached from chewing the leathery meat and he gave up. Instead he began packing his pipe with tobacco. "I guess we should get back to work pretty soon."

"Aww. Let’s take a rest for a while. Those dead men ain’t goin’ nowhere." Jeb slumped down in a chair and waved his hat to create a breeze.

"It's not the dead men I'm thinking about." Joseph pointed to the sky. "It's that storm. I expect it will dump on us within the hour."

"Damn." Jeb jumped up and the two began assembling their photographic gear from the wagon. Twenty minutes later they began to set up shots of the numerous breastworks surrounding the town.

"Nasty lookin' fortifications." Jeb referred to a series of heavy logs sharpened to deadly points, crisscrossing a long trench.

"After three long years of war, we've made an art form out of building battlements. Let's move some of the bodies over here. Make a powerful backdrop."

Twenty minutes later, they had five dead soldiers strewn in different positions with the trench in the background. Joseph peered through the camera lens.

"Prop that musket by his knee, that's right." Joseph motioned. Satisfied with the day's work, he stretched and yawned. Rain began to fall, long slivers of drops that bounced on the hard ground.

"Guess we’re done for today,” Joseph said. “It'll take a while to develop these anyhow."

Jeb looked across the field. "Say, ain't that your Major friend?"

Joseph stopped packing and looked up. He grinned at Sean O’Connor marching toward him. “Well, I’ll be. . .” Slapping at his trousers to shake the dust off, Thornhill stretched out his hand. "Sean, good to see you again."

"By God, it's hot here. Even in the rain. How can you stand it?" Sean unbuttoned the top button of his jacket.

"I don't have any control over the weather." Joseph plucked at his damp shirt. "Maybe you should take that jacket off."

"I can't. I'm on official business. Got to interview General Grant."

Jeb said, "Now that he's whuppin' ol' Bobby Lee?"

"I wish that were the reason." Sean smiled. "Excuse us a minute, Jeb." He pulled Joseph aside. "Have you run into that civilian again since we last met?"

"Not since Fredericksburg. Haven't noticed anything unusual --no mysterious bodies, at least."

Sean looked over his shoulder. "I don't like it. Ever since I saw your photo, I've been watching for him. But it's like he disappeared, or never existed."

"Did you check the hospital records in Gettysburg?"

"Aye. Nothing."

“Maybe he’s dead.”

“That would take care of the problem,” Sean said.

“What did you find out about him?”

“The sutler gave his name as Jack Cade. Records show a Jack Cade licensed as a sutler, address listed as National Hotel in Washington." Sean shrugged. "Keep your eyes open, Joseph. If the civilian and the sutler are the same man, as I suspect, he’ll know you took a picture of him. He may be gunning for us both."

Joseph’s throat suddenly went dry.

*

Jack Cade slipped into his wagon and dropped the canvas flap across the back for privacy. He propped up a stained mirror atop a trunk and pulled out a small box of makeup, dyes, and face paints that he'd borrowed from a theater manager he knew. Damn his arm hurt from that wound. He touched it gingerly, sighed. Then he set to work creating a disguise that he hoped would pass muster with that photographer as well as O'Connor, who would surely recognize him now.

With a thin artist's brush, Cade delicately painted gray steaks into his dark hair and mustache. He glued on a short beard of similar brown and gray color. Inhaling the strong chemicals, his nose twitched, and he sneezed, causing the beard to shift. Cade peered in the mirror at the crooked beard and smiled, then readjusted it on his chin.

Next, he smudged some makeup on his face and with a fine, sharply pointed tool, etched some lines in the thick paste, giving the appearance of wrinkles. A pair of rimless spectacles completed the transformation. Last, he revisited his wardrobe and finally decided on a plaid shirt, loose black trousers with suspenders, and brown boots, creating an overall look very different from his own. Cade stood back to study his new image in the foggy glass.

This is the last face Sean O'Connor is going to see.

He tweaked his suspenders, smiling.

Now if only the damn heat would let up, so this makeup won't run down my face.

He fanned himself with an old newspaper.

I'd better keep a safe distance from that photographer just in case my nose droops.

Cade stepped out of the wagon. A pale quarter moon and tens of stars were already visible in the humid night sky. The men had finished dinner and doused the cook fires. Many sat around, drinking the last of their chicory, smoking and listening to the sweet strums of a soldier's guitar.

Cade pulled out a pocket watch and realized he had been in the wagon almost two hours.

"Hey, sutler, how about some cigars?" a voice called out.

"Sure soldier." He completed the transaction then moved on.

Strolling the camp, he kept his eyes watchful for O'Connor. He crouched by his wagon and pulled a pipe from his pocket. He ambled to the far side of the encampment and back again. About to give up, O'Connor's face flashed before him from across a campfire.

Hell. He's with that damn photographer. Cade steeled himself to remain motionless. No sense getting close to the both of them. Just wait. Slowly, he rose and moved behind his wagon.

By midnight most of the troops lay in their sleeping rolls, a few remained talking quietly in clusters. Cade gazed at them, pacing back and forth outside his wagon. He drew out his pipe, lit a match, and threw it quickly to the ground. Once again, he checked his pocket watch. An hour before dawn. Cade crept through the camp, alert for the slightest sound. Except for a few guards, the camp slept. He stole quickly toward the tent a private had earlier pointed out as O'Connor's.

Heart thumping, he sucked in a deep breath and held it as he warily carved a slit through the back tent wall with a sharp blade. He hunched over, sheathed the knife. An owl screeched in the distance and he thought he heard a twig snap. He waited, nerves on edge. Nothing. He wiped a sweaty hand on his pants and drew out the ice pick. He snuck into the tent, pausing only to slow his breathing. Moonlight shone through the tent flap, casting a milky glow within.

The fake beard slipped and he pressed it to his chin with one hand. Makeup dripped into his eyes and he blotted them with his sleeve.

He crouched and waited. On the cot, a man slept with his head turned away. Cade's heart began a slow steady thrum. He crept to the cot, his arm raised, gathering strength, and rammed the ice pick deep into the back of O'Connor's neck. O'Connor gasped and convulsed, his arms and legs jerking crazily. After what seemed like an eternity, he stopped moving. With relief, Cade heard the final exhalation of breath, like a deep, restful sigh.

Cade yanked the ice pick from the dead man's neck and rolled him over. He stood above the dead man and looked down into his face. A young, dark-haired boy with brown eyes glazed in death. Choking down a startled cry, Cade dropped the weapon and toppled backward to the ground. His pulse roared in his ears.

Wrong man. I've killed the wrong man.

Rising to his knees, he groaned, fought to regain control of himself then swayed to his feet.

Retrieving the ice pick, Cade heard footsteps behind him. He held his breath.

"Hey, what the devil are you doing in my tent?"

Cade turned to face Sean O'Connor. This time he would not make a mistake. He sprang at O'Connor with the weapon raised, but the major managed to parry the blow, and the two men fell backward rolling in the dirt floor of the tent. Cade lunged for O'Connor's throat but couldn't get a firm grip. The ice pick flew out of his hand in the scuffle.

Cade had little time to complete his mission before others would hear and come to O'Connor's rescue. Then all would be lost. A new burst of adrenaline shot through his body and, reaching for a handful of dirt, he threw it into the Major's face. At the same moment, he spied the ice pick, grabbed it and fell upon O'Connor plunging it deep into his chest.

A soft gurgling noise spilled from O'Connor's lips and his eyes bulged in their sockets. His mouth moved silently then he fell still, a surprised stare in his vacant eyes.

Cade quickly yanked out the weapon and felt for the major's pulse. This time no mistake. Sean O'Connor was dead.

The next morning, Joseph poured himself some chicory, grimaced at the taste. Jeb raced over from the officer's tent, face red, eyes brimming.

"What's the matter with you?" Joseph said. He stood. "What is it, Jeb?"

"Joseph, ya' ain't gonna like this."

"Go on."

"I'm sorry, really. It's. . ."

"What?" Joseph stood.

"Yer Major friend's dead. So is some young soldier who slept on his cot."

"Dead? What do you mean dead?"

"Doncha think I know what dead means?"

"How?" Joseph threw down his mug and started moving toward O'Connor's tent.

"Hey, wait up. They's investigatin' now. Ya cain't go in there."

Joseph reached the tent, but several officers waved him off. He caught one's arm. "What happened to Major O'Connor?"

"We don't know yet, but he sure as hell didn't die in battle."

Joseph gripped his stomach as the rage flowed through him. "He's back."

"Who? What?" Jeb said.

"The civilian. He's back."

Chapter 19

Concord, Massachusetts

October 29, 1864

Joseph knocked on the door of 225 Chestnut Street in Concord. The rain of the last two days had stopped. The air hung heavy and damp and his shirt clung to him wetly under his arms and across the back. The door opened and Joseph found himself looking down at the petite and even more fragile, Louisa May Alcott. She was dressed in a Stewart plaid dress with lace collar. Her skin looked pale, but when she smiled, as the first time he'd met her ten months ago, her whole face lit up.

"Joseph. Please, do come in." She opened the door wide and stood aside, then led him into the parlor and a large emerald green divan. "I'm pleased to see you again. In her last letter Sara told me you'd be stopping by. She said something rather obscure about an investigation. It's all rather disconcerting."

Joseph squeezed his lanky frame into a tight-fitting high-back chair, narrow even for a slight man.

"Can I get you a drink? Tea?"

"Yes, thank you."

Louisa May leaped from the sofa and hurried off, minutes later returning with a china tea service on a tray.

He stood, took it from her and set it down on the small table in front of them.

“Please, sit here.” She patted the seat next to her then poured a cup of tea. Her crinolines swished on the velvet sofa.

"Charming house."

"I grew up here. It's small, but familiar."

"Family?"

"Parents. And an older married sister. Mother and father are away for a few days, visiting friends in Boston." She sipped her tea. "Let me congratulate you on your wedding-- goodness, six months ago? I'm so sorry I wasn't able to attend, but even now I'm still not completely recovered yet from my fever. I did send a note to Sara."

"She told me. I'm very sorry you couldn't be there, Louisa. Sara thinks very highly of you."

“I'm much better now.” The dark circles under her eyes told him otherwise.

“Was it a lovely wedding?” she asked, her eyes dreamy and faraway. “How did Sara look? What did she wear?"

"A simple wedding, really, with the war still on, you know. Very warm but at least it didn't rain. April, of course. But Sara . . . well, she looked very beautiful in a dress of pale blue satin. She wore a wreath of flowers, orange blossoms, on her head with a sheer veil of, er, something or other."

Louisa May sighed. "Did you have photographs taken?" She giggled. "What a silly question."

"My best man, Alex, took the photographs. I brought one for you. Sara insisted."

Joseph took out a folder from his pocket and handed it to her. She opened the cover.

"Lovely." Her voice was breathy and tears formed in her eyes. "I can envision her walking down the aisle with a bouquet of white gardenias in her arms.

He smiled. "A nice thought but not true. Affordable flowers are much too hard to find."

"Let my imagination run wild," Louisa said. "I'm a writer, you know. Words are like paintbrushes to me. I try to visualize places and people, in my mind, so that when I describe them, others can see them as I do. Quite like you do with a camera."

"You seem to have a natural talent for it, then. I, on the other hand, am forced to see things in black and white, through the eye of a lens."

"Oh, I've seen your photographs. They may be limited in color but in depth are emotionally arousing. Perhaps too much so, considering the subject matter."

"Have you completed your *Hospital Sketches*?"

"Soon. I shall send you a copy as soon as it's published. Wishful thinking on my part." She paused, waited.

"Did Sara write you very recently?"

"A few weeks ago."

Joseph smiled. "Then you know she's with child."

Louisa nodded. "I didn't want to mention it until you did, I felt . . . never mind. Congratulations. You must be so excited."

"Yes, I am. Thank you."

Louisa set her cup down. "Sara also told me that you are on a special project for the army and might be in need of assistance." She glanced at Joseph conspiratorially. "That is why you're here, isn't it?"

He lowered his voice. "Yes, in fact, it is. I'm acting as a reporter, assuming a role, that is, not as a photographer."

"Oh, goodness. Why?"

"That's a secret."

"How can I help?"

"Actually, I'm afraid to get you involved."

Louisa May frowned. "Because I'm small and frail? Or because I'm a woman?"

"Because it could be dangerous."

"Nonsense. It's my duty to help my country in any way I can." Her eyes shone with patriotic pride. "Recovering from a long and tedious illness, I've been utterly bored the last few months and need a diversion." She looked at his expression. "Oh dear. I didn't mean to trivialize this."

"I'm not sure what to make of you, Louisa May Alcott."

"Why don't you tell me what you'd have me do."

Joseph cleared his throat and leaned forward. "Tell me what you know about Concord Armaments."

She fixed her eyes on his. "They produce arms for the government and employ most of the working men in this town."

"What about the owners?" Joseph named them.

"I know *of* them. Mr. Lindsey, of course, is a generous contributor to the hospital." She paused, brow furrowed. "Might I ask why the interest in Concord Armaments?"

Joseph studied her intelligent eyes. "I'm sorry but I can't tell you."

She searched his face. "You should know that Concord Armaments used to be a factory which made pots and pans, kitchen utensils, that sort of thing. Before the war, they were struggling and the workers started leaving town for better jobs elsewhere. Once the war started, the company turned its manufacturing to guns, ammunition and artillery. Orders poured in from the government.

The men's wages were raised. They stayed. More men arrived. Now they produce arms and ship them daily. I see the wagons all the time, coming and going."

"Where are they going?" Joseph asked.

"To the railroad depot, I assume. I don't know."

"I see."

"Joseph, you will have a difficult time finding out anything. The men won't talk to you. They want to keep their jobs. They need to keep their jobs."

He nodded.

She reached for his hand. "I do hope you'll consider using me for whatever you need. I'm acquainted with everyone in this little town. Perhaps you'll need introductions, or letters written or delivered? Anything."

"I may very well do that. First, I must learn what I can on my own then determine the next steps."

"This is all so terribly intriguing. I hope to write a novel about it someday. I've been writing an outline already. It's about a family who lives through the war--mother, father and four daughters-–haven't decided if there will be a son yet." She looked at him. "Girls, you know, have a terrible time during war."

He didn't know what to say but a new respect seeped into his heart for her. "A book, then?"

"A book, pure fiction, of course, but with a hint of the truth. No need to worry. I'll wait 'til I learn the outcome of this affair before I publish."

"Good heavens," he said, eyes wide.

She laughed and it sounded like music, like Sara, to his ears.

He stood and they walked together to the door.

"I do hope to hear from you soon, Joseph."

"You'd better start calling me Christopher Meeks, reporter extraordinaire."

She giggled. "Oh yes, indeed."

As the door closed, the scent of lavender remained with him. His sense of dread dampened the pleasant sensation.

Chapter 20

Concord, Massachusetts
October 30, 1864

The next morning, after a light breakfast, Joseph left the hotel. An Indian summer sun shone and warmed his cheeks. He checked his pocket for his notepad and pencil. He rehearsed again in his mind what he would say if he ran into Samuel Lindsey. Lindsey had invited him, after all, and he had camera equipment with him if he needed to pretend to take photographs as well as write a story for the papers.

As he sloshed through the muddy streets, his boots took on a new color. As did the lower leg of his pants. The earth here seemed to be darker and redder than he was used to. The walk stretched his legs and he flexed his shoulders a few times to stretch out the kinks from the hotel mattress then rolled his sleeves up against the damp heat.

On the outskirts of town, he came to his destination: Concord Armaments. Housed in a large, four-story red brick warehouse, Joseph approached slowly, organizing his thoughts for the interview. The sound of machinery: cutting, brazing, hammering, tumbled out of the large warehouse doors, and he could see men working, sparks flying within. He looked around for the entrance to an office, changed his mind, and walked directly into the plant itself. One of the men looked up.

"Somethin' you want?" the man growled, wiping his thick hands on a grimy apron.

"I'm looking for the foreman."

"You found 'im."

All two hundred and fifty pounds of him, Joseph guessed.

He stuck out his hand. "Christopher Meeks, reporter for the Bangor Gazette in Maine. And you, Sir?"

"Wright. Harrison Wright." The foreman gave his hand a brief jerk.

Joseph cleared his throat as he studied the burly man. "I understand this armory has been the predominant supplier of arms and ammunition to the Union front."

Wright stood silent, head tilted, scratching at his bushy black beard as if fleas lived there.

"I'd be real interested in doing a story on the company. Maybe even sell it to the Boston Herald."

Wright's lip curled in a scowl. "Don't know 'bout that. Real busy here. No time for

chattin'--"

"Mr. Lindsey said it would be okay." Joseph watched the foreman's brow scrunch up in uncertainty. "How about if I tour the factory, see how the weapons are made, talk to the men."

"Can't talk to the men. They got jobs to do."

"All right then, how about if you take me on a tour yourself, and I'll give you top billing in the story."

Wright shook his head.

"Look," Joseph pressed, "how would it sound if I write an article and say 'Concord Armaments foreman refused to accommodate reporter'?"

"Hmmph." Wright snorted, then turned and looked at the workmen, who seemed intent on their jobs.

"Let's make it quick," the foreman said finally, and led Joseph into the huge, noisy plant.

Ceiling-high windows lined all four walls, providing the primary light, but certain areas of the warehouse were brilliantly lit, as if on fire, with gas lamps. In these areas, workmen assembled the finer parts of the weapon: springs, tumblers, locks and screws, using magnifying lenses to aid them. The strong smell of pig's grease permeated the air, thick and heated from the machinery and hundreds of sweaty bodies.

"What?" Wright shouted above the din.

"I said, is the foundry here too?"

"Next door. We just produce the stock and assemble the weapons here."

Joseph stepped carefully around the men and machines, ducked as some sparks flew at him. He stopped at one contraption to watch the man working it. The workman did not turn or even slow down.

"That's the rifling machine." Wright pointed.

Joseph stared at a long table attached at the far end by belts to a huge wheel. As the wheel turned, the gun barrel, held steady in a vise on the table, rotated as spiral grooves were cut into its bored interior.

“What does the ‘rifling’ do?” Joseph asked.

“Projects a bullet with greater distance and accuracy.”

Joseph jotted notes as the foreman moved on. Hurrying to catch up, he shouted, "How many weapons can you produce in a day?"

"'Bout three hundred. Now this here's where we turn the stock."

Wright kept moving. "Here's the boring machine. Barrel comes straight from foundry and we bore the holes in 'em."

Joseph caught the eye of the workman, who immediately turned back to his job.

"Can I see the foundry?" Joseph wiped his sweat-streaked forehead.

"What for?"

"To have the complete picture of the manufacturing process. Got to see where the guns are cast."

"Hot as hell in there."

"Won't stay long."

Wright looked at him and swiped the dripping sweat off his chin. He turned and marched to the far end of the room and the back doors. For a big man he moved fast. Joseph raced after him. Outside, he breathed in several gulps of fresh air before following Wright through a set of double doors which led to another oversized red-brick warehouse. When these doors opened, however, Joseph stood on the edge of an inferno.

Surely, this was what Dante meant.

A blast of heat hit him, searing his skin. He choked back a cry as he moved his head slowly from left to right, taking in the nightmarish scene. The huge space loomed dark and cavernous with few windows compared to its sister building next door. Fires roared from monstrous stoves, their stygian bellies spitting and coughing flames and bilious clouds of smoke. Towers of coal surrounded them and inky soot streaked the walls, floors, ceiling . . . and the men who fed the flames. They hunched, sweating, skin blistered red from exertion, black from soot, scooping up shovelfuls of coal, again and again without stopping. Others, blank-faced, unblinking, stood over giant cauldrons of bubbling, fetid-smelling liquid, stirring the soup with long-handled spoons.

The heavy doors slammed shut behind him. Joseph swallowed hard and suppressed an impulse to turn and run.

"This way." Wright smiled for the first time.

Joseph followed him deeper into Hell. He moved past the men stirring and shoveling, toward others hammering and brazing. This time the men looked up from their work. Some even stopped to watch him, their eyes an eerie white glow in blackened faces.

Sweat poured off Joseph and soaked his shirt. He had difficulty holding onto his pencil with wet fingers, and he kept wiping them on his clothes. Breathing took effort. His heart raced unevenly, struggling to pump oxygen through his tired lungs. Suspicious eyes stared at him from every direction. And a twinge of fear crept up his back.

Do they know who I really am?

A hand touched his shoulder. He jumped.

"Lookin' fer a job, mister?"

"Uh, no, no." He faced a pencil-thin man, with several missing front teeth. "How long have you worked here?"

"'Bout a year, maybe. Dunno 'zactly."

Suddenly Wright intervened and the skinny man ran off.

"Told ya not to bother the men. They's got work to do."

"Sorry." Joseph paused. "I think I've seen enough."

"No more questions?" Wright asked.

"A few. But how about if we go outside to talk?"

The foreman shrugged, led the way back to the giant doors. Joseph followed closely on his heels, feeling the men's eyes bore into him. His skin crawled.

Wright immediately headed into the first plant again and Joseph dogged his heels. "How do the orders come in? Do the quartermasters send--?

"Don't know 'bout paperwork. Ask the manager."

"Who's he?"

"Henry Nelson. Upstairs." Wright pointed to a staircase on the far wall that led from the plant floor to a series of open offices off an upstairs balcony.

"Could I see him now?"

Wright shrugged. "Up to him."

"Thank you, Mister Wright, I appreciate . . ." Joseph watched Wright's back disappear into the plant. He headed for the stairs. As he walked through the production areas, one man in particular seemed to be tracking him. An older man working on the planing machine. Joseph stopped and looked around. The foreman was nowhere to be seen. He approached the older man.

"Something you have to say?" he spoke quietly.

The man's eyes darted around. Abruptly he continued his work, ignoring Joseph.

"I told you not to bother the men," Wright bellowed from behind.

"Right." Joseph turned and headed toward the stairs. He knew the old man had something to tell him.

Chapter 21

Concord, Massachusetts

October 30, 1864

Henry Nelson, the plant manager, a nervous, twitchy man sported a waxed handlebar mustache that reminded Joseph of steer horns. Nelson wore his hair oiled, shiny and parted in the center. Clothes hung on his thin frame as if passed down from an older brother. But his eyes were truly disconcerting. Pale and almost transparent blue, the left one had a life of its own. It moved around the socket loosely as if scanning all directions at once.

Studying the office, Joseph noticed a large window behind Nelson's desk, overlooking the street two stories below. The furnishings were sparse and cheap and he wondered why the manager of such a wealthy concern didn't have an office befitting his station. He turned his attention to Nelson and focused on his right eye, the one that seemed to be watching him. Will Nelson believe in his ruse?

"Be happy to talk to reporters." Nelson tipped his chair back and tucked his thumbs in his waistcoat pockets. "Been with Concord Armaments since the start of the war, I'm proud to say. You may know that we switched a few years ago from manufacturing other products to producing the finest in arms for our government." His smile revealed small, pointy teeth.

Joseph addressed his original question about ordnance.

"Our orders come directly from the Quartermaster Officers who send us the paperwork. We fill the orders and ship to the location requested, or as near to as possible. Sometimes when the army is on the move, you can't always get the order to the original location, you understand?"

"How are they shipped? Rail? Wagon?"

"Wagon to Boston Harbor then by cargo ship down to Baltimore. From there, wagon or rail."

"Any chance I can see some of those orders? I'd like to make this article as authentic as possible."

"Sounds like you're new at this job?"

Joseph nodded. *You wouldn't believe how new.*

"Let me check my record books." Nelson opened some drawers in a nearby cabinet and pulled out a large ledger. From the back of the book, he withdrew several loose documents. "Here are some orders from the 91st Pennsylvania and the 44th New York. Have a look at those while I check on a few things. Be right back." Nelson carried the ledger with him.

Joseph flipped through the documents. Some of the dates had been crossed out and new dates entered. These were not the originals. As soon as Nelson was out the door, Joseph sprang up. He raced to the cabinet and drew out another ledger. On immediate inspection everything seemed in order. He pulled open a second drawer. Nothing out of the ordinary. The third drawer was locked.

Damn.

He heard footsteps, raced quickly to his chair and picked up the documents.

"Those help you out any?" Nelson opened the door.

"Yes, thanks. Any chance I can talk to the men?"

"You can talk to the men, but after work. We don't want to get Wright all riled up, now, do we?"

Joseph half-smiled. "Definitely not."

"The men go down to the Quincy Pub most every night. You can meet them there."

"What about the owners?"

"None of them are in town right now."

Thank God.

"Any other questions?"

"Tell me, Mister Nelson, do you ever have any complaints about the company's products from the field?"

Nelson narrowed his good eye. "Complaints? Well, a few, to be sure, but our record is relatively unmarred by major dissatisfactions. Naturally, when you produce such large supplies of high quality arms as quickly as we do, there's bound to be some manufacturing flaws. Why do you ask?"

"No specific reason." Joseph jotted a note down on his pad. "I understand you're experimenting with new alloys here to make stronger, more efficient weapons. Can you comment on that?"

"Yessiree. In fact, we are the only private arms company working with these new materials."

"And how do these new metals work?"

Nelson leaned over his desk. "We're collecting data from the field even as we speak. I'd be happy to share the results with you once the information is tallied."

"Are these new amalgamates cheaper to produce? I mean, will the ordnance be cheaper for the government to purchase? What about reliability? How will they hold up under action?"

"Yes, er, to your first question. They will be considerably cheaper to produce. Again, we don't know yet how they will withstand fire, but we have every confidence they will prove far superior to those that came before."

Joseph looked down at his notepad. "From some of the records I've checked, it appears that an order filled over a year ago was only about half the cost of one of the same quantity filled a month ago. That tells me that this new alloy is, indeed, twice as expensive to purchase. Can you explain that?"

Nelson bristled. "Well, er, naturally other costs go up. The price of shipping, and men's wages have risen greatly over the year."

"Sounds like they've doubled."

"In some instances." Nelson glared at him with his one good eye.

"One other thing. The men I've talked with in the field have bitter complaints about the ordnance. They say that they've had more problems with their weapons, artillery and ammunition than is usual, and that the ordnance is getting progressively worse as the war goes on. Can you comment on that, Mister Nelson?"

The manager stood up, almost knocking his chair over. "It sounds like you're trying to find a story that doesn't exist. Fabricate a controversy to sell papers. Is that how you plan to make your mark as a reporter? Well, you won't get any help from me. Concord Armaments is a reputable concern doing business for years with the United States government. Never been a problem before. And I resent your implication that there's one now."

Joseph was sorely tempted to respond but held his tongue.

"This interview is over. I'm a busy man. I must get back to work. I assume you can find your way out?"

"Thank you for your time, Mister Nelson. I'll be sure to send a copy of the article when it's published."

On the street, Joseph sucked in a few deep breaths.

Guess I won't be taking up acting anytime soon.

He started down the muddy street toward the town Pub. Had he looked back at Concord Armaments and up toward the window next to Henry Nelson's, he would have seen the pinched and tight-lipped expression on Samuel Lindsey's countenance.

Chapter 22

Concord, Massachusetts

October 30, 1864

The Quincy Pub stood like a welcome sentinel at the east end of town. Built around 1770, its walls, inside and out, were made of a flat, gray stone grouted with mud. The Pub had survived surprisingly well over the years and as Joseph entered, he admired the heavy chestnut beams that crisscrossed the ceiling and the thick, knotted pine that planked the floor. Dark and smoky, the air was saturated with various aromas of pipe tobacco, cigars, beer and hard liquor. Joseph wound his way through countless unwashed bodies to the bar. He did a slow scan of the pub, wondering which of the men worked at Concord Armaments.

The barkeep regarded him somberly. "New 'round here?"

"Name's Meeks. Reporter from Maine."

"Ahyup."

"Doing a story on Concord Armaments."

The barkeep wiped the bar but raised an eyebrow.

"I heard that some of the workmen might be found here after hours. I'd like to interview them for the story. Can you point any of them out to me?"

The man hesitated. When he spoke, his lips barely moved. "That table there." He tilted his head toward a table in the far corner of the tavern. Three men sat in their work clothes, a bottle of whisky on the table.

"Much obliged." Joseph took his drink with him and introduced himself to the workmen. They ignored him, went on talking with each other.

"Mind if I sit?" He pulled a chair out. "Let me buy you gents drinks." He called out to the bartender for another bottle.

The men's eyes were fixed on their drinks.

"That's quite a factory you work in. Mister Wright gave me the ten-cent tour today. Have you been there long?"

No reply.

"Look, gentlemen, you have your jobs, and I just want to do mine. Find out more about Concord Armaments. After all, they are the leading supplier of weapons for the army."

The three men looked at him.

"Something you're hiding?"

One man finally spoke. "You'd better get your story somewheres else. We like our jobs here mighty fine."

"Why would you lose your jobs because of me?"

"We just do what we're told," another said.

"And you were told not to talk to me."

Joseph sensed the hostility rolling off the men in waves.

He leaned into the table. "Help me out here. This could be good for all of us. You know, get your names in print?"

They glared at him. He glared back.

"Enjoy your drinks, gentlemen. On me." Joseph stood, kicking the chair out of the way. He walked back to the bar. Out of the corner of his eye he recognized the old timer he had seen at the planing machine earlier. The man leaned against the unlit stone fireplace and watched him closely.

Joseph laid some money on the bar, turned to leave when, unexpectedly, the man bumped into him. In the confusion of spilled drinks and apologies, the older man whispered, "What room you stayin' in?"

Joseph peered into his rheumy eyes. "Room four, top of the stairs."

He left the pub and walked quickly back to the hotel. In his room, second thoughts crept in. He gathered the revolver and ammunition that Sara had insisted he bring, checked the barrel and stuffed it in his pocket. If the old man noticed it, so much the better.

At midnight, Joseph heard a soft knock. He gripped his pistol and opened the door slowly. The old man stood there, grinned a gap-toothed smile and held up a bottle of whiskey and two glasses. "Didn't think this dump would have glasses," he said and stepped into the room. The stranger set the bottle on the dresser, yanked the cork out and poured the whisky. Joseph watched him: scraggly beard, gray-brown hair, thin to the point of emaciated, age anywhere between forty-five and sixty.

The man gave him a glass, downed a third of his own in one swallow.

"Name's Otis Redburn. Saw you at the plant today. Then I hear'd you askin' the other workmen 'bout the company." The word company had a peculiar emphasis. "That true--you a reporter?"

Joseph nodded and sat down on the bed as he gestured for Redburn to sit in the only chair in the room. "If you overheard my conversation with the workmen, then you know that. Why do you want to talk to me? Aren't you afraid of losing your job?"

"Well, I'll tell ya. I know work's hard to get, but there's more important things in this world than money. I'll get by. Cuz, ya see, if I don't get fired, I'm gonna quit. I can't work for a company that's killin' our men what's fightin' and dyin' for us. Nossir."

Redburn jumped to his feet, and Joseph reached for his pistol. But the old man just went to pour another drink. He sat back down with his glass. "See, it's like this. I been workin' for the company for goin' on two years now. All along they been doin' some funny things."

"Funny things?"

"They been cheatin', ya know, not using the best materials, leaving parts out of the weapons, fillin' the cartridge boxes only half full, stuff like that. But now it's gettin' worse-- these new metals they're using don't stand up to firing, and they know it. They've been testin' 'em over and over. But they still make 'em out of this junk metal. Why? Cuz it's cheap, that's why. And the company's makin' money by the barrelful, but our boys are gettin' kilt, for nothin'." Redburn let out a pent up breath.

"Something more?"

"I got me a son. He's fightin' for the 116th New Hampshire. Last year I got this here letter from him." Redburn reached into his jacket pocket and pulled out a rumpled piece of paper. He held it a moment, looked at it, offered it to Thornhill. "Since then I've received 'bout four more letters, all similar, all describin' the same type a' problems with weapons. Saved 'em all but I brought this one special so's you'd know what I mean." Redburn shrugged his bony shoulders. "He's a smart boy--much smarter'n me. Educated, ya know? I can't read too good myself. Had someone read me the letters. Go on."

Joseph unfolded the letter, looked up at Redburn, who stared down at his glass.

"Read it aloud, Mister Meeks."

"July 18, 1863

Dear Dad,

I'm writing this letter a few weeks after a fierce battle at a little place called Gettysburg on the Pennsylvania-Maryland border. Folks here say it used to be a peaceful town but it will never be the same again. Still, we can only hope this is the beginning of the end. I was one of the lucky ones, only a few scrapes, no real injuries. But some of my good friends are gone. Remember Lloyd Axel? He passed in front of a Minié ball, and it took him in the eye--blew him right off his feet. I tried to help, but he was dead instantly. It was an awful sight--part of his head blown away, but he still had that same half smile that he always wore, you know, like he was funnin' the Lord or something.

And, Dan'l Crooks--my friend from the 25th Infantry Regt, Ohio. . . he didn't make it neither. He was whomped to smithereens by cannon debris. Strangest thing, that. The cannon seemed to heat up red hot and the shell exploded as it left the muzzle. It blew up the barrel and bits of hot metal went flying everywhere. Dan'l wasn't even firing the cannon, just standing nearby. This isn't the first time one of our guns has blown up like that. The shells we've been supplied with are faulty--the fuses are too short or are duds, and even when the fuses are fine, the shells fall short or go long. There's nothin' the gunners can do about it. Some of the cannon projectiles are not weighted properly and can't be aimed with any semblance of accuracy."

Joseph stopped, cleared his throat. He looked at Redburn who was staring into the air. He continued reading.

"I've been mighty lucky, had some near misses myself. My musket nearly fell apart after one battle. Had to exchange two of them now and finally got myself an Enfield, which seems to be of far better quality. I guess you'll find it amusing that my defective muskets were manufactured at Concord Armaments. Ha Ha.

"Dad, I truly miss the cool green and blue North, and believe it or not I even miss doing chores around the house. (I'll bet you'll remind me of this when next I complain!) The blasted heat and bugs down south are vicious in the summer and that's where we're headed. Home seems very far away and my old life seems like a dream these days. I will try to write as soon as I can. Have someone write your words to me. I'll know it's you. Your loving son, Edward."

After a long silence, Joseph spoke. "Mister Redburn, how serious are you about helping me?"

Redburn looked at him with fire in his eyes. "'Bout as serious as a man can be."

"I mean, well. . . helping me could be dangerous."

"Don't make no never mind to me, nossir. My boy's out there fightin' with our weapons. He could've been one a' them casualties."

"You're still an employee in good standing at Concord Armaments? And no one has any reason to think you'd suspect them of doing anything illegal?"

"No reason I can see."

"Too bad you can't read or write," Joseph said almost to himself.

Redburn's face fell.

"Wait a minute. There may be someone who can help. She can read and write." Joseph stood up and walked to the window, looked out. His heart felt swollen with empathy for Redburn.

"A woman?"

"Yes. An intelligent woman."

"I got me a real good memory," Redburn said. "If I get the information to her and she writes it down--that good enough?"

"Can you remember names and dates? Of shipments from Concord Armaments?"

"Yep. Sure can. Trust this ole brain." Redburn tapped his head with a finger. "Now who's this lady that's fixin' ta be my secretary?"

"Miss Louisa May Alcott. She lives in town, 225 Chestnut Street."

"Well, I'll be . . . I know Miss Louisa. She used to help my boy with his writing. Good woman. That's fine, jest fine. What do I do?"

"Bring her the information and she'll get it to me at the newspaper office. I'll let her know it's an old friend she'll be working with. Now there's one . . ." Joseph stopped.

The old man screwed up his eyes. "There's somethin' else, ain't there?"

"When I was in Nelson's office today, I found a locked drawer in one of the ledger cabinets. I need to get into that. Any way you can sneak me back there tonight?"

"Now? Jaysus." Redburn scratched his head.

"It's important."

"They's got a crew workin' all night, but it's spare, 'bout six men. Might be we can try sneakin' up the side fire ladder to the office floor. I don't know--if we get caught--"

"Not we, Mister Redburn, me. Just show me the way."

"I can do that. Sure you'll be okay? I mean, if you get caught . . . " Redburn stomped his foot. "Nossir. No--"

"What do you mean no?"

"I'm goin' with ya."

"You can lose your job for this," Joseph said.

"Hell. Lindsey and his cronies need to be brought up by their bootstraps, by God. I cain't sleep for thinking about those boys dying out there. My boy. I'm going with you. Come on." The old man headed straight for the door, not looking back.

Joseph tucked his gun in his waistband and hurried after him.

Chapter 23

Concord, Massachusetts

October 30, 1864

They stood across the street from Concord Armaments and watched from behind a sprawling elm. The main plant cast a feeble yellow light out into the street, but the upstairs windows were dark. A dog bayed in the distance, sending chills up Joseph's spine. A low-lying fog blanketed the deserted street and his feet disappeared below the ankle.

"This way." Redburn skittered to the side of the building, looked over his shoulder, leaped, and grabbed hold of the fire ladder. He climbed halfway up to the second story as Joseph pulled himself up to the first rung. When Redburn reached the window, he held onto the ladder with one hand and slid the window up. Then he threw his leg over the ledge and scrambled in. Joseph followed.

He and the old man stood and listened. Satisfied no one had heard them enter, Joseph headed straight for the locked drawer in the old wooden cabinet. Pulling out his knife he began to pry at the hook which held the drawer locked, while Redburn lit a lamp that he found on the desk.

"That's better." Joseph continued to play with the lock until he heard a snap. He looked at Redburn. Then he flipped through the drawer, searching the documents. He pulled out one file, then another and began skimming through them. When he finished each, he slid it back in the drawer. Until he came to one called Cape Lookout. He opened it and began to read. "Where's Cape Lookout?" Joseph said. "Ever heard of it?"

Redburn shook his head. "Nowhere around here. Wait, there's a map on the wall."

Joseph grabbed the lamp and held it in front of the map. He ran his finger down the eastern coast starting at Boston. It took a few minutes but his finger finally came to rest on Cape Lookout. "Cape Lookout. North Carolina."

"The South?" Redburn whispered. "I'll be damned."

Joseph continued shuffling through the notes. "Large quantities of goods being shipped from Concord to New Bedford Harbor--onto a ship called the Blackhawk." The same name mentioned in the logbook, Joseph recalled, when he'd rummaged through Lindsey's desk during the New Year's party. "According to this, the side-wheel frigate makes frequent trips from New Bedford to Cape Lookout." Joseph stared at Redburn. "Nelson told me they shipped goods out of Boston to Baltimore. Sounds like they use New Bedford Harbor to ship to the South. Damn."

"Thievin' traitors." Redburn sniffed in indignation.

Joseph continued to sift through the books. He stopped abruptly when he came to one manifest. "Looks like the Blackhawk takes delivery in New Bedford in a few weeks." He stared into space. "I've seen enough. Let's get out of here."

"Sssh." Redburn hissed. Footsteps ascended the stairs. Both men froze. Redburn blew out the lamp then licked his fingers and damped it. Joseph pulled the old man toward the desk, and they both crawled under it, pulling the chair in front of them just as the door opened.

A harsh yellow light from the hallway sliced through the blackness. Joseph squeezed his body back as far as he could in the tight space and held his breath. He could smell whisky on Redburn's breath. Sucking in a deep gulp of air, he held his breath until he thought he'd explode. But surely whoever was there would hear his heart pounding?

The door closed and the footsteps moved away.

He noticed it then. The cabinet drawer was still open.

A voice shouted from outside the door. "Whadya doin' now?"

"I heard somethin' up here."

"Let's go, for chrissakes, Jocko. Ain't nothin' there."

"Yeah, lemme just check."

"I wanna drink. Let's get outta here."

"Just a minute, will ya?" Footsteps stopped down the hall and the adjacent office door opened with a squeak.

Joseph touched Redburn's arm then dashed out from beneath the desk and softly closed the drawer. A door slammed shut. Joseph scurried under the desk again, Redburn tugging at his sleeve.

"Jesus, Jocko. Let's go."

The door to their office opened once more. Joseph bit his upper lip to keep from exhaling.

"Jocko."

"Yeah, yeah, yeah. Aw, what the hell." The door slammed closed.

Joseph exhaled, touched Redburn's arm. "You okay?"

"Nearly shat my pants. Son of a--" Redburn stood shakily.

"Let's get out of here." Joseph quickly put the files back in the cabinet, carefully arranging them in the original order. Then he closed and locked the drawer and the two men hurried out the way they came in. Someone was bound to notice the knife scratches on the cabinet drawer in the morning. Nothing could be done about it now.

Back in the hotel room, Redburn poured two whiskeys. He stared at Joseph.

"What?" Joseph said.

"I got me a suspicion that you ain't no reporter."

A minute went by before Joseph answered. "And you'd be right. I'm a photographer with the Union Army. I, er, do a little investigating as well."

Redburn arched an eyebrow.

"Right now I'm looking into complaints of defective arms. Trail led directly to the door of Concord Armaments."

"A Union photographer? Jaysus." Redburn gave him a somber look and swigged down the last of the whisky. "Thanks for bein' honest. Truth's important, least to me."

"To me too, Mister Redburn."

Redburn stood up and held out his hand. "I do thank ya Mister, er, Meeks yer right name?"

"Thornhill, Joseph Thornhill."

"Thank you for givin' me the chance to help my son. . .and my country, by God." The old man smiled. "Yessir, we're gonna catch them no-good sumsa bitches at their own game."

Joseph held the old man's hand a moment. "Dammit all, Mister Redburn I do believe you're right."

"What we gonna do now?" Redburn asked.

"I want you to get all the information you can from the company and get it to Miss Alcott right away. Ordnance orders, numbers, places, where it's being delivered and how. Names of the Quartermasters, anything you can learn. Can you do that?"

"I can do that, yessir."

"My job will be to find proof of their treason, Mister Redburn. And to do that, I need to begin at the end--the port of departure: New Bedford Harbor.

Chapter 24

New Bedford Harbor, Massachusetts

November 11, 1864

Joseph felt at home in this small New England coastal town. New Bedford Harbor was not unlike Portsmouth, New Hampshire, a town he had visited with his dad often as a boy. Strolling the docks, he savored the cloying smell of fish and saltwater. He slipped on the seaweed covering the dock like so many wet snakes, and he took pleasure in the shouting and swearing of the seamen as they hoisted their loads aboard the ships. Dozens of crates waited on the dock to be hauled aboard the vessels. Sailors, merchantmen, and even young children ran about ducking and dodging horses and wagons.

Joseph hoped that his memories of the fishing town would provide adequate preparation for this role so he wouldn't immediately betray himself as a landsman.

He dug his hands into the pockets of his blue duck trousers that fit tight around the hips and flared at the bottom. A white and blue checked shirt matched the trousers. He considered his hat the most important accessory. Made of black tarpaulin, the tam sat pushed back on his head so that half a length of black ribbon hung over his left eye. Joseph tied a red bandanna around his neck. The costume was used and well-worn. His complexion and hands were already weathered from traveling the road for so long. He'd left his satchel with Louisa and purchased an old haversack, which he slung over one shoulder. He looked passable for a sailor.

Joseph sauntered up and down the dock and kept a sharp eye for the Blackhawk. He'd sent a dispatch to Pinkerton about his discoveries at Concord Armaments and had hoped to have new instructions by now. But there was no word and no time to wait. The Blackhawk would be sailing soon and with it, its cargo of high treason.

Three ships, fancy-rigged schooners, had anchored at the south side of the dock but none bore the name Blackhawk. Joseph stood a moment, taking in the salt breezes, feeling almost elated despite his perilous mission. At the end of the pier he came to a seedy-looking pub. A paint-chipped sign creaked above the door as it swung in the light wind: *Her Mistresses Chains*. Joseph entered, tripping on a step that he missed in the dimness. He peered into the gloom and inhaled the heavy scent of tobacco smoke.

"What'll it be, sailor?" a barrel-chested bartender asked, his tone friendly as he stretched blunt fingers on the bar.

"A cold brew if you've got one."

"That we do." The bartender's hairy hand pulled on a spigot, drawing beer into a large pewter mug. He set the mug down in front of Joseph and held out a hand for coins.

"New around here, then?" the bartender asked.

"I am."

"Where from?"

"Portsmouth. Looking for some work shipboard. Know where I might find some?"

The barkeep eyed him closely then motioned to a man seated at a corner table. The man finished his beer, and wiping his mouth with a sleeve, walked over. Large, stooped-shouldered, his face weathered with a thousand folds and creases, the sailor leaned on the bar.

"Lem, this young feller's lookin' for some work. Kin 'ya use a strappin' lad such as this?"

The man screwed up his eyes at Joseph. "An' what be yer qualifications?"

"First, whom do I have the pleasure of addressing, and might I buy you a drink, Sir?" Thornhill stalled answering the question.

"Aye, I'll take a drink, that's fer sure. Lem Jacobs." The man held out a callused hand. "Second mate on the California."

"I saw her dockside. She's a beauty." Joseph studied Jacobs, and then as three men entered the pub, turned his eyes to the door. The men sat down at a table and called out for beers. They didn't seem a threat so Joseph returned his gaze to Jacobs.

"She's a beauty all right, the California." Jacobs agreed. "And just three years aloft."

"Actually, I've heard a lot about a ship called the Blackhawk. Might you know anything about her?"

Jacobs raised an eyebrow at the bartender. The other three men fell silent, and their eyes remained unflinching on his.

Jacobs shrugged his shoulders and said, "We got nothin' to do with that one. Now are ye interested in sailing on the California, or ain't ye?"

"Might be. When does she sail?"

"Week from tomorrow. If ye be wantin' a job aboard, be here that mornin'." Jacobs nodded to the bartender and left.

Joseph raised his eyebrows. "Something I said?"

"Aye. Blackhawk." The bartender moved to the other end of the bar, clearing mugs along the way.

Joseph looked around. The three men at the table sat silent, staring at their drinks. After his experience at the Quincy Pub, he knew he wouldn't get information from these men. He chugged his beer and headed to the door.

Outside, a thick fog rose up to meet the dusk. At the end of the dock, he rounded the corner to the inlet side. Peering through the ghostlike film, he could make out the shape of a ship. Moving closer, through a curious gap in the fog, he spied a large, sleek vessel--a side-wheel frigate with three masts--sitting tall, almost regal in the water. The huge vessel disappeared then loomed into view like an ethereal spirit. Painted glossy black with crimson trim, the ship stood apart from the others, like the Prince of Darkness in Gabriel's Valley. On the bow, in large red letters that looked painted with blood: *Blackhawk.*

Goosebumps covered his body as he stared at the blockade runner. Must be two hundred-fifty feet long and can probably top twelve knots.

He noticed that even with her sails still furled, scores of men sprinted about readying the Blackhawk for a journey.

He heard a shout, "Move ye bloomin' ass, by God!"

"Who ya be tellin' what ta do, ya son of a whore," came the reply.

At that moment, a high pitched squealing sound caused Joseph to spin around. A sailor pointed to the sky. Joseph tilted his head upward and watched a rope hoisting a large wooden crate aboard the Blackhawk. The crate swayed and shimmied twenty feet off the ground as the rope creaked and groaned from the weight. Joseph could see the rope fraying as it carried the weight.

"The rope! It's going to snap!" he shouted to the seamen. Too late, he looked up again in time to see the crate come careening down toward him. Diving to the dock, he tucked and rolled, his shoulder coming to a painful thud against the side of a barrel. The crate hit the deck with a shattering crash and broke apart.

Jesus. He exhaled and stood up, trembling, and brushed himself off.

"Son of a bitch. Now look what ye done," a sailor shouted.

"Ain't my fault the rope tore, is it?" another one argued.

A crowd formed.

Joseph looked back to the place he had been standing just seconds before. The wooden crate lay broken in splinters and its contents strewn across the boardwalk. Guns. Rifle muskets, pistols, carbines.

Joseph pushed his way through the throng to get a closer look. He had to identify the manufacturer. Sailors collected the weapons, piling them into barrels to be repacked for the voyage. His eye caught some words on a broken sliver of crate and he bent to pick it up.

He ran his fingers over the black letters: Concord Armaments.

On it its way to Cape Lookout, no doubt.

Joseph looked up at the Blackhawk. He could make out the shape of a man standing on the bow, but in the light of dusk could not see his features. Suddenly a light appeared next to the man. A sailor had lit a lamp and held it up. Joseph made out the face: weathered brown skin, a beak-like nose, an unpleasant scowl curling his top lip. Across his left cheek, an ugly red scar tore its way down past his chin to his neck. Spiders crawled under Joseph's skin.

A young boy came up beside him and stared up at the ship. The boy stood shoulder-height to him, barefoot and shabbily dressed. Joseph stepped back wondering if the child would pick his pockets. But the boy only looked up and waved.

"Do you know who that is standing on the foredeck?"

"That's the ship's captain, Cap'n Farrell. Ain't that scar on his cheek a bee-yoot? He had a fight with this guy. . . killed him, he did, but not before he got slashed with a broken bottle."

At the sound of a long, low whistle, the boy raced off.

The Blackhawk made ready to sail.

Joseph moved aside as two men pushed a heavy crate past him. Skirting around some large trunks, he watched the men labor for a while, keeping his eye on the captain. In the moonless night, the only light was from oil torches scattered around the deck. He stumbled on some burlap bags and small containers waiting to be loaded.

Joseph was relieved that he no longer needed to find his way aboard. He knew exactly what cargo the Blackhawk was shipping. He would report to Pinkerton as soon as he reached his hotel. He stepped away from the activity.

What was that? He stopped, listened. A creak? He moved again. Stopped. A footfall?

Joseph turned. An indistinguishable shape approached.

"Who's there?" he shouted.

No answer.

The shadow emerged from the blackness, revealing a craggy-faced seaman, long knife gripped in his right hand.

"Hey now mister, what do you think you're doing? I don't have any money." Joseph held his hands in front of him, palms forward, hoping the man would see he was unarmed.

Short and powerfully built, the man lashed out with muscular arms and thick hands, knife slashing within inches of Joseph's gut. Joseph jumped back and turned, expecting to run but found the way blocked by two more men. He recognized them from the pub. One grinned a feral smile of jagged teeth, while the other chewed a wad of tobacco, brown muck oozing out the side of his mouth. Joseph rotated in a tight circle watching them close in. His brawn wouldn't get him out of this mess. He had to use his brain. Maybe a surprise offensive. With a swift kick he trounced the first man in the groin.

"Argh," sounded from the sailor as he doubled up then breathlessly muttered, "get 'em."

Joseph darted through the opening left by the downed man and ran, legs pumping and feet pounding across the wooden dock. Footfalls closed in behind him. *Jesus, it's no use. I'm cut off.* He guessed the land's end of the dock would be only a few hundred feet away. Maybe, he'd lose the men in the maze of town streets and alleys, get back to his room where he'd left his haversack and gun.

A two-story structure reared up out of the darkness. He raced toward the warehouse, the men's footsteps close behind. Crashing into the large doors, he pounded and pushed at them.

Locked.

He turned and realized the men slowed down. They hadn't seen him. He held his breath, ran around to the other side. No entrance. He looked up, wishing he could fly to the roof. A window on the second floor had a fire ladder suspended from the sill--about eight feet off the ground. He'd have to jump high enough to grab the lowest rung. Could he make it? Did he have enough time to try? Pressing himself against the wall, he listened for the sound of running footsteps. One on the left. One on the right. They had split up, circling.

Joseph sucked in a deep breath, wiped the sweat from his face, and lunged for the ladder. Missed. He lunged again, this time fingers grabbing the bottom rung. Just as he wrapped his second hand around the bar, he felt arms tugging at his legs. He couldn't hold on and tumbled to the ground.

The three men were ready for him. Each held a knife.

Joseph held up his hands in surrender. "Whoa, easy now. You win. What the hell do you want with me? I'm just looking for a job." He panted, leaning over bent knees.

"So, ye're interested in a job? Aboard the Blackhawk, eh? Well, that's jest what yer gonna get, eh mates? Captain Farrell needs more able-bodied men."

The men surrounded him and held his arms as they dragged him to the loading ramp.

"Take him aboard and tie him up in steerage 'til we set sail," the first man ordered.

The others grunted. Before Joseph could utter another sound, a sharp thunk to his head came from behind. The pain caught him short and lights blinked before his eyes. His stomach heaved its contents onto his shoes. The world fell dim and fuzzy. As he sank to his knees, he lifted his head to gaze up at the Blackhawk. Captain Geoffrey Farrell smiled down at him. A boot to the head put him out.

Chapter 25

Cape Lookout, North Carolina
February 12, 1865

Joseph Thornhill woke in a daze. No longer asail, the ship was docked somewhere.

But where?

He sat up and shifted his bruised and scarred body. For almost four months, he'd kept track of every day by using his thumbnail to scratch a mark on his belt. His home had been the steerage compartment of the Blackhawk, an exceedingly uncomfortable area not fit for man or beast, filled with coils of rigging, spare sails, ship stores and various other baggage. At times he'd sweltered in the heat or shivered with cold and damp. Food was scarce and what he'd eaten was unfit for human consumption: worm-riddled bread, greasy broth, and to drink: tepid water teeming with suspicious-looking particles. But then prisoners weren't human. As a reminder of his status, his chains rattled noisily when he tried to rearrange his position.

Joseph often wondered why Farrell hadn't killed him. Now he assumed he was alive because the Captain wanted to torture him instead. On rare occasions he could visit the deck but only when the ship was far out at sea without land in sight. Ten times in four months his chains were undone when the ship battled fierce storms and they needed all hands. The only thing that kept him going were thoughts of Sara. They'd been married six month before he disappeared. And she was with child. The thought of a son or daughter had kept him going.

My poor Sara. You must certainly think I'm dead.

Joseph wiped his nose with the back of his hand. He examined his aching body, probing black and blue bruises gently with his fingers. But his will remained strong and came back in a rush when he spied gulls flying overhead. He was near land. Where? Now he could put into practice what he'd been rehearsing for weeks--slipping his hands and feet out of the chains by greasing them with pump oil. He'd lost so much weight that the manacles fit loosely around his wrists and ankles.

Sliding back as far as his chains would allow, Joseph reached behind some crates for the oil tin he had stowed away. He spilled some out on his left wrist, and with his right hand twisted and turned the chain bracelet. The pain made him dizzy and his wrist began to tear and bleed. Stubbornly he kept spinning the metal band and after five minutes his left hand came free. A far shorter time than when he first starting practicing. Wiping blood on his trousers, he began working on the right wrist and had it free within minutes. He then tied strips of cloth from a torn sail nearby around his wrists to stem the bleeding and went to work on his ankle. He winced at the mere thought of sliding the manacle over an ankle bone, but he took a deep breath and began to push and twist at the metal fastener. The pain made his eyes water and he bit his tongue to keep from crying out.

An hour later, exhausted, he dropped the chains on the floor. His ankles throbbed, swollen and bloody. Again, he tied strips of canvas around the joints. Gathering all his strength, he leaned on the crates and pulled himself to his feet. One of his knees buckled under him, and he collapsed to the deck with a groan. He lay there a moment then tried to rise again. Finally, breathless and lightheaded, he stood holding onto the crate. He tried to stretch the muscles in his legs, but sharp pains shot through them as if punishing him for their long imprisonment. He shook out one leg, then another and stretched his back to loosen the kinks. Every movement agonized him.

He held his breath and listened for voices. Evidently, he had slept through much of the unloading, because only a few shouts could be heard and no footsteps aft and stern pounded above. Still he waited in the dark, stuffy steerage hold.

Is it night or day? He lost track of time and couldn't even be sure what season it was.

All quiet above. Joseph reached up to the hatch and slowly pushed upward. He blinked sweat out of his eyes and murmured a silent prayer. The hatch was unlocked. Joseph lifted it slightly, enough to peer about the deck. Dark and still.

Ahhh, the cool, fresh air felt wonderful. He inhaled deeply and looked around again. No one. Again he listened but didn't hear a sound. Gently he lifted the hatch all the way and slipped silently onto the deck. Closing the hatch behind him, he crouched low and slithered over to the ship's side ladder. He threw his leg over and caught the top rung with his toes then quickly shimmied down into the sea. Once in the cool water, he swam around to the far side of the dock, away from the moored ships and the tavern lights. The freezing water felt astonishingly good, the salt soothing his wounds.

Joseph floated under the pier for a few minutes to catch his breath. His arms and legs felt maddeningly weak. He swam a bit, treaded water, swam some more. Buoyed by the sea and his return to freedom, strength began to creep through his muscles. He swam for longer periods, deeper strokes.

When he returned to the pier, Joseph decided not to risk climbing up. Instead, he began swimming toward a small coved inlet. By the time he dragged himself onto the sandy beach, he was exhausted and beaten. He hobbled toward some trees out of sight of the beach and through sheer force of will hauled some dead leaves and branches to cover himself for protection and warmth.

Just need to catch my breath.

He lay on the ground smelling the sweet fragrance of ferns and pine needles beneath his head and closed his eyes. More comfortable than he had been in months, he fell asleep.

Rustling jolted him awake. He sat up, pain racking his side, fear of being captured gnawing at his gut. Leaves crunched lightly and Joseph crouched and held his breath. Two eyes blinked at him in the darkness--eyes circled by a white and brown mask.

Raccoon. Jesus. He exhaled deeply as the animal scurried into the woods.

The dark night enveloped him with safety, and he gazed up thankfully at the bright pinpoints of light in the sky. At least he hadn't slept until daylight. He felt stronger now. The swim had stretched his muscles and pumped his blood. He had to find food. Peering into the darkness he noted with surprise how good his vision was. After being chained in the dark for so long he had become a creature of the night. Now he saw the vague outline of trees and brush. In the distance the water glistened with moonlight, and the Blackhawk bobbed and swayed gently at the end of the pier.

Joseph rested a moment longer, listening intently. Satisfied he was alone, he stood up and brushed the dirt and leaves from his bedraggled clothes. He noticed smells other than saltwater and seaweed, smells of tall oaks near the shore and the mulberry bushes a few yards inland. This brought a small smile to his lips. When was the last time he had smiled? He rubbed at his stiff jaw and was reminded he now had a thick, scratchy beard.

The war! Christ! What about the war?

It hadn't ended, he knew that for certain. If it had, the gunrunners would be out of business. But what was the status? And where was he? He had to reach Alex, then Pinkerton or Colonel Baxter in Washington. Had Redburn gotten those documents to him? No time for questions now.

Joseph hobbled stiffly toward campfires in the distance. Crouching low he crept up on a small encampment of soldiers. Confederate soldiers. Hell. The South. The port must be Cape Lookout, the one port of call the blockade runners seemed able to get through to. He slumped wearily, the realization of how far he had to go hitting him like grapeshot.

But I'm free and somehow I'll make my way north, even if I have to crawl.

He stole up to the encampment and watched. Only a few guards sat by the fire, talking quietly. One stood up and started moving in his direction. Joseph dashed for cover behind a heavy thicket of ferns. He held his breath as a young soldier came by to relieve himself. That uniform--he needed it. But how? His hands shook. He had never killed a man before. Quickly, he scanned the ground at his feet and found a heavy rock about the size of his palm.

Now, before he gets away! Joseph took a deep breath and pounced on the man. He raised his arm and brought the rock down on his head. The sound of rock upon bone caused Joseph's whole body to vibrate with dread. The soldier uttered a soft whimper and crumpled to the dirt. Joseph knelt by the boy and rolled him over, hoping he had only wounded him. But the private was dead, eyes staring, mouth agape.

Joseph squeezed his eyes shut and murmured a silent prayer. Dead bodies were familiar to him. But there was something different about a man he had killed himself. In disgust, he quickly stripped the body of its rag tag uniform and boots and prayed they would fit. Finally, Joseph dragged the body and hid it in the bushes. It wouldn't be long before the soldier's friends came looking for him. Maybe they'd think he deserted.

The clothing fit adequately, not a uniform really, just some beat up trousers, shirt and torn jacket. But the boots were too large. Better large than small. He ripped his old clothes into strips and used them as rags to stuff the boots. They'll do. The soldier had a knife and, grateful for any weapon, Joseph tucked it in his back pocket. He looked around once more and bolted through the woods and away from the enemy.

During the day he rested and at night, Joseph walked and walked, stopping only for a few minutes at a time. Early one morning, near a shallow brook, he pulled out the knife and began to painfully scrape away his beard. Nicked and cut, nonetheless his bare face felt cool and wonderful.

The barren landscape reminded him of winter. The heavy underbrush crunched under his feet as he zigzagged his way north. His lungs hurt but he gained wind with each step. During the day, he found shelter under tree branches, between large rocks or in small caves. Come dusk, he would move, ever-cautious until night blanketed his escape. His stomach reminded him how hunger weakens the body and he stopped often to eat berries. He was lucky enough to catch a fish in the clear, cool streams that crisscrossed his path. This he ate raw, not wanting to take time or the chance to light a fire.

Joseph stayed away from roads and heavily trodden paths, winding his way through dense woods and undergrowth. His skin was scratched and lacerated, his clothing torn. He followed a river north and when the sun began to rise, he estimated he had covered about fifteen miles. But it was a long way to Washington, especially traveling alone. He yearned to talk to someone, anyone. Well, anyone in blue. That is, if he didn't get shot first. A Union soldier would think him a Reb, a Confederate soldier would think him a deserter.

His thoughts meandered but always returned to Sara and the baby. A lump closed his throat as a terrible sadness came over him. He'd have to get word to her as soon as he was able. It gave him the edge to push on.

Three weeks passed as Joseph trod his way north. His thoughts were on Sara a good deal of the time. He wished he had paper and pen to write her with. He missed his satchel. Fortunately, he'd left it with Louisa before he trekked down to New Bedford. He wished he had that satchel and gun now.

One morning, bitterly cold and exhausted, he finally came to the outskirts of a town. Concealing himself behind a majestic oak, he watched as Confederate soldiers stacked crate upon crate in front of the depot station. An old wooden sign swayed in the wind announcing the railroad stop: Richmond, Virginia.

God. The southern capital. Joseph's pulse quickened. Those crates! His hands trembled on the rough tree bark.

He had seen those crates aboard the Blackhawk. He had lived with those crates, slept with them, rested against them. They contained artillery, guns and supplies from Concord Armaments.

Now they were being delivered into the hands of the Rebels. Right here in Richmond, to be distributed to Lee's Army in Northern Virginia.

Hellfire! He balled up his hands into fists. The very proof I need, right there. What I wouldn't give for a photograph of this scene.

At the sound of conversation, he ducked further behind the gnarled trunk.

"So whut we gunna do with these here munitions now?"

"I hear'd they's goin' down the road apiece to Petersburg. Genul Lee needs guns mighty bad with the siege goin' on."

"That Grant is one stubborn sum' bitch, I guess. He ain't likely to quit for a spell."

"Aw, shit, when's this damn war gunna end, anyways?"

Joseph's mind raced. Damn, I can't just let this evidence disappear. He crept through the woods and looked back. He stopped suddenly as an idea began to form in his mind. Alex had planned to leave the gallery to his apprentices and head back out to the field by January of '65. And if that was the case, Joseph knew his friend would be where the action was.

He moved with a newly tapped energy. This time instead of marching north, he headed southwest--to Petersburg.

Chapter 26

Petersburg, Virginia
March 2, 1865

Alexander Gardner dipped his pen in the jar of ink on the small writing table in front of him. He'd been back out in the field again for two months. At first, he'd worried about leaving apprentices to oversee the gallery, but now that he had, he was pleased to be in the open air again. He wrote:

. . . Four railroad lines and several major roadways make Petersburg the strategic key to taking Richmond. General Ulysses S. Grant knew this as fact when his army arrived in mid-June, 1864. Cut these lines and the city of Richmond would be cut off from much needed food and supplies. But Lee and the Army of Northern Virginia stood staunchly guarding the road to Richmond, despite the fact that they were outnumbered almost two to one. Grant outmaneuvered them. For eight long and tedious months, he lay siege upon the city of Petersburg for eight fearful months of fighting, artillery and mortar shell fire, constant drill and for the Confederate army, barely subsistence conditions.

Now, months later, Lee's army consists of only about 60,000 hungry, tired, ill-equipped soldiers, while Grant has 110,000 well-equipped men. It seems the end is in sight, but Lee has not yet surrendered.

Early in the siege several coal miners from the 48th Pennsylvania came up with a plan. They began digging a tunnel toward a rebel fort southeast of the town. They intended to explode four tons of gunpowder under an area called Pegram's Salient and send a large number of troops through the open gap. The tunnel took a month to dig and was over five hundred feet long with sidelong wings at the end to hold the powder. On July 30, the Federals set off the gunpowder; it blew up a Confederate artillery battery and left a crater about one hundred seventy feet long, sixty feet wide, and thirty feet deep. Rather than go around it, the Union troops dove right into the crater and were trapped by Confederate counterattacks. More than four thousand Union troops died or were wounded . . .

"Letter home?" Jeb Reilly asked.

"No, journal entry," Alex said, laying his pen down.

"You're turnin' into a regular historian, now," Jeb said. "Picking up where Joseph left . . ." His voice trailed off.

Alex murmered, "Och, never mind, Jeb."

Jeb rose. "Let's get somethin' to eat."

They sat by the cook fire, warming themselves in the chilly dusk as they prepared dinner.

"Sure do miss Joseph, though," Jeb said.

"Aye." Alex stared into the fire.

"Do ya think he's alive, mebbe?"

"I'd like to believe that."

"I think he is. Don't know why. Just do."

They fell silent for a while.

"Shit." Jeb spat suddenly. "Salt pork, burned beans, corn cakes and bad coffee. Don't ya jest love field work?"

Alex smiled and replied, "Don't complain. Just think what the poor Rebs have got to eat down there in the town."

"Well, and that's all they deserve, by God. Why the devil don't they just give up and let's all of us go home? Ain't there enough dead?"

"You know I've heard the count of dead since the war began to be as high as over half a million," Gardner said. "Christ, I just cannot conceive a' so many."

"Jaysus. What a bloody mess." Jeb poured himself some more coffee and stood up. "Well, I'm gonna develop some pictures for a while, lessen I start to bawl. I'll jest see how that old brick mill came out."

"Right, good night, then." Alex looked around at other campfires and men sitting around them. No rowdy jokes and laughter issued from the encampment. Everyone seemed in a melancholy mood. He reached in his pocket and pulled out a packet of letters from Sara to Joseph. She continued to write and send them to him in the hopes he could locate him. How long had he been gone? Time seemed to have no beginning, middle or end in war. Since the end of October, was it? And his friend was now a father. Joshua. A fine young lad. This brought a tiny smile to Alex's lips. Joseph a father, and he, his very own self, a godfather.

I should write the dear lady again, he told himself, but what more can I say? She just waits and prays for his return, or the news that he's dead.

"Jesus in heaven, Joseph, where are ye, man?"

Alex stared into the fire and watched the flames kick sparks into the air, when he caught his breath. Through the smoke and flicker he saw a man. His eyes were playing tricks on him for he swore it was Joseph and surely that was only because he was thinking on him tonight.

The man hissed and waved him over.

Alex leaped to his feet, looked around. Most of the campfires were dead and the men asleep. He walked cautiously over to the man hidden behind the trees. When he approached the edge of the woods an arm reached out and grabbed him. In the pale full moonlight, Alex found himself looking at an emaciated and utterly disheveled Joseph Thornhill.

"Oh, me dear departed Mother."

Joseph pulled a teary Alex some distance from the campsite and the two men hugged for several long moments. Finally, stuttering and shaky, Joseph briefed him on his misfortunes.

"Good heavens, man. Let me get you some food, ye must be starvin'."

"Please, yes, food."

Alex led Joseph to the cook fire, piled some leftover stew on a plate, added a chunk of stale bread and handed it to his friend. Joseph practically shoveled the food in his mouth and held the plate out for more.

"I must say, ye're the first man I've seen actually enjoying army food." Alex grinned.

At that moment, Jeb stepped down from the darkroom wagon and a new reunion began.

“By God, Joseph,” Jeb said, after hearing Joseph’s story. “We surely thought you were gone.”

“So did I, Jeb. So did I,” Joseph said.

“Go on, eat,” Jeb said. “Yer lookin’ like you need it bad. Even this crummy army food.” Jeb stood. “I’ll let you two gents catch up. I’m going to get me some sleep.” He touched Joseph on the shoulder. “Welcome back.”

Joseph smiled up at him. He finished eating, drank two mugs of coffee and exhaled deeply. "By God, it's good to see you, Alex. I knew I'd find you here."

"This is where the siege is, so, of course--" Alex stopped when Joseph reached out and clutched at his sleeve.

"Sara? Did you hear from Sara? Is she--?"

Alex took Joseph's hand. "She's fine."

"And the baby?"

"Fine. A boy, a lad named Joshua."

"Joshua," Joseph whispered. His eyes filled.

"I have some of her letters . . . she'll be very happy to hear . . . thank God you're safe." Alex's voice cracked.

"Although I must say I've seen you looking better," Alex said.

They grinned at each other.

Joseph leaned close to his friend. "Listen Alex, I need your help. There's no time to lose. There are photographs we must take. I must prove that Concord Armaments has been selling arms to the South and they are--."

"Whoa, slow down. Tell me everything."

Joseph took a deep breath and began. His story took twenty minutes to unfold and brought him back to his mission.

"I think I found a way to do it, Alex. To prove their treason. You must help me."

"What can I do?"

"The company has shipped crates of arms and munitions to the railway depot in Richmond. They're stacked a mile high with their name stamped on the outside. If we could get a picture of that next to the station that says clearly Richmond, it would be proof."

"Are ye crazy? How the devil will we get pictures there? First of all, how would we cross the lines? We could get shot at by either side. It's not like we can just waltz up and shoot, you know." Alex stopped short. The two men looked at each other, both remembering the Rappahannock experience and burst out laughing.

"I'm not saying it'll be easy," Joseph said. "We'd have to circle around the flank and head into Richmond from the south. Then, I figured we'd pose as southern photographers as cover. How's your southern drawl?"

Alex arched his eyebrows.

"Well, a Scottish burr will do fine. We could fake a license or something. Shit, I don't know. This is terribly important, Alex."

"Jesus." Alex wiped his brow. "Let me think. A license. I suppose I could fake one."

"Two."

"Er, two." Alex thought for a moment. "I can try." He started to shuffle back to the wagon, turned. "You're sure about this?"

"I'm sure," Joseph said. He smiled at the big man. "It's good to be back, Alex."

"It's good to have you back, Joseph." Alex held up a hand. "Let me get something from the wagon." He returned with Joseph's satchel. "Here. Miss Alcott kept this for you. Inside are letters from Sara. You read these while I get to work on the licenses." Alex climbed back up into the wagon.

Joseph opened the satchel and withdrew a packet of letters tied with a string. He pulled one out at random and read one from last December.

December 18, 1864

My Dearest Joseph,

It has been nearly three months since I've heard from you or about you, my love, and my heart is wrenched with worry. Alex has been checking with Mister Pinkerton and Colonel Baxter daily to make every effort to locate you and yet to no avail. It is my secret prayer that you have taken it upon yourself to conduct a secret operation without the knowledge of Mister Pinkerton. It is not unlike you to go off and do something rash if you believe it is the right thing to do and you have no choice.

Still I have been barely able to sleep at night or think during the day, without feeling your loss keenly in my soul. I try to remain positive, if only for son, Joshua. He's a fine boy, healthy and strong like his father. He tells me, without words, how much he wants to come into a world that is free from war and strife, free from prejudice and hatred. A world that values every man and woman for who they are, no matter skin color or background. I wonder how much of this rather liberal attitude he would get from his father. . . and his mother.

I have written many times to Louisa. She, too, has not heard from you, nor has Mister Redburn, the gentleman from Concord Armaments you recruited to assist you. He continues to provide information to Louisa and she in turn has been forwarding that directly to Mr. Pinkerton.

Oh my dear, what has become of you? I know you are not dead. You cannot be, for that I would feel in my very being, down to the tiniest bone in my little finger. No, you are in danger but you are alive. If only I could help you. Somehow. Perhaps my prayers will bring you back, safe, to the ones you love and who so terribly miss you.

For now, I will assume with great optimism, that you are reading this letter, so will write the news of the day as I have for the three years past.

First and foremost, President Lincoln has been reelected to a second term over General George McClellan. With Andrew Johnson as his running mate, Mister Lincoln won over 55 percent of the popular vote and carried every state except Delaware, Kentucky and New Jersey. In the electoral college, he drew 212 to McClellan's 21. Father has been extremely pleased that the country has finally 'seen the light of day,' as he puts it.

Mister Lincoln also formally established Thanksgiving as a national holiday. Mother is already searching for a large bird to cook and to inviting neighbors and dear friends, like Alex and Jeb, to join us. By the way, Alex has your satchel with your letters and journal and will keep it safe for you.

My love, if only you could be with us.

I send our deepest wishes now from all of us. Come home soon.

All my love, Sara

A few minutes later Alex returned.

Joseph wiped tears from his eyes. "Thank you for saving this."

"And why wouldn't I?"

"It means a lot to me. Tell me, Alex, about Joshua, my son. What's he like? Does he look like Sara, or me?"

"He's a fine babe with a healthy set of lungs."

Joseph grinned, pulled the grin back. "Alex, do you have a toothbrush I could use? I think Sara would faint if she saw me now."

"We'll fix you up. For now, what do ye think of these? Pretty good forgeries if I say so meself." He held out two documents.

"How do you know this looks like a real southern license?"

"Oh, I saw one once."

"Once? You forged a pass from something you saw once?" Joseph gulped.

"Trust me. I've got a memory like an elephant. Now here are some civilian clothes that should fit. Go ahead, get them on." He threw a bundle of clothes to Joseph. “And here’s a toothbrush.”

Joseph gratefully tore off his clothes and threw them aside.

"Och, I hope we can pull this off."

"Let me do the talking.” Joseph patted him on the shoulder. “You just pretend like you know what you're doing."

"Pretend to be a photographer?" Alex raised his eyebrows.

About to climb into the wagon, Joseph stopped short.

"What's the matter now?" Alex asked.

"Do you think General Longstreet is in Richmond?"

Alex whistled. "Good God. Longstreet?"

"He'll know me for sure."

"Aye, Joseph, that he will. Maybe you should think about this some more."

"No, it's too late now. I'll just have to risk it."

Alex grabbed his arm. "Listen, if Longstreet's there, we'll get out in a hurry. You have me word. All right?"

"I’ll leave a note for Jeb and then we’ll get going. We need to get to Richmond before the evidence is gone. Assuming it isn't already too late." Joseph climbed up beside Alex in the wagon.

Alex turned to him and in a hoarse voice said, "May God be with us, Joseph, as we enter the mouth of the dragon."

Chapter 27

Petersburg, Virginia
March 3, 1865

"What a beautiful day," Joseph said. "All the more exquisite for my freedom."

The two men gazed appreciatively at their surroundings as the wagon bumped along the dirt road. Surprisingly mild for early March, sunlight cut through wind-spun clouds creating golden beams on the brown landscape.

By the time they pulled the wagon to a stop outside the railway depot in Richmond, Alex and Joseph had caught up on each other's lives. Joseph practiced his southern accent on Alex whose Scottish lilt needed no sharpening. They'd encountered no army units along the way but now Joseph's confidence waned as he realized he was on enemy ground, with no Union backup.

The scene before them was one of disarray. Soldiers, dressed in homespun, butternut rags, wandered aimlessly around the depot. Many had no weapons, but most still wore the CSA kepis on their dusty heads. Their boots appeared as broken down chunks of leather, stuffed with rags or newspapers to fill the holes.

At their arrival, shouts echoed around the depot and several armed soldiers rushed over to them. When the men realized this was a photographer's wagon, they whooped and hollered. Few opportunities in the south existed to get their picture taken, so Joseph and Alex were most welcome.

"Gentlemen." Joseph jumped down. "Ah do hope you'll allow us to take your photographs this fine day." He surveyed the area, eyes wary for Longstreet. Then he studied the depot and the crates stacked in front. A number of them sat empty, tops leaning aside, just where they had been unloaded. He stared at the imprinted name: Concord Armaments.

We're in luck.

He approached the circle of Confederates around Alex.

"These boys would like to get their pictures taken today. Where shall we set up?" Alex winked at Joseph.

"What do y'all think about posing before that depot? Make a good backdrop."

The men agreed cheerily.

"All right, now, dust yourselves off, boys," Joseph said, and he and Alex began pulling equipment out of the wagon. They stopped suddenly when a voice called out, "Sirs, I must ask to see your license, please."

Joseph's heart kicked in his chest.

A hand rested on his shoulder. Too late.

But Alex's voice whispered, "It's only a Lieutenant."

Joseph fought to compose himself as he turned to face a short, heavyset man with handlebar mustache.

"Certainly, Lieutenant, we're most happy to accommodate." He straightened in relief. When he flashed the license before him the Lieutenant grabbed and studied it.

"And who is this gentleman?" he asked pointing to Alex.

"This is my assistant. You know, Sir, a photographer cannot take pictures by himself. By the way, Lieutenant, I'd be very happy to take your picture, if you so desire. Does your wife have a recent photograph of you? Or your children? We can set it up right over here, if you wish."

"I don't like this one bit," the Lieutenant said. "We haven't seen a photographer around here in months, now two of you turn up. No Suh, I don't like it."

"Sir, we've been on the road a mighty long time and just want to be of service to our soldiers. Now, what can possibly be wrong with that?"

"Ah don't know. . . this is highly irregular."

"Well, if that's the way you want it, I guess we'll just mosey along, head back toward Petersburg. I'm sure General Lee will allow photographs to be taken of his brave troops."

"Say, Lieutenant," offered a private, "why not let 'em take our pictures? Cain't be no harm, now, cain it?" The Confederates chimed in with yays and hoots.

The Lieutenant's cheek muscles twitched. "Where y'all from?" he asked Joseph.

Joseph blinked at him a moment. *It's all over now.* He smiled. "Maryland. A little town called Churchton."

"On the Chesapeake Bay?"

Joseph choked back a lump in his throat. "Yes, you know it?"

"Never been myself. Wife's cousin used to live. . . never mind." The Lieutenant waved a hand.

"And where are you from, Sir?" Joseph asked.

"I'm from right here in Richmond." The Lieutenant looked

around at his men who were staring at him, then stammered, "Well, Ah don't. . . oh all right." He handed back the licenses. "Go on now, take your pictures."

The men cheered.

The photographers set up their equipment facing the depot and had the soldiers pose in front of the crates.

The light is perfect.

Joseph centered the crates in the lens.

"Let's get a close up shot, boys. Alex, you pose those men --no, to the right a bit, good."

Alex moved behind Joseph. "Let me see, Joseph."

Joseph let Alex look through the camera lens. Then he angled the camera close enough so the writing on the crates could be read. By exposing two plates simultaneously using a stereo camera, he could process one as an ambrotype to give to the soldier and keep the other as a negative. He hoped the Confederates understood little about the photographic process.

A few hours later, the photographers had taken and processed a dozen photographs. They distributed the ambrotypes to the men, but kept all the negatives in a box inside the wagon.

Anxious to be out of enemy territory, Thornhill turned to the men and said, "Well, gentlemen, glad we could be of assistance. Now we must head to Petersburg where our comrades are engaged by that little tyrant, Grant. I bid you good day and God speed."

The southerners waved a hurried goodbye then exchanged photographs to compare images, arguing who looked best.

Alex headed the horses south out of sight of the railroad depot. He turned the wagon right and snapped the reins.

"This is far enough," he said. He steered the horses on a well-beaten path in the reverse direction.

"Joseph, me dear friend. It's time to go home."

Chapter 28

Dumbarton Street, Georgetown

March 27, 1865

The long trek home from Richmond had taken nearly three weeks. Joseph and Alex were forced to skirt around southern camps and Rebel scouts, travel minor rough roads, off the beaten path. Joseph was worn out and bedraggled from his sea journey and the arduous tramp through the South.

"Stay with me one night," Alex said. "Get yourself prettied up for Sara. You can shave and bath, get some new clothes. . ."

"No. I must get home. I must see her."

"But she will be frightened at your sudden appearance, and the way you look, man."

"I pray she will be glad to see me, no matter how I look."

"Aye. That she will."

Alex dropped him off at the Dumbarton Street home on the morning of March 27. He stepped down from the wagon now and smiled up at Alex.

"No goodbyes, man," Alex said. "Now get in there and hug yer wife and child."

Alex whistled and the horses took off down the street, leaving Joseph standing in front of his house with its newly red-painted door.

He wished he could have sent word to Sara in advance. Despite her pluck and resilience, Sara might actually faint at the sight of him unannounced.

Suddenly the door opened and there she stood. Exactly as he remembered. Her red hair tumbled loose around her shoulders; there were a few more lines around her eyes and mouth but the warmth of her smile lit her face like a hundred suns. His Sara.

No words were spoken, none were needed. He took her in his arms and they stood, embraced in their love, until both stopped crying. Then they pulled apart and gazed at each other.

She didn't say he looked thin beyond belief, or that his hair had turned gray or his skin appeared leathered by the elements. All she said was, "Would you like to meet your son?"

*

The Executive Mansion, Presidential Office
April 12, 1865

Two weeks passed before a meeting with the President could be arranged. Since the surrender of General Lee to General Grant on April 9 at Appomattox Court House, Mr. Lincoln had his days and nights filled with appointments. Messengers hurried in and out of the President's office with dispatches, and secretaries waited for the President's signature on scores of documents.

Joseph Thornhill stood next to Alexander Gardner, both behind U.S. Army Colonel Sanford Baxter and Allan Pinkerton, in front of President Lincoln's desk waiting for his acknowledgement. Joseph's eyes took in the room and he noted with dismay the shabbiness of the furnishings: dark, heavy woods filled the office, bookshelves crowded with legal tomes, dismal eighteenth century paintings on the walls, and a huge worn desk occupying the center of the space.

Joseph stiffened to attention as the President removed his spectacles and rubbed his eyes. He noted how much older Lincoln looked, the weariness in his sunken cheeks and hooded eyes evident, the stoop in his posture more pronounced. Mountains of documents sat piled in front of the commander-in-chief, in need of his attention. Four photographs rested on top of the mound. Joseph knew these were the photographs he and Alex had taken at the Depot in Richmond. He shifted on his feet and felt a rivulet of sweat making its way down his back. A sideways glance at Gardner revealed an amused smile on the big man's face.

The President spoke and Joseph recognized the distinctive voice of the man who had been the subject of his portraiture in past years. Lincoln looked ten years older.

Pinkerton and Sanford moved to the side, parting like the Red Sea to allow the photographers to step forward.

"Mister Thornhill, Mister Gardner, it is good to see you both again," the President said, standing, hand outstretched. He shook with both men. "My wife tells me your photographs of me and the family are the finest we own."

"Thank you, Sir," Alex said. "However, it's the subject that makes the photograph."

Lincoln rubbed his distinctive chin and chuckled. He sat back down behind a massive wooden desk piled high with papers.

"I understand you've been through some difficult times these last few months, Mister Thornhill, and I thank you for risking your safety to bring me these documents and photographs." He reached back to his desk and brought forward the images. "These are, indeed, damaging."

Lincoln adjusted his spectacles back on his nose and looked down at the pictures in his hand. "I cannot fathom how you two managed such a charade. Posing as southern photographers and strolling blatantly into the Richmond depot. Astounding." He paused. "But then you are remarkable men."

Joseph opened his mouth but Lincoln waved a hand. "I know you've been working undercover for Mister Pinkerton, of course. Very brave and terribly useful work. I am deeply grateful. And your photographs . . . truly remarkable recreations of reality." Lincoln gazed out the window for a moment. "The way you've captured death, not only its finality, but its infinite sadness. Perhaps they're too real."

He rose, stepped from behind his desk and gazed at the photographers. “In any event, I've given these documents only a cursory inspection right now and need more time to examine them thoroughly and to assess how best to deal with the traitors responsible for so many lives." Lincoln shook his head. "These are powerful men who won't go down without a fight. They also have many allies--allies who still consider themselves my enemy. No, the best way is the legal way. We will gather all the evidence and convict them in a court of law. It is the only way in a democracy. Let their peers decide."

"But, Mister President--" Joseph said, unable to hide his disappointment. “How long is that going to take?”

Lincoln took off his spectacles. “Pinkerton will get right on it.”

"Can't you, I mean, why couldn't you, as President, bring the traitors to justice?"

"Mister Thornhill, I understand how you feel." Lincoln stood up. "At the beginning of the war, I suspended the writ of Habeas Corpus and, although I believe to this day it was the right thing to do, I nevertheless suffered the criticism of one who abandons the law for his own convenience. I am not about to let that happen again."

Baxter spoke up, "But, Sir, you have no doubt that they will be convicted?"

"No doubt, once we make our case. And thanks to these men," he smiled at the photographers, "we appear to have the proof we need. Gentlemen, I plan to set aside time early next week to review these reports." He looked at Joseph. "And photographs. Then we shall meet again and discuss them in detail. I'm sure I'll have many questions for you. At that time you'll need to give sworn testimony as well."

"Of course," Joseph said.

"In the meantime, Colonel Baxter, I leave it to you to put everything in good order. We will need to have all our t's crossed and our i's dotted when we confront the conspirators." He looked at each man in turn. "Good. Now, you must excuse me. My wife has dinner plans for us this evening." The President smiled and laid a gnarled hand on Joseph's shoulder. "Have faith in me, Mister Thornhill. The war may be over but I will not let these treasonous acts go unpunished. I can promise you that."

Chapter 29

The Ebbitt House
April 12, 1865

Samuel Lindsey sat in a booth at the Ebbitt House. The air hung thick and murky from cigar smoke and he swigged down a second whisky to wet his dry throat. His jaw clenched when he reflected on the conversation he'd had last night with Jack Cade. Was it true? Did the man speak the truth when he claimed he was courting his daughter? Damn his insolence. How dare he think he's good enough for Rebecca?

Porter Hobbs approached. Lindsey would have to deal with this conundrum later. And deal with it, and his only child, he would.

Hobbs heaved his bulk into a seat and ordered a drink. "And bring the bottle," he said to the waiter. To Lindsey, "If only we could wrap up this abominable business. But here we are, ready to enlist that, er, assassin's services once more. I say, quite a fix, eh?"

Lindsey merely nodded. He grew irritated as Hobbs nervously thrummed his fingers on the table, beads of sweat dampening his thick mustache. Hobbs had grown obese from overindulgence in food and liquor the last few months. His jowls drooped to his collar.

Lindsey remained fit and trim, hair graying to silvery white, but otherwise not showing his age. He betrayed his own anxiety, however, by continually twisting his beard between his fingers. He reached for the bottle of whiskey, which had arrived and now sat in the center of the table, and considered making small talk. He changed his mind. At least Harlow wasn't here tonight. His brother-in-law's foolhardy questions would have sent Lindsey into a rage. No. He needed to remain calm, in control. Particularly in front of Cade.

Where the devil was he? Lindsey slid his fingers under his collar and tugged. At that moment he saw Hobbs's face redden as the fat man stared across the room. Lindsey turned and saw the reason for Hobbs's anxious expression. Jack Cade had just entered the tavern. He wore a dark waistcoat, top hat and gloves and appeared quite the dandy. A beautiful blond woman wrapped in a shawl of crimson lace, draped his arm. It seemed to Lindsey that the air suddenly electrified.

He grabbed Hobbs's arm. "Get a hold of yourself."

"Let's just get this over with."

Lindsey watched as the maitre d' assisted the stunning golden-haired lady to remove her shawl and escorted her to a table. Then he drew in a deep breath as Cade's head spun around and his piercing eyes drilled right into him.

Cade walked to Lindsey's table, removed his hat and gloves, and pulled out a chair. He waved to the waiter to bring him a glass. "Well, gentlemen, it looks like you're a few drinks ahead of me."

Hobbs began, "Uh, what about the young lady?"

"She'll wait," Cade said. "Most women will wait for me." He aimed this remark at Lindsey.

Lindsey wanted to throttle the man, but, as luck would have it, he still needed him. So, instead he spoke in carefully chosen words, "Jack, we must talk to you."

"It's probably time to call me by my right name," Cade said. "After all, my job is done. And very well done, I may add."

Lindsey opened his mouth, but the waiter arrived and spoke to Cade, "Ah, Mister Booth, so nice to see you again. Are you back in the theatre again after your travels?"

"Hello, Stephen, and thank you. I've only taken a sabbatical from acting, you see. The war and all."

"Of course, of course. I'll bring your favorite brandy." The waiter hurried off.

"Hmph," Hobbs said. "John Wilkes Booth, the actor. How did you come up with the name Jack Cade?"

Lindsey exhaled. *Who cares?*

"Mr. Hobbs," Booth said. "You're not familiar with Shakespeare, then?"

"I, well, somewhat, I suppose."

"Let me enlighten you," Booth said. "Jack Cade was, indeed, a real person. He lived in fifteenth century England and led the peasants in the Kent rebellion."

Hobbs just blinked.

"Cade is a character in Shakespeare's Henry VI Part 2."

"Oh," Hobbs said.

"That play, in case you're not familiar, is most famous for the quote, 'The first thing we do, let's kill all the lawyers.'" Booth burst out in a hearty laugh.

"Ha, yes. Ha," said Hobbs.

"John," Lindsey prodded.

Booth held up a hand. "Drinks first, my good man."

The men were silent as Stephen set down a brandy snifter in front of the younger man.

"Now. What is this all about?" Booth said.

“We need your help,” Hobbs blurted out. “Once more."

Lindsey shot Hobbs a dagger. That was not the way Lindsey had intended to approach Booth.

But Booth responded with an impish grin. "Of course. I am at your service."

"This is serious, John," Lindsey said.

"You mean it hasn't always been? What a shame. Tell that to the four agents." Booth smiled more broadly.

"This is no joking matter. The photographer, Thornhill, the one who’s seen you out in the field--he’s free and he's here in Washington. He and Baxter have been to see Lincoln."

Booth's eyes widened. "I know who Joseph Thornhill is. He’s free? Imagine.” Booth’s gaze rested on a point over Lindsey’s shoulder. “So, Thornhill managed to escape from the Blackhawk. Geoffrey Farrell has fallen down on the job.”

“The failing of the ship’s captain is not our concern now.”

Booth drained his glass and murmured to himself. As if taking new measure of Thornhill he said, “That photographer must be one tough son-of-a-bitch.”

"Be that as it may,” Hobbs said. “He's here in Washington and he’s already presented evidence against Concord Armaments."

"What sort of evidence?"

Lindsey twisted his lips. "We don't know for sure, but some documents and photographs--."

"Photographs? What photographs?" Booth straightened in his chair.

Lindsey shook his head. “We don’t know.”

Booth slammed his glass down on the table and the remaining brandy showered the air.

"Thornhill certainly gets around, doesn't he?" Booth's jaws clenched.

"Lord knows what Lincoln will do with the evidence," Hobbs blustered. "But I know for sure he won’t let it go, war ending or not."

Booth leaned forward. "The war is not over yet," he hissed between his teeth.

Hobbs threw his hands up casually. "It doesn't matter whether the war is over or not, there's still danger of exposure and I'm--"

Booth grasped the tablecloth in his fists, bunching it up and drinks fell with soft thuds. Wine, blood color, spread across the linen. "The war is not over." His face had gone white.

"All right, all right, man." Hobbs sat back.

Lindsey waved away a waiter who had appeared to clean up the spill. "Listen to me, Booth. We’re in this together. You could just as easily be implicated as we can."

"What would you have me do."

"There’s only one thing that will save us. It won't be an easy task and may require quite a bit of underground reconnaissance."

Booth's eyebrows shot up.

"But my sources can help. Whatever you need," Lindsey said. “I can get--”

“What,” Booth interrupted, “would you have me do?"

"We need to eliminate all possible links to our activities." Lindsey dropped his voice, eyes darting around for eavesdroppers.

Booth held his hand up for silence. His eyes moved from Lindsey’s to a point across the room. "Damn the man to hell," he snarled. With a quick motion, he donned his hat, pulling the brim low and grabbed for his gloves. He bounded out of the establishment, skirting waiters and tables on the way. In his hurry, he left his lady friend behind.

"Christ almighty," Lindsey said.

"Now what the devil was that all about?" Hobbs muttered, mouth opening and closing. "Where did he go? Is he coming back?"

Lindsey laid his hand on Hobbs's shoulder and nodded in the direction of the maitre d'. A handsome couple sat in a booth near the front of the restaurant. The man's hair was long and loose, not slicked back with perfumed macassar oil as the fashion, and he wore a fine brown tweed suit; the lady commanded attention with her dazzling red hair and delicately chiseled bones. She wore a striking gold brocade dress with a soft fringe of lace at the throat. The two seemed intent only on each other, sharing wine and holding hands.

Hobbs gulped. "Joseph and Mrs. Thornhill, I presume?"

Chapter 30

Washington City

April 14, 1865

In the early morning hours, John Wilkes Booth tossed and moaned in bed. He awoke finally, soaked in sweat, covers rumpled and tangled around his feet. Sitting up, he swung his legs over the edge of the bed and rubbed his face.

Photographs. He dreamed of photographs. Did Joseph Thornhill catch him on the battlefield? At Antietam? Fredericksburg? No. Impossible. But was it? What did it matter? He'd been in disguise.

Booth dragged himself out of bed, sponge-bathed in cold water and dressed. Staring in the mirror, he stroked his full mustache with his fingers. Then he lathered his cheeks with foam, and raked it with a long blade razor. Patting himself with a damp towel, he continued to gaze in the mirror. He must take extra care with his hair. Slicking it back first with a French pomade, he then carefully fluffed it into its natural curls.

A knock on the door gave him pause. He opened it to a bellman who handed him a letter. Booth gave him a tip, scowled as he ripped the envelope open. He recognized the paper. Rebecca.

Hadn't Lindsey talked to her, made her understand? He read the short note:

My Dearest John,

I've not heard from you since I confided my news. Please, dear, we must not let this tear us apart. I pray you contact me soon. There are decisions to be made.

Lovingly,

Rebecca

Booth crumpled up the note and threw it on the floor.

Decisions have already been made, my little strumpet.

He shook his head and thoughts of Lindsey's daughter flew out of his mind. He returned to his reflection in the mirror. He must look his best. After all, this was the day. Details had been finalized with Lindsey and Hobbs. The last and most important task in his career as assassin. This was what he'd be remembered for, his name on everyone's lips.

Suddenly, as if on cue, the sun burst brightly through the windows and dissipated all remnants of his ominous dreams and worries about Rebecca. The hotel room looked almost elegant in the morning light with its rich cherry woods, an oriental rug of umber hues, and a lightly patterned wallpaper.

After dining at the hotel, Booth felt positively cheered. Whistling, he stepped through the lobby and into the street.

Wearing a riding outfit, dark suit with close fitting trousers, calf-high boots and a new pair of spurs, Booth left the hotel and walked quickly the few blocks to the Herndon House. He smiled and tipped his hat at several ladies passing by.

Ah, the smell of lilacs.

They stared at him and giggled.

That's what the handsomest man in America, as Harper's had named him, must deal with. For now, he must set his plan in motion. And the first step was to gather his collaborators.

At the Herndon House, Booth made straight for Lewis Paine's room. Paine, a muscular, square-jawed tough brightened visibly when saw Booth enter.

"John, come in, glad ta see ya. How'sa 'bout a drink?"

"No thanks, I just want to talk. Are you sober, Lew?" Booth flopped down in a plush chair of gold velvet. He grimaced at the disorder in the room. Clothes strewn on the bed and draped over chair arms.

"Why sure. Talk about what? Another kidnapping?" Paine said, referring to the wild scheme Booth had about kidnapping Lincoln.

"No, this time assassination. This time for good."

Paine immediately sat up. "Yeah, really? Aw'right. What's the plan? Whatdya want me to do?" Paine asked, eagerness softening his hard features.

Booth outlined his plan. "The Lincolns will be at Ford's Theatre for the performance tonight. General Grant and his wife were supposed to accompany them, but unfortunately they're leaving town." Booth sauntered around the room, hands in his pockets. "Too bad, we could have killed two birds with one stone."

Paine laughed.

A knock on the door startled both men. They looked at each other. Paine jumped off the bed and opened the door to George Atzerodt and Davie Herold. Booth realized he'd been holding his breath.

"Glad you're here, boys," Booth said.

"What's goin' on, Johnny?" Herold said, taking off his crumpled hat and tossing it on the bed.

"I've come up with a new plan. Tonight will be our night to win victory for the South." Booth lit a cigarette, puffed, watching his collaborators through half-closed lids.

"Are ya gunna tell us?" Herold prompted.

Booth smiled, "Patience, Davie. Patience is a virtue."

"What's a virtue?"

"Never mind. My plan is in three stages. Three men must die in order for us to achieve success."

Herold's mouth dropped open.

Booth turned to Paine. "Lew, your target will be Secretary of State Seward. He's recently been hurt in an accident and is bedridden."

Paine grinned boyishly, "An easy mark wouldn't ya say?"

"Listen now. You'll gain entry to Seward's home by pretending to be from the druggist with some new medication for him. You need to give him the medicine yourself, remember-- you're simply following the doctor's orders. Then you'll proceed to Seward's bedroom upstairs and kill him. Simple. . . and elegant."

"Sounds too easy," Paine nodded. "What'll I use? Knife, gun?"

"Whatever will do the job."

"My choice?"

Booth nodded, turned to Herold, "Davie, you'll escort Lew to the Seward House. Know where it is?

Herold bobbed his head.

"Then wait for him and the two of you make your escape together. George," Booth instructed the foreign-born Atzerodt, "at the exact same time Paine is taking care of Seward, you'll go to the room of Vice President Andrew Johnson. There you will shoot and kill him. Do you understand?" *Lindsey will not like this but I know what's best for the Confederacy.*

Atzerodt gulped and licked his lips.

"Damn it George, are you drunk again? I need you sober for this job." Booth grabbed Adzerodt's collar and shook him.

“I don’t know, John, I’m scared.” Adzerodt's voice cracked.

“Now look here, you fool, you’re going to hang either way. You’re in this with me too deep.” Booth growled. “If you back out now, it means our deaths too. You don’t want that on your conscience, do you?”

“No, no, I vill do it. Don't worry, John.”

“All right then. Where's your gun?”

Adzerodt showed him a Colt revolver.

"Good." Booth paced like a nervous cat. “I’ll be at Ford’s Theatre taking care of the Old Man himself.” He spun around and looked at them. They all stood at attention. “Now listen here. It's very important that each of these men die, for the sake of the South. Do you all understand?"

He waited for each of the men to give assent.

"All the killings will take place at exactly ten-fifteen tonight. Check your watches now. After it's done, we meet at the Navy Yard Bridge, ride to Surrattsville to pick up extra arms that Mary Surratt hid for us, and hightail it to Port Tobacco, where our money will be waiting.”

“How much, Johnny?” Herold asked.

“More than you can count, Davie,” Booth said.

“That’s not much,” Paine added with a laugh.

Booth shot him a dagger. “Remember, ten fifteen.”

“Did you get any money in advance?” Paine asked.

“Don’t worry, my business associates will be there with the money."

"How do ya know ya can trust 'em?" Paine asked.

"Just trust me, boys. Have I ever let you down?"

That afternoon, Booth strolled into Ford's Theatre. He needed to survey the Presidential Box. Slowly he walked up the steps to the dress circle and made his way around to the far right of the house, facing the stage. He glanced over his shoulder then moved behind the caned seats proceeding down the south aisle of the dress circle until he came to a door. Opening it, Booth walked through a narrow hallway with two more doors, the entrances to Box Numbers Seven and Eight.

Well, isn't that convenient. Booth grinned when he found the locks of all three doors broken.

As Booth entered Box Number Seven he saw at once that the partition usually separating the two boxes had been moved. Now one large box stood ready for the presidential party. He walked to the front of the box and gazed down over the balustrade to the stage twelve feet below. Actors on the stage were rehearsing for the evening's performance.

Yes, this will work very nicely.

As he headed toward the stage door exit, he eyed a two by four board, propped up to support a music stand; eyes darting around, he pulled it away from the stand and carried it with him back to the Presidential Box. In the box, he took out his penknife and carved out a niche in the wall of the corridor. Then he played with the board, jamming one end of it into the niche and the other against the door. It worked. He could prevent someone from pushing the door open once he got inside. Tucking the board away into a dark recessed corner, he slipped out of the Theatre and rode back to the National Hotel.

After supper, alone in the dining room, he went over the plans again in his mind. He must not fail, not just for Lindsey and his partners, but also for the South, his home.

He leaned back in his chair, lit a cigarette.

I will change history, he thought, and his heart pounded with new energy. He blew ribbons of smoke into the air.

John Wilkes Booth will be a name revered and remembered for all time.

Chapter 31

Ford’s Theater, Washington City

April 14, 1865

Returning to his room, Booth loaded his .44 caliber pistol, a single-shot derringer, and tucked it away in his pocket. He slipped a hunting knife into the waistband of his trousers.

Just for good measure.

He left the hotel by the back entrance and picked up his horse at the livery stables on the next street. He set out for Ford's Theatre on horseback.

Once there, Booth gave his horse over to a handyman and walked beneath the stage where he exited a side door into a corridor that led to Taltavul’s saloon. At the bar, he checked his pocket watch frequently.

"Got a date, Mister Booth?" the bartender asked.

"A very important appointment." Booth grinned. "With fate," he added. As he downed his drink, he felt a sharp slap on his shoulder. When he turned around he faced a short, splotchy-faced man.

“Sa. . . ay. . . aren’t you John Wil. . .Wilkes, huh, Booth? Yeah, I know you. You’ll never be as great an actor as, as your father was, huh?” The drunk stammered.

Booth's face reddened. He took a deep breath and said, “Mister. When I leave the stage, I will be the most famous man in America.”

Leaving the saloon, he made directly for the theatre lobby. He stopped abruptly as he heard his name.

"Booth," the drunk had stumbled after him.

"Sir, you're drunk," Booth said.

"I never get, uh, drunk." The man tripped, fell into Booth, who backed up in disgust.

"Get out of my way," Booth spat.

The man teetered after him down the hall. "How's 'bout doing that famous scene from Julius, uh, Caesar. You know the one where--"

"Sir, I have an appointment. Now go back to your booze." Booth tried again to escape. This time the man grabbed his arm and swung him around.

Booth slapped him with his open hand. "I told you, leave me alone."

The drunk swayed, drooling in a daze. Booth took the opportunity to move away fast and headed for the stairs to the dress circle. Quickly he checked his watch.

Still time.

He stopped to survey the audience a moment, estimating the size of the house he would play to tonight then checked the time again.

Paine and Adzerodt should be in place now.

Breathing hard, Booth moved swiftly to the door leading to the Presidential Box hallway. Once there, he positioned the pine board that he had hidden, into the niche he'd carved in the wall earlier that day.

Ha! Let them try to follow.

Booth held his breath and listened for his cue on stage.

I must be ready at exactly the precise moment.

The audience expected the moment too, as Laura Keene sailed offstage and comedian Harry Hawk spoke his line, "Heh, heh. Don't know the manners of good society, eh? Well, I guess I know enough to turn you inside out, old gal--you sockdologizing old man-trap."

Boisterous laughter erupted in the theatre.

Now.

Booth's senses slipped into sharp focus. He moved purposefully, mechanically toward the Box. The door seemed tilted, out of kilter, somehow.

Not like that this afternoon, he thought dimly.

He reached for the knob, but it moved out of his grasp. His fingers wrestled with the air. Finally, he caught the knob and it fell cool and smooth in his hand. Like a porcelain egg.

Turn, he instructed his hand.

Slowly the knob turned and the door cracked open as if on its own.

Did he open it?

At once he pushed the door far enough to allow entry and with his other hand pulled the derringer from his pocket. It felt slick, warm from his own body heat. But it gave him strength. He stared at it, ran his fingers over the polished steel. Finally, he looked up. The Presidential Box. With a soft click, he closed the door behind him, leaning back on it for support. In a glance, he took in the familiar surroundings. He knew other people occupied the Box, but Booth noticed only the tall, imposing figure seated before him. The President leaned forward toward the stage, one hand on the railing.

Booth's eyes blazed. The enemy. His blood began a slow boil.

No one existed inside that Box but Abraham Lincoln. Not Mary Lincoln. Not the couple seated at the far right of the Box. As if he wore blinders, his peripheral vision faded into a reddish blur, the scene a surrealistic vignette. His heart pounded and thrummed in his head, obliterating all sound.

Silently, he approached, his feet rising and falling as if in a dream. The world stopped spinning. Life crawled in slow motion. No one in the Box seemed to hear or see him.

Incredible.

Beads of sweat dripped down the sides of his face, and his shirt felt sticky and damp. The curls on his head tightened into ringlets from the wetness, and his eyes glimmered in wild anticipation.

Now is my moment. Just one tiny flick of the finger.

Booth drew in his breath and raised the six-inch long pistol. He steadied the weapon with his other hand and aimed it at the President's head.

I am God's instrument of His Punishment, he rejoiced.

This is for you, Lindsey. And for me.

He squeezed the trigger.

The .44 caliber bullet exploded and vanished into Lincoln's head. The President's right arm jerked up reflexively and within seconds, he slumped in his chair, unconscious.

Mary Lincoln's shrieks shook Booth out of his trance.

A sense of giddiness washed over him. "Freedom!" he cried over her screams. He threw down his gun, useless with only one shot, and pulled out his knife. Crazed with exaltation, adrenaline racing madly through his body, Booth rushed to escape.

I am invincible.

Suddenly, hands clutched at his sleeves and he landed hard on the floor, a man's full body weight upon him. The other man in the Box. He struggled to hold onto the knife. More screams filled the Box. Women's screams tore at his brain.

"I will kill you," Booth growled through clenched teeth. He slashed at his captor in several vicious strokes. Blood spurted from the man's arm.

"You cannot stop me. No one can stop me."

The man fell backward, moaning.

Booth leaped to his feet and raced to the railing, still clutching the bloodied knife. Without a moment's hesitation, he vaulted from the balustrade onto the stage. But the twelve foot flight was imperfect. He caught his right spur in the flag draped over the balcony and landed heavily on the platform. Pain seared through his left leg.

It's broken, he sobbed inwardly. He forced himself to stand, eyes smarting.

My greatest performance!

Booth lurched to stage center, playing to a shocked and horrified audience. He raised the bloodied knife, his face red with exultation, his voice impassioned with a fervent hatred.

"*Sic semper tyrannis*!"

Chapter 32

Washington City
April 14, 1865

"Whoa, hold up there. Halt, now."

John Wilkes Booth brought his horse up short and swallowed the pain of his broken ankle. He beamed at the sentry of the Navy Yard Bridge. Dressed for an evening at the theatre, he knew he appeared respectable. If only hc could calm his hammering heart and settle the roaring of blood.

"Bridge is closed after nine, mister." The sentry held Booth's lathered horse by the bridle and studied the rider closely.

"I understand, Sir." Booth steadied his voice. "I'm heading toward Southern Maryland. I've been on an errand in Washington and am running a bit late--trying to get back home. Do you suppose you can make an exception and let me cross?"

"What's your name?"

Booth smiled again. "John Wilkes Booth."

The guard squinted at Booth in the moonlight then waved him on.

Booth knew Davie Herold followed a short distance behind. He prayed Davie would pass through the sentry point as easily. He needed him.

He squinted at his watch in the moonlight. Less than an hour to midnight. He rode across the bridge then pulled over to wait for

Herold. His leg broiled with fire and nausea rose and fell in waves. He sat slumped in his saddle and closed his eyes briefly. Despite hot and cold flashes that raced up and down his body, he nodded off. Pounding hoofs jolted him awake a few moments later.

"Hey Johnny, I made it." Herold gave him an imbecilic grin.

Booth adjusted his weight in the saddle and turned his horse with difficulty. Slowly, he made his way down the road, southeast toward Surrattsville. Herold followed.

"How'd things go, Johnny?"

"We'll know soon, Davie. We'll know soon."

"What're we goin' to Surrattsville for, Johnny?"

"To pick up a few things at the tavern." Booth's head lolled against his chest. "And to get some whiskey to kill this bloody pain."

"Jeez, Johnny, maybe you should get to a doctor."

"I intend to, Davie, I intend to."

Booth pulled up in front of the tavern and swung his bad leg over the right side of the horse so he could dismount, tied his horse to the rail and hobbled inside. His eyes burned from the smoke-filled room and he peered around to find John Lloyd, the operator. He limped past several farmers drinking at the bar. No one paid him any notice.

Booth spotted Lloyd, head down on a table, reeking from liquor.

"Lloyd, wake up, man." Booth shook him and pulled him up by his thick black hair.

"Yeah, yeah, I'm up, whaddya. . . oh say, Booth, how the devil are--? Lloyd's words slurred.

"I'm great. Now listen here." Booth sat down next to Lloyd and leaned into his ear. "I am pretty sure we have assassinated the President and Secretary Seward."

Lloyd's jaw dropped and he stared bleary-eyed at Booth.

"Now, get me those carbines and field glasses that Surratt is holding for me. Hurry, man." Booth pulled Lloyd up and pushed him toward the back of the bar. The drunken man returned with the weapons. Booth grabbed them out of his hands, examined them, and his lip curled when he noticed the CA on the wooden stock. Concord Armaments.

Shit. I hope these fucking weapons work.

A few minutes later he and Herold had loaded up their horses. Before they could move on, the road vibrated with galloping hoofs. Booth grabbed the reins of his horse and pulled the animal behind the tavern.

"Davie, quick, here."

Pressed against the cold stone, he could hear men talking and laughing on the front porch. He dared a peek in the dirty window and held his breath at the sight of three Union soldiers clomping their way to the bar.

"Jaysus," Herold whispered. "That was close."

Booth blew out a breath, remembered the pain in his ankle.

"Davie, help me up. I've got to get this ankle set. It's torture."

Herold boosted him onto his horse, and the two rode quietly away from Surrattsville.

"Where we goin'?" Herold asked.

"Remember Dr. Mudd? Samuel Mudd? We'll head that way to his house. . .near. . . near Bryantown."

"Okay, Johnny, yeah, we'll go there."

Booth rode slowly ahead and dropped off to sleep a few times in the saddle. At four o'clock in the morning they arrived at Mudd's house. Herold got off his horse and ran to the front door, thumping on it with his fists like the devil chased him.

"There's a hurt man out here. We need a doctor bad," Herold shouted.

Booth sat lopsidedly on his horse waiting for the signal. He didn't want to dismount again for nothing. He lifted his head heavily when he saw a sliver of light beam through the open front door, and Herold came bounding down the porch steps, calling out, "Doctor's here, Johnny, come on."

"Help me down, Davie," Booth rasped.

Herold half-walked, half-carried his friend into the house, where Mudd ushered him into a bed in an upstairs room.

Booth stared at the doctor, not sure whether Mudd recognized him as a Shakespearean actor or not.

I'll not say anything. Better for both of us, he thought in a daze.

With a surgical instrument, the doctor slit his left boot and examined the swollen leg. Diagnosing a fractured fibula, Mudd fashioned a makeshift splint.

"How about the pain? Something--?"

"I'll get you some laudenum for the pain," Mudd said. "I'll also have my farmhand make you some crutches. You can't go anywhere like that."

"Doc, I need to send a note to someone. Do you have some paper and pen?"

"Why, uh, yes, sure. I'll get them."

Booth pulled himself clumsily to a sitting position and leaned back, exhausted and perspiring from the effort. He gazed around the room. Comfortable, well-appointed, greens and yellows, it reminded Booth of his room as a child on his family's farm in Maryland.

Mother, he thought. It's been so long.

The doctor handed him some paper, pen and a jar of ink, and left the room. Using a book to lean on, he wrote the following note:

The job is done. We have struck a blow for the South and I have given up all that was holy and sweet. Now for your promised assistance in departing this country. Perhaps your Captain Farrell can ferry me down the Rappahannock and out into the Chesapeake Bay. From there I can pick up a freighter to foreign lands. I will leave the details to you.

A good friend of mine, William Jett, will find refuge for me temporarily, somewhere near the town of Port Royal, Virginia. I will await word from you there at the General Store in his name. Do not fail me. If I am captured, your name will be on my lips. Yours and Rebecca's.

Booth blotted the note and inserted it in the envelope. On the outside he wrote:

Samuel Lindsey, Front Street, Georgetown, Washington.

*

Potomac River, Maryland
April 20, 1865

I have too great a soul to die like a criminal. . . Booth dotted his I's and closed his small leather bound diary wearily. His leg still pained him, but despair wore down his spirit. He felt so tired all the time. He lay flat on a soft cushion of grass in the Maryland countryside gazing up at a luminous sapphire sky.

I've got to get out of here. I can't keep hiding in the woods like a common thief. The anger made him weak, and minutes later he fell into a deep sleep.

"Johnny." Herold shook him gently by the shoulder. Booth started awake.

"Johnny, wake up. You're sleepin' again. You sleep too much."

Booth knew Herold spoke the truth. He had to get moving soon or he would plunge into a lethargic haze, unable to shake off this apathy. He struggled to sit up and held out a hand to Herold.

"Help me up."

Herold pulled him to his feet. "Want to read the paper, Johnny? I got one here. It's the--"

"No," Booth said sharply and Herold immediately shut up.

"No, Davie," Booth spoke more gently. "I've seen enough." He staggered as he shook out his legs and circled about. "Imagine. The tyrant is dead and the whole world mourns. And, dammit all, Paine never managed to kill that old man Seward. He bungled it. And that Hessian fool, Adzerodt, completely abandoned his job. Never even got near Johnson. Coward." He rubbed his three-day growth of beard. "And me?"

Herold waited, chewing his bottom lip.

"I've made Lincoln a martyr. That dictator, now I've done it." Booth put his face in his hands and groaned. "I'm a hero, don't you see?" He looked at Herold, eyes wild.

Herold recoiled from his idol.

"I'm the one who killed the old man and saved the South. So why doesn't the world acknowledge it? Instead I'm hunted, no better than an animal, how can that be?"

“Booth.”

He stopped short at the sound of a voice.

"Booth," a man called out.

Booth and Herold walked slowly out of the woods to meet their friend. Thomas Jones dressed like the farmer he was, in stained coveralls and oversized, floppy boots to help him wade through the muck in the stables.

"Thomas, my friend," Booth said. "I can't tell you how grateful I am for your help. Without you, we would never have made it."

"Well, Booth," Jones crinkled his weathered face in a grin, "you'll be really grateful when you hear the latest news on your bounty."

"What do you mean?"

"You're worth a good deal of money these days."

Booth waited.

"The Feds are offering a hundred thousand dollars for information leading to your capture."

"A hundred thousand dollars?" Herold whispered, mouth open.

Booth narrowed his eyes at Jones. "I see, and are you telling me that--?"

"No, Sir, I surely am not. You have nothing to fear from me. But the Feds are closing in. They've already arrested most of your friends."

"What? Who?" Booth reeled around, agitated.

"Well now, let's see," Jones scratched his head. "Sam Arnold, Paine, Atzerodt and Mary Surratt."

"Mary? Good God."

"John Surratt skedaddled off to Canada. Fine thing. Doesn't want to risk his skin, not even for his own mother." Jones shook his head.

Booth looked at him. "I've got to get to Virginia, Tom. Help me."

"Sure, sure. I've already arranged for a rowboat. Davie here can get you across, no problem. I've got some contacts who'll meet you there and get you hidden away."

"I must be in Port Royal soon. I'm to get an urgent communication there, one that will help me depart the country."

"You'll get there, don't worry. Now let me gather up some supplies and get you ready to travel tonight."

Jones turned and walked briskly back to the large gray farmhouse that completed the picturesque landscape. A red barn and silo stood on either side of the house, with stables to the right and in front, a huge pen for breaking and training horses.

Hours after dark, Booth sat on pins and needles waiting for Jones' return.

Can I trust him? A hundred thousand dollars is a lot of money. What if he calls the Feds? No, he wouldn't. God, I'm going mad.

When Jones finally arrived, he helped Booth mount a horse and the three men headed toward the Potomac. They passed through swamps and thick underbrush, even crossed a public road. As they neared the river, Jones hurried off to scout ahead and whistled them on.

Booth climbed down clumsily off the horse and hobbled over to the riverbank where Jones untied a small rowboat.

"Thomas," Booth clasped his friend's hand. "Thank you. Please let me pay you."

"No, Sir. The boat cost eighteen dollars. I'll take just that if you please."

Booth nodded and gave him the money while Herold scrambled aboard and manned the oars. Jones helped Booth into the boat and waved them goodbye.

By daybreak, after hours of rowing in the fog and dark, Booth studied the terrain surrounding the river.

"Christ, Davie, we're going nowhere. The incoming tide must've carried us several miles upstream, but this is still Maryland. Damn."

"Let's go back, Johnny."

"Wait, what's that?" Booth squinted through the mist at the Maryland shoreline. It looks like horses. I think those may be the same men we saw at Surrattsville."

"Oh no," Herold's voice rose.

"Ssh, quiet. They can't see us. Pull ashore over there." Booth pointed to a jet of land visible in the dawn light. "If I'm not mistaken there's a farmer lives there. Peregrine Davis, a true Confederate. He'll help us. We've got to get off this river now. Go on. Row, man, row."

Chapter 33

Port Royal, Virginia
April 25, 1865

John Wilkes Booth sat up and bumped his head on a low hanging branch of the locust tree. He swatted at the flies that buzzed around him and sucked on a daisy stem.

When will this end? He sighed.

He looked across the meadow to see Davie Herold running toward him waving a piece of paper. Davie wore the same filthy brown trousers and torn shirt that he'd had on for days.

Booth rubbed his head and pushed his greasy hair back. He hadn't shaved in a long while or barbered his hair in weeks and felt disgusted with life as an outlaw. He tried to tuck in his grimy shirt, snapped his suspenders and stood up, leaning on the tree for support.

Damn this ankle.

"A letter," Davie shouted.

Booth grabbed the envelope out of Herold's hand.

"Postmaster said it come two days ago." Herold grinned as if he were responsible for the good news.

"Two days ago? Why didn't I get it earlier?" Booth looked at the envelope addressed to William Jett, Port Royal General Store, Port Royal Virginia. He tore it open:

Am in receipt of your letter and feel it necessary that we meet and make final arrangements. Everything is under control, have no fear, but I did not want to chance sending you money in the post. I shall arrive on the afternoon of the 25th and will meet you at the same place this letter is addressed.

SL

Booth blinked. The 25th. That's today. He stuffed the letter in his pocket and pulled out his watch. Nearly two o'clock.

"We're going to the store, Davie." Booth tried to straighten his clothes and ran his fingers through his tangled mat of hair.

"Jeez, I just come from there."

The General Store sat in the middle of the only street in town, housed in an old brick building. The wooden porch out front sagged and tilted but somehow managed not to fall down. Inside, the small space overflowed. Barrels of sweets, sugar, flour and rice took up much of the floor. Sacks of barley and grain leaned carelessly in a corner. Shelves were packed with cans and jars of jams and molasses. One customer, an old lady, occupied the owner's time. Booth bought some tobacco and rolled a cigarette as he waited outside. Across from the store he could see the town's only saloon. Next door sat the Post Office, and next to that the Town Hall. Both civic buildings appeared deserted. Only the saloon sported some life, with men coming and going, laughter and the sounds of an out-of-tune piano tumbling from its swinging doors.

By the time he finished his fourth cigarette, his nerves twitched, and he paced in front of the porch, his bad ankle paining him. He stopped and turned at the sound of a horse and carriage clopping down the road. Moments later, the driver climbed down and opened the carriage doors. Samuel Lindsey stepped out, slapped the dust off his suit, and approached Booth.

"Ah, John, you appear the worse for wear," Lindsey smiled thinly. "Where shall we talk?"

Booth took his elbow and ushered him across the street to the bar. They sat at a table in the far corner and ordered two whiskeys.

"You don't look well," Lindsey said.

"What do you expect? I'm on the run, an outlaw. Instead of a national hero, I'm a pariah. Hated by everyone." He picked up his glass. "You wouldn't look your best under these circumstances, hiding in the bushes every night. Now let's get on with it." Booth slugged down his drink, eyes flashing.

Lindsey waved a hand, "All right, no need to get testy. I'm here to help you, remember?" He cleared his throat. "I have secured the means of travel to remove you from this country. However, my associates and I feel that it's imperative to convince the Federal authorities that you have not just disappeared, but, indeed, have perished."

"Brilliant. So I'm dead am I? And how will that be accomplished?"

"We have arranged the following scenario: a man, by the name of Lucas, of limited mental capabilities, but of similar height, weight and coloring to yourself has been retained by Mister Hobbs as a ruse to lead the Federals astray. Another man, a Union Sergeant by the name of Boston Corbett, has been bribed to shoot the man assumed to be you."

"But it's *not* me, they'll know, they'll recognize--"

"He will shoot you," Lindsey said with a flicker of impatience, "and destroy the evidence. Several other cavalrymen will assist him. They have also been paid."

"What about the ones who haven't been paid?"

"They will be kept away from the body. Believe me, only certain officers will be allowed near the dead assassin, for security reasons. It's all worked out."

"And have these officers been paid?"

"Handsomely."

Booth screwed his eyes up at Lindsey. "Go on."

"Tomorrow afternoon, you will lead your friend, David Herold, to the Garrett barn. You know it?"

"Of course I know it."

"This is important." Lindsey leaned forward. "You must convince Herold to wait for you inside and not to leave for any reason. Can you do that?"

"I can convince Davie the sky is orange if I've a mind to. He has little mind of his own."

"Herold must be captured so that the authorities are convinced that the dead man is you."

"Will Davie know the truth?"

"What do you think?"

"No," Booth said. "If he does, he'll never be able to keep it secret."

"Correct. He must think you're dead. That will convince the authorities as well."

Booth waited. "So, you want me to give up my friend?"

"To save your own skin, yes," Lindsey said. "Is that a problem?"

"No."

"I didn't think so."

"Go on."

"You will then hide on the back side of the Garrett farmhouse, where my carriage will escort you back to Washington."

"What? Washington? The whole damn Army is searching for me--"

"You'll be dead, remember? No one will be searching for you."

Booth narrowed his eyes. "Why do I need to go to Washington?"

"So you can kill the last two men who are a threat to us. The men that know who you are and what you've done. The only men that can tie you to Concord Armaments . . . and to me." Lindsey leaned back in his chair.

"Sanford Baxter and Joseph Thornhill," Booth said.

"Once they have been dispatched, you will then be escorted to a riverboat and out to the Bay. From there you'll board a frigate sailing to Portugal."

"Why Portugal?"

"We have friends there who can help you get, er, adjusted."

"And my frigate abroad--Captain Farrell to the rescue?"

"At that time, I will hand you one hundred and fifty thousand dollars. . ."

Booth raised his eyebrows.

". . .which should see your way comfortably for a long time on the continent. That will end our relationship and my debt to you."

Booth stared into mid-space. That night would be his last in hiding. Tomorrow someone in his place would be dead and a few days later he would be on his way to Europe and a new life.

"Now, is everything satisfactory?" Lindsey spoke softly. "Are you clear on your final mission and the events of your, er, demise?"

Booth gave a quick nod.

"Good," Lindsey said. "After you sail, our relationship is over. I do not expect to hear from you ever again."

"Ever again. Now that's a long time, Samuel," Booth said. "A very long time."

*

Garrett's Farm

April 26, 1865

"Hey, what? Who are you?" Davie Herold reached for the carbine he'd propped up against a bale of hay. He looked at the man who had just ambled casually in through the barn doors and was struck by the resemblance to Booth.

"Hi," the man said simply in a deep voice.

Herold walked over to him, noticing he was unarmed and said, "Who are you? What d'ya want here?"

"Oh nothin'. My friend told me to come in here and wait. Said I'd know what to do when the time come."

"Time come for what?"

"Dunno." The man smiled.

"What's your name anyway?" Herold asked.

"Lucas. What's yours?"

"Uh, Davie. Davie Herold." He screwed his eyes at the stranger. "Who's your friend?"

"He said his name's Booth."

"Jaysus. Don't you know your own friend's name? You have ta' wait 'til he tells ya'?"

"Uh, whatdy'a mean?"

"Agh. Never mind, never mind, forget it. Just sit down and we'll both wait for Johnny." Herold rubbed his forehead in frustration.

Herold thought about making conversation with the man, decided not to. He wasn't much of a conversationalist anyway. He lay back down against a bale of hay, watching the dust and bits of hay cavorting around the air in the sunlight streaking through the window. The barn felt warm and safe. He looked over at Lucas. Asleep.

Herold's eyelids drooped and within minutes, he too fell asleep. He didn't know how long he'd been sleeping, when confused and dazed, he awoke to the sounds of men shouting and horses braying.

He noticed Lucas lift his head up off the hay sleepily then lay back down, ignoring the ruckus outside.

"What the hell?" Herold jumped up and ran to look out through a small opening in the barn board. "Holy Christ, Holy God. It's the whole of the Union Army."

"John Wilkes Booth, come out with your hands up. Surrender or we'll have your damned head."

Herold's eyes bugged out. He looked around him for escape, saw none.

Trapped!

"Come out with your hands up," the voice bellowed again.

"Wait, wait," shouted Herold. "I want to surrender. Please, don't shoot. I'm comin' out."

Herold kicked open the door and walked out, hands above his head, face knotted in fear. Several cavalrymen rushed over and ushered him away, as Herold cried and groaned over and over, "I didn't do it, I didn't do it."

"Booth, come out," a lieutenant yelled.

Herold screamed, "He ain't in there. That ain't him."

The lieutenant yelled back. "Oh, he's there all right. I saw him with my own eyes."

Oh God, Johnny, why did you come back? Herold thought in despair.

In a panic that Booth had returned to face a firing squad, he shouted, "Johnny, look out, don't come out. Run, Johnny, run."

One of the soldiers thunked Herold on the head with the butt of his rifle and he burst into tears. He watched the scene in front of the barn through blurry eyes.

"This is your last chance," the Lieutenant ordered. He turned to one of his men and gave a signal. The man hurried around to the back of the barn and, grabbing a handful of hay, set it afire. Then he threw the burning hay into the barn and in moments flames burst inside and thick gray smoke billowed through the doors. The fire snapped and crackled as the dry barn boards lit up in an inferno.

"Nooo," Herold moaned.

As the soldiers bent on one knee, took aim at the front of the barn, Lucas, finally recognizing the danger, rushed out the front doors. He slapped at sparks on his arms, screaming at the top of his lungs. His face and clothes streaked with soot, he appeared an apparition from a slave colony.

Tied to a tree, Herold couldn't get a clear view of the man running from the barn. But he gaped at the sergeant who deliberately took aim and fired. The screaming man fell. The sergeant and his men rushed in and dragged him away from the burning barn, carried him to Garrett's porch and lay him down.

"Johnny," Herold sobbed, shrieked at the troops, "Why'd ya have ta kill 'em?"

Soldiers scurried around, rounding up the other accomplices from the farm house and escorting them to a wagon nearby. But Herold couldn't take his eyes from his friend, lying on the porch.

He squeezed his eyes shut. No, not Johnny. He can't be dead.

"Get that saddle blanket over here," the lieutenant ordered a soldier. "You," he instructed his sergeant, "get needle and thread from the house and sew up the body in the blanket."

Herold watched, drool hanging in threads from his mouth, as they carried the remains of the body to a wagon. Guarded by soldiers, tears streaming down his cheeks, Herold rode alongside the wagon.

Goodbye, Johnny. I'm sorry I couldn't save you.

Chapter 34

Dumbarton Street, Georgetown

April 26, 1865

Late that night, Joseph sat in his study working on captioning his photograph albums. His suit jacket hung on a hook nearby, and he had removed his tie and loosened his collar. Lighting his pipe, he leaned back in his chair, content, thinking about Sara and his son. He still had trouble imagining himself as a father. He'd have a hundred photo albums dedicated to him, and his brothers and sisters, when they arrive. And I'll teach him to take photographs, learn the profession. In Joshua's lifetime, the science will have advanced. Maybe, action photographs will be just as commonplace as still-lifes are today.

He puffed on his pipe and looked around the comfortable room, lined in books, mahogany wainscoting and rich leather furniture. Mostly Sara's heirlooms but he loved them. His eyes rested on a photograph on his desk. One he had personally taken of Mister Lincoln. Such an interesting face, always changing. Sometimes young, sometimes old. Often homely, occasionally handsome. Lincoln. And now he was dead. God in heaven.

Sara knocked softly then entered. She sat across the desk from him.

"I still can't believe he's dead, Sara. I was in his office just two weeks ago." Joseph dropped his head in his hands. "Why didn't I see it?"

"What could you see, Joseph? That John Wilkes Booth was an assassin? That he was the civilian who killed those agents in the field?"

"Including Sean. He was my friend, Sara. My God. Why didn't I recognize him? I should have. I'm a photographer, for heaven's sake, I am trained to see things others don't."

"Booth is a master of disguise, an actor with all manner of ways to mask his real identity. No, dear, you couldn't have known."

Sara picked up the picture of Lincoln that Thornhill had taken a year ago. "Very sad. For us, for the country, for the future."

"He would have done something. Lincoln. He would have punished Lindsey and his cronies. Put Concord Armaments out of business." He paused. "So many deaths, needless deaths. Even though the President was generous to a fault, he wouldn't have shown mercy. Not for these crimes."

Restless, Joseph sprang out of his chair and walked to the large floor-to-ceiling window draped and valanced in heavy green brocade. He stared down at the rain bouncing on the wet macadam. A carriage was parked across the street, and the driver sat on top, bearing an oversized umbrella to shield himself. Joseph realized he could not see the driver or the carriage very well in the dark. Then he noticed the gas lamps were not lit in front of the house. Hmm, he'd have to see to those in the morning.

Sara stood, went to him. He bent, kissed her forehead. "Go to bed, love. It's late."

"What about you?" she said.

"I'll be up shortly." He turned back to stare out the window, heard the door close softly behind her.

Joseph's mind tried to grasp the immensity of the situation. How could he right this terrible wrong? If Pinkerton and Baxter couldn't convince the new President, Johnson, to act, then what could he do? And Johnson wouldn't act. He felt sure of it. Johnson was weak. He claimed the country needed to heal, and that there was no point pursuing profiteering and treason when he had a Presidential assassination and conspiracy to deal with.

Joseph banged his fist on the window jamb. His mind was so caught up in his thoughts that he never registered someone entering the room and stealing up behind him. Until he saw the man's image shimmering in the wet glass. Those black, insolent . . . triumphant eyes.

Too late.

Maggie

Chapter 35

Dumbarton Street, Georgetown

Monday, June 10, 2000, 8:00 a.m.

Maggie heard the doorbell but it took a few minutes to register. She was on her bed, propped against three pillows with her laptop on her legs and Joseph's journal opened at her side. She pressed Save and shut down the Mac, then scurried out of bed. "Coming," she yelled.

A moment later she opened the door to Frank Mead and Charlie Byrd, his sergeant. Mead held up a bag of bagels.

"Gentlemen." She smiled and led them into the kitchen where she poured three cups of coffee.

Mead and Byrd dug into the bag, brought out bagels and a container of cream cheese. Maggie got out plates and utensils then sat down at the kitchen table.

"What's the occasion?" she asked.

Mead sliced an onion bagel and spread cream cheese on it. Byrd did the same with a cinnamon raisin.

"Anything on the DNA?" Maggie said.

"You know how long that takes." Mead's smile displayed dimples, which she always thought rather counter-productive for a homicide cop. "I've called in a few favors. We'll know soon."

"You think it's Joseph?" Byrd said. He reminded Maggie of a stork with his gangly limbs and beak-like nose.

"It's got to be Joseph," she said.

"Have a bagel," Mead said. "Actually, we came for two reasons. First, to tell you the crime lab team found no significant evidence from the site that would lead us in any helpful direction. Dead end. Two, I wanted Charlie to hear about the diary. He's a Civil War buff. Got a whole battle scene, what--Gettysburg?--set up on his dining room table, soldiers in full battle regalia and all."

"Awright, awright," Byrd said.

Maggie smiled and regaled Byrd with Joseph's spying activities.

"So Joseph assumed the government agents were murdered," Byrd said. "But how, with no visible wounds? And, more important, why?"

"I can answer the why easier," she said. "These majors were investigating allegations of shoddy arms and equipment. Guns, ammunition, ordnance in general, of an inferior quality, produced cheaply and quickly to make a profit."

"Profiteering," Byrd said.

Maggie nodded. "Joseph also left damning photographs of crates and guns stacked in front of the Richmond Depot." She looked at Byrd, waited.

"Richmond, Virginia. So the arms company sold guns to the South as well as the North."

Byrd leaned back in his chair and smiled. "Treason."

"Treason," Maggie echoed.

"Do we know who the company is?" Byrd said.

Maggie smiled inwardly at Byrd's use of *we*. He'd bought into Joseph's mystery.

"We do, in fact. The name was printed on the crates."

"Convenient, "Byrd said.

"A company called Concord Armaments, located in Concord, Massachusetts."

No one spoke for a few minutes.

"You think all this is tied in to the body?" Byrd said.

"I do," Maggie said.

"Well, it was a long time ago. I mean who are we going to prosecute today, a hundred and fifty years later?" Byrd paused. "This company, Concord Armaments. Are they still around?"

"They're now called Concord Provisions," Mead said. "On the surface, they look legit. May be. They sell camping gear, survival equipment and--"

"And guns," Byrd finished.

They fell silent, sipped their cold coffee.

"Well, hell," Byrd said. "Maybe we should contact Robert Redford and make this into a movie."

"I don't know about Redford," Mead said, "but I contacted a feebie friend who said Concord Provisions has a number of big government contracts. Right now they're under investigation. All hush hush." He raised an eyebrow.

"You think they're carrying on the old tradition?" Byrd said.

Mead shrugged. "Lotta' money in guns."

"Selling guns to who, al Qaeda? Iran?" Byrd asked.

Maggie said, "Makes my skin crawl."

Byrd got up and poured himself more java, sat down.

"There's more," Maggie said. "At the end of the war, Joseph and his Army boss, Colonel Sanford Baxter, brought all this evidence to the President."

"To Lincoln? Holy shit," Byrd said.

"Lincoln promised to look into it," Maggie said. "To launch a full-blown inquiry into Concord Armaments."

Byrd sat on the edge of his seat. "And?"

"He was assassinated a few nights later," she said.

"Convenient," Mead said.

Byrd stood, walked around the kitchen and back again. "Go on, tell me there's more."

Maggie smiled. "The last entry Joseph made in his diary spoke of a report that Colonel Baxter wrote, outlining the whole conspiracy. The report was supposedly kept sealed for thirty years. The country was in such turmoil that President Johnson decided to muffle it."

"You're sh--, kidding me?" Byrd said.

"I'm not and I don't think Joseph was. I think he was murdered for what he knew."

"Where is this report?" Byrd said.

"I wish I knew," she said. "But I'm going to find it. Somehow."

Maggie tapped a spoon on the table. "And I'm also going to find out who that civilian was."

"How the hell you gonna do that?" Byrd asked. "Got a time machine you can crank up?"

"The answer's already here," Maggie said with a faraway look. "In the photographs."

Chapter 36

Georgetown University

Monday, June 10, 2000, 10:00 a.m.

Charlie Byrd left but Mead lingered in Maggie's kitchen. "You going down to the lab to analyze the photographs?" he asked.

"Yeah." She started cleaning up the kitchen. Mead picked up some plates and cups and set them in the sink.

"Forget the dishes," she said. "Come on down to the lab with me and I'll show you how it's done." She looked at him. "If you have time."

"Hey, I'm on a case. A cold case." His broad smile made her think of a kid with a new bike.

"Just let me collect everything." She headed straight for her bedroom and gathered all the photos, letters and the journal into the satchel.

Mead's car was parked on Dumbarton Street.

"I think you just want me along for *the ride*," he said.

The Georgetown University's Digital Photography Lab on the fourth floor of the Arts and Humanities Building was state-of-the-art worldwide. As director, Maggie was often called in by law enforcement to digitize images and documents on local and federal cases.

A dozen students were busy on projects at their stations. Equipment hummed and an iPod hooked to a Bose receiver cranked out *Indigo Girls* in the background. Maggie waved and zoomed straight into her office, Mead tailing behind. The students knew enough not to bug her with questions when she was in a tear like this.

She switched on the computer first, and while it booted, turned on the scanner, printer and finally, the office lights.

"Grab a chair."

Mead rolled a chair next to Maggie's. She typed at warp speed and within minutes, the civilian's face was ready for analysis.

"So here's Joseph's civilian. Now I download my facial recognition software."

"You use that a lot in serial rapist cases, don't you?"

"Oh yeah. Come on, come on," she said. "Takes a while to load."

Finally, all was ready. She cracked her knuckles and shook out her fingers.

"Okay. Joseph's photograph caught the civilian at three-quarter view, so I'm going to turn him frontally and fill in the missing features. Since human faces aren't symmetrical, it'll take a little artistic license."

"Human faces aren't symmetrical, huh?" Mead said.

"No, if you cut your face in half and morph two right sides or two left sides together into one face, you'd have two different people."

She angled the face on the computer to a frontal view, studying him with her photographer's eye.

"Anything strike you odd about the face?" she asked.

"Yeah," Mead said. "It's like there's something artificial about him. Staged."

"I agree. But what? His coloring?" She tapped some keys. "Yes. His blond hair doesn't match the dark eyes, mustache and eyebrows."

"Right," Mead said. "Maybe he's wearing a wig."

"All the more reason to suspect him of something sinister. Who wears a blond wig on the battlefield of the Civil War, for heaven's sake?"

With the Mac's artist's tools, Maggie copied the features from the visible left side of his face to the blank right side. Then she began to re-shape those so they looked more realistic. She narrowed his new eye, changing the slant slightly.

"Fill in the eyebrow," Mead said.

"Want to do this?" But she filled in his eyebrow, making it thicker and darker.

"The mustache is easy," she said. "At least the two sides look like they belong together now."

Maggie pushed her chair back and examined him.

"Well, it's better, more realistic. But the shape of the face doesn't seem right."

"You'd know better than me," Mead said. "I can see why you need artistic license here." His cell rang and he grabbed it off his belt, walked into the outer room.

For the next few minutes she adjusted the civilian's cheekbones and forehead lines. His hair seemed full and thick from what she could see, but maybe it's parted on the side and his hairline is actually receding? She tried that. Then she sat back again. Tried again.

Mead returned. "Can't stay long."

"Frank, I think you're right about the coloring. Those black eyes don't fit."

"I don't think they had contacts back then, so he didn't change his eye color. I still say it's a wig."

"Handsome devil, though, whoever he was," Maggie said. "Now for the next step. Thanks to Professor Homer Catesby, a pre-eminent Civil War expert at the competing University, I have a program disk that could be the answer to this identification dilemma."

"What's the expert's solution?"

"Homer's graduate American History class is digitizing all the Civil War photos that they could access for a new database. This includes not just famous Civil War celebrities but even the common soldier. In the end, there could be hundreds of thousands of photographs available for study."

Mead whistled.

She slid the disk into the drive and waited. After a few whirrs and bleeps she tapped the keys to give instructions.

"Old Mac here will now attempt to match the civilian with the students' archives. She pressed Enter. "Go, Baby."

Maggie stood and stretched her arms in the air.

"Coffee?" She made a beeline for the Mr. Coffee at the other end of the room, as if she needed a wire in her blood, and brought back two steaming mugs.

"Did I miss anything?" she asked.

"Nothing's changed. Still searching," Mead said. "How long will it take?"

"Truthfully?" Maggie sighed. "This could take hours, even days, depending on the size of the database."

"Uh, days?"

"Well, there are so many photos. Plus, it might never find a match."

Mead's cell buzzed. He listened a while then clicked off. His look told Maggie he'd learned something big.

"That was the ME. She found a small puncture wound in the back of the mummy's neck. A wound caused by a tool like an ice pick."

"I knew it," she said.

Mead sat down in front of the computer and watched.

The caffeine combined with her restless night of sleep made Maggie jittery and her body buzzed with a tingling sensation. She held her hands out in front of her. "Yikes. I'm shaky from anticipation."

"And twelve cups of high-test."

She caught T.J. out of the corner of her eye.

"One of the students beamed me in," he said. "Hope you don't mind my stopping by." He nodded to Mead.

"Not at all." She turned around to accept a light kiss on the lips.

Maggie explained what they were doing.

"Amazing technology."

"Hmm, we'll see how amazing."

"Nothing yet?"

"It's really foolish to sit around waiting. It will probably be days," she said.

At that moment a beeping noise from the computer drew them to the monitor. Maggie rolled her chair close. Mead and T.J. leaned over her shoulders. The screen flashed the words over and over again: A match has been found.

"You know what this means?" she said. "The reason that the computer found a match this soon?"

"What?" Mead said.

"The civilian is a match to someone famous."

"Let me guess. Robert E. Lee," Mead said.

Maggie rolled her eyes. Then she swallowed hard and pressed a few keys. She minimized the civilian's face and moved it to the right half of the screen. On the left a new photograph began to emerge, pixellating, dot by dot, line by line in agonizing slowness. Maggie tapped her fingers on the desk, heartbeat escalating with each passing second.

"Where's the drum roll?" T.J. asked.

And then it was done. Except for the hair, the two pictures matched. Two men stared back at her from the screen, both had dark, penetrating eyes, but one was blond, the other dark-haired.

In a quick flurry of motion her fingers signaled the computer its final commands. Within seconds a name appeared under the matching photograph.

She stared in disbelief at the three words, color draining from her face and let out a small moan.

"Holy shit, holy shit," T.J. said.

"Holy shit," Mead said.

"John Wilkes Booth," Maggie whispered.

"The civilian in Thornhill's photo was John Wilkes Booth."

Mead dropped into the chair next to her. "What does this mean?" he said. "Booth assassinated Lincoln. Did he kill all those agents too? How? Why?"

Maggie shook her head as if to clear a fog. "What do we know about Booth? He was a Shakespearean actor, wasn't he?"

"He was also a southern sympathizer, a zealot, in fact," Mead said. "He hated Lincoln with a vengeance and everything he stood for."

Maggie stood up, almost knocking her chair down. "This isn't possible. Could I have made a mistake."

"You don't make mistakes," Mead said.

"This isn't a perfect science. Maybe the features I attributed to him--"

"Look," T.J. said. "Look at the photos. It's him. The face is the same, Maggie."

She stared at the monitor, knowing he was right. "How can that be?"

Mead gazed off into the past. "Booth was said to be the mastermind of a conspiracy to wipe out the government. The Vice President, Secretary of State, and Secretary of War were all targets that night. Only Lincoln died."

"I should know this," she said. "After all I come from a Civil War background."

"Me too," T.J. said. "Mom and Dad are Civil War descendants. They have all kinds of memorabilia, old muskets, minié balls, photo albums around the house."

Maggie looked at him a minute, realizing she'd known that but never paid attention.

"So what now?" T.J. asked.

"If Joseph's diary is a credible source," Maggie began piecing the story together, "then John Wilkes Booth was not merely an assassin who believed vehemently in his own cause as history has portrayed him."

Mead spoke quietly, "He was a hired assassin. He killed four officers as well as the President of the United States."

Maggie's mind spun like a cyclone trying to swoop up every bit of information in its path. "He may have killed Joseph." She threw her well-chewed pencil down and stood. "How could this have been kept secret for so long?"

"The men who hired Booth certainly would have wanted it kept secret," T.J. said. "Maybe they had a lot of power to bury it."

"Yeah," Maggie said. "And I'd bet my life that those same men were connected to the company involved in the profiteering."

"Makes sense," T.J. said.

"Maybe it started as profiteering," she said. "Manufacturing weapons on the cheap to save a buck. It escalated into gunrunning." She folded her arms around herself. "Why sell just to the North if the South could pay too?"

"Profiteering and treason," Mead said. "High crimes. Adding murder and assassination wouldn't be much of a stretch."

"It had to end in murder," Maggie said. "Those four agents had to die or the profiteers' dirty little secrets would've gotten out."

"But they did get out," TJ said. "Through Thornhill."

"Right," she said. "Joseph and Baxter went straight to the top."

Mead said, "And Abraham Lincoln had to die."

"Jesus, Maggie," T.J. said. "If you're right, do you know what this means? It changes history."

Maggie slumped into her chair. "And Joseph was the last thread that could unravel them all. He'd seen the civilian and could identify him."

They fell silent, each roiling in thought.

"This is going to throw the textbook publishers into a tizzy," T.J. said. His cell beeped and he walked off to speak.

"Where does that leave us?" Mead said. "Call the history police, report it?"

"There's more I need to research," she said.

She steadied her gaze on Mead. He waited.

"If we can connect Booth and Concord Armaments then we have a new motive for killing Lincoln. Before going public with this, I need to know if there's a link and what that link is."

Chapter 37

Library of Congress

Tuesday, June 11, 2000, 11:00 a.m.

Maggie's eyes scanned the reading room in the Library of Congress without seeing it. Her hand unconsciously stabbed at the notepad in front of her. In the last two hours, she'd gone through a dozen books and articles and found no reference whatsoever to the sealed government file that Joseph wrote about.

It's got to be here.

She rubbed her eyes and settled reading glasses back on her nose. Slowly she turned her attention to the book in front of her, a heavy volume about the Lincoln years written by John Hay, one of Abe's trusted secretaries. If anyone knew what happened after the assassination, Hay did. In the index, there was only one mention of a Special Services investigation. She couldn't give up. Thirty minutes went by and then there it was. Her wandering eyes caught it--a sealed portfolio. She straightened in her chair. Her blood began to percolate.

So as not to cause further dissidence and disunity to the fragile United States of America, the Cabinet under President Andrew Johnson and with his approval, heretofore secures the information regarding the Executive Mansion Investigation (during the years 1861-1865) in a sealed portfolio, not to be opened before thirty years have passed.

How could she locate that file? Professor Homer Catesby.

Rather than call, Maggie took a taxi to GWU. She prayed the Professor would be in his office, not teaching a class, but she'd wait if she had to.

His office was on the third floor of the History and Political Science Building. She knocked, tried the knob and it opened. A woman sat at a desk in the front office. Maggie was about to inquire after the Professor when the inner office door opened and Homer Catesby walked out.

"Maggie, what a nice surprise. Come in, please." He looked at her face then said to his secretary, "no calls or interruptions, Susan."

Maggie seated herself in a leather high-back chair across a large mahogany desk from Catesby. She wore a white silk blouse, slightly wilted from humidity and anxiety, and black slacks. She crossed one leg over the other to keep them still.

"Professor, I need your help." She explained her mission.

He leaned forward, mouth slightly parted as if he might salivate on his desk.

"My God, a document written by a Union Army Colonel and sealed by President Johnson."

"Do you have any idea where it might be?" Maggie asked.

Catesby sank back in his chair and rocked. "We have a collection of Civil War documents, waiting to be digitized. Most of the originals are preserved at the National Archives."

She waited.

"1865? Sealed for thirty years?" He thrummed his fingers on the desk. "I don't know. I just can't imagine such a valuable item being filed away here."

"Were there other documents that were sealed? Sensitive information that the government wouldn't want made public?"

"There were soldiers' war records."

"Excuse me?"

"Maggie, in any war, soldiers do, uh, bad things. When they're caught, if they have influence--"

"You mean money?"

"Of course. To keep from being exposed, they can have their records either expunged or filed away until all the principals are dead. That way nobody in their time knows what they did."

"What *did* they do?" Maggie asked.

"Went AWOL for the most part. Deserted. But there are some cases of cruel and unusual treatment of the enemy. Massacres of innocent civilians, torture, horrible things."

Maggie pondered this. "I never thought. . . what other documents would be sealed for thirty years?"

"Knowledge of any conspiracies against the government. There were many of those during the Civil War, besides the Booth conspiracy, of course. There were also many spies. For both sides. Some double agents, to use a James Bond term." He paused. "You told me yourself that your ancestor was an agent. One of the good guys, of course, working for Lincoln, but nevertheless a spy." Catesby sighed. "No, those were ruthless times and ruthless men. Terrible things happened and not just on the battlefield."

"So what are the chances this document that John Hay mentioned could really exist and be mixed in with these other sealed files?" she said.

"One way to find out. Search through them." Catesby stood. "Follow me."

Maggie felt her hands go clammy. Was this really happening? Was she going to find the missing document?

She followed the Professor down long, winding hallways, upstairs and across another hallway, which ended at two double doors. The doors opened into an immense library with no windows to the outside. The walls were rich dark wood, and books lined every shelf from floor to ceiling. Rolling ladders moved across each wall for access.

She stopped and gaped. "This is stunning, Professor. I had no idea there was such a library outside of the Library of Congress."

"It is pretty impressive, isn't it?" He hurried to one corner, where he started running his hands over a shelf of large reference books.

What's really impressive, Maggie thought, is that he probably knows every book in this library.

"So here," he said, pulling a book from the shelf. This lists all the files, folders, special boxes of loose documents that have been collected over the years, over the centuries."

Maggie swallowed the dryness in her mouth.

"Should we use the year it was sealed, 1865, or the year it was to be released, 1895?" he asked.

"Can't we try both?"

He chuckled. "If you have a few months to go through them all, yes."

"Oh God, really?"

"Now don't lose faith. We may find it first thing."

Or we may never find it at all.

"What was the Colonel's name again?"

"Sanford Baxter," she said.

He handed her the volume. "This lists everything in the collection. You start here. I'll get the second volume." He smiled. "It's research, dear, not entertainment."

It was Maggie's turn to laugh.

She began scrutinizing page by page the lists of files in the library. Catesby did the same with his book. Hours flew by, students and faculty came and went, voices rose and died, still they found no reference to the sealed portfolio in question. Throughout the day, Maggie texted with T.J., Mead and her contractor amongst other communications. Catesby left a few times to attend to business. They both skipped lunch. By dinnertime, they were starving, so decided to grab a bite at a nearby café. Following dinner, they were back again at the library.

"What time does it close?" she asked.

"It doesn't. Not for me." He grinned like a school boy.

They lowered their heads into their books and kept going.

At nine-thirty, bleary-eyed, Maggie was ready to stop for the night. She worried that the Professor would get worn down. That's when she saw it. *Executive Mansion Investigation, 1860-1865. Do Not Open until the year 1895 under penalty of Article 2113.*

"Professor?" she rasped out, her breath coming fast.

"The White House wasn't called the White House during the Civil War, was it?"

"No. It was called the Executive Mansion."

"You need to look at this."

He scooted out of his chair and leaned over her shoulder, read the entry. Neither spoke for a few moments.

Finally, he broke the silence. "This may be it."

"Where would we find it?"

"Give me the numbers that are next to that entry."

Maggie called them out, while he wrote them down.

"Come with me." He took off down the corridor into a small anteroom. There he examined the shelves, then pulled over a ladder. He climbed to the top shelf, began searching.

Maggie chewed her lower lip and paced below.

“Yahoo,” Catesby cried. He pulled out a file folder, climbed down.

Catesby slid out a yellowed document sheathed in a special coated plastic-like material. “Ah, good, already been conserved.”

He laid it down on the work table and they both leaned over.

"Why do you think it was never acted upon, even after the thirty-year time limit?" she asked.

"My guess is that they forgot about it,” Catesby said. “Perhaps the principals involved were dead, many administrations had come and gone. Maybe only a few people knew about it. No doubt some government bureaucrat stuffed the envelope away somewhere, forever forgotten."

"God, look at my hands,” she said. “They're shaking."

"Move that lamp closer.”

She did.

He looked at her, clasped her hand a moment then said, “Read it out loud.”

Her voice sounded hoarse and feathery to her ears.

“To Whom It May Concern,

The documents and photographs contained in this packet and my narration of the events that occurred between 1861-1865 regarding the Executive Mansion Investigation will be sealed by the present administration under my protest. I fervently trust that thirty years hence, the future administration will uncover these documents and confer justice where it is due.

The terrible events of the past two weeks have precluded an end to the investigation that spanned the entire war. However, I must lay down the facts that came to my attention near the war’s end and warranted the President’s full deliberation. Mister Lincoln set up a special task force to investigate allegations of profiteering in private arms and munitions factories after the second battle of Bull Run. I headed up that investigation in which four U.S. Staff majors were charged with the task of proving or denying those allegations specifically to one ordnance company: Concord Armaments.

Each of those officers either disappeared or died under peculiar circumstances. Before his untimely death, the fourth operative, Major Sean O'Connor had engaged the help of one Union Army photographer, a Mister Joseph Thornhill, who worked on occasion for the U.S. Secret Service under Mister Allan Pinkerton. Mister Thornhill carried on the investigation at that juncture, but in September of 1864, disappeared for a period of nearly four months. Fortunately, he resurfaced prior to the Confederate surrender at Appomattox. Attached is his affidavit to the effect that he had taken photographs on the battlefields of Antietam and Fredericksburg of two government investigators, Major Randall Sills and Major Philip Malone, both dead; he also photographed an unknown civilian on said battlefields, who might have been the agent of death for both officers."

Maggie's eyes popped. "Agent of death?"

"Keep going," Catesby said.

"Mister Thornhill brought with him to Washington the documents, herein enclosed, and related the disturbing news regarding the company Concord Armaments."

"Who's that?" he asked.

"Concord Armaments was thc ordnance company under investigation for profiteering and possibly treason. The foundry, operated by Concord Armaments, was where the weapons were actually manufactured."

"Unbelievable," Catesby said. "Go on, please."

"Not only have these companies been guilty of deliberately manufacturing defective and inadequate guns, munitions and artillery for the sole purpose of increasing profits, but, in addition, they were selling same arms to the Confederacy. They are guilty of the most heinous of all crimes. . . treason.

"Mister Thornhill managed to obtain the photographs, in separate package. . ."

"Those were in Joseph's satchel," Maggie said.

". . . proving beyond a reasonable doubt, that Concord Armaments did indeed ship arms and munitions to the South."

"Those were the photos at the Richmond Depot?" Catesby said.

Maggie nodded. *"Thornhill rushed this documentation to me and we immediately brought it to the President's attention. That was on April 12 of this year."*

She turned to the Professor and they both sat open-mouthed.

"The course of events that followed that night and for the next several weeks is now a sad part of American history. The documents regarding this investigation have been buried by the present Johnson administration under the guise of sensitivity. It seems there is fear that, since the principals involved are prominent and powerful businessmen, uncovering such a scandal would only add to the present government turmoil. I, therefore, wish to set the record straight here and now, and pray that justice will inevitably be discharged.

The company in question is owned and facilitated by: Samuel Lindsey, Porter Hobbs and Harlow Knox. These are wealthy men who have no scruples, no ethical or moral standards, and it is not unlikely that they arranged for the death and disappearance of the four agents.

The documents herein relate as I know it, the story of the profiteering, gunrunning, and treason of the aforementioned parties. I leave it to the reader to see that amends are made and justice prevails.

Sanford T. Baxter, Colonel

United States Army,

April 24, 1865

Maggie scrambled to find her notes. "Wait a sec. When did John Wilkes Booth die?"

"April 26, in Garrett's Barn. Why?"

"Coincidently, Baxter suffered a heart attack in the dining room at the Willard Hotel on April 26."

Maggie fixed Catesby with a hard stare. "There's a lot more to tell you, Professor. You'd better sit down."

Chapter 38

Arlington, Virginia

Friday, June 12, 7:30 p.m.

Maggie took a moment to study Senator Wade's *plantation* from the street as the cab dropped her off. An historic colonial from the 18th century, the clapboard siding was freshly painted a pale blue with white trim and black shutters added to the affluent look. As she lifted her hand to knock on the cinnamon-colored door, Maggie's throat tightened. She had spent many of her high school and college days here after her parents died. Fitz and Dorothy had stepped in as surrogate mother and father.

She swallowed a lump of nostalgia and knocked.

Fitz opened the door himself.

"Maggie, love, come in. This is such a treat. Dorothy's at her bridge club, so it'll be just you and me." He turned to a woman waiting in the wings.

"Jenna, would you bring us some iced tea and maybe some of your famous butter cookies?"

The woman nodded and left. Fitz ushered Maggie into a large living room.

Beautiful as always, Maggie thought. Several new pieces of furniture since she'd last been here--elegant leathers and fabrics,

Persian rugs and stunning paintings to add color. She moved closer to one. It was signed Edouard Manet.

"Lovely." She turned to face him. "It's been a while since I've been here," Maggie said.

"I know. You spend more time at T.J.'s. Sit, sit." Fitz lowered himself on a flower-patterned loveseat.

Maggie sat close to him on a deep russet leather chair.

"You're not here for a casual visit," Fitz said. "It's about the body in your basement, isn't it?"

Before she could think, the words were out. "What do you know about a company called Concord Armaments, now known as Concord Provisions?"

Just then Jenna brought a tray and served them iced tea. Maggie reached for the sugar, dropped it, picked it up and dropped it again.

Fitz leaned over and patted her leg. "Relax, Maggie. I know all this stuff about the mummy has made you a bit, er, jittery. It would make me pretty damn anxious too, I can tell you." He sipped his tea.

She wasn't sure how to respond.

Fitz went on. "Too soon for a DNA match, I guess? I watch CSI, like the rest of the world." He winked and smiled. "So, what you know so far is that the body was male and estimated to be about a hundred and fifty years old."

"The age wasn't in the papers."

"Come on, Maggie. T.J. and I talk."

"Sorry, of course," she said.

"Tell me what you really want to know."

For the next twenty minutes, she relayed the information about the sealed portfolio and what she'd learned about Concord Armaments, aka Concord Provisions. Fitz asked questions from time to time, and she let him draw his own conclusions.

She asked, "Did T.J. tell you about my digital analysis of the civilian in the photograph?"

"He did. John Wilkes Booth. Pretty fantastic, if you want my opinion."

"You don't believe it?"

He exhaled. "I don't know what to believe." He stayed silent a long while. "I know you're the best in your field. Still, John Wilkes Booth? Everything we know about him says he was an overzealous madman who hated Lincoln and the government. This claims he's a hired killer. Hired by who? Concord Armaments? Why? To hide their crimes?" He stopped, searched her eyes. "You really think the photograph is Booth?"

Maggie stared at her shoes. "I'd stake my career on it."

"Good God, Maggie, if it is Booth--"

"If?"

"It's beyond fantastic. Do you realize that history will be rewritten?"

"Yes."

"The country will go nuts."

"Yes."

"Aren't you stunned?" he asked. "You seem pretty casual about it."

"I've gotten over my shock, Fitz. Now I need answers. If Joseph was right about this, then there was a conspiracy of massive proportions, Lincoln's assassination only one part of it."

He leaned forward, elbows on knees. "What can I do? That's why you're here, right?"

"I need to know about Concord Provisions. A friend in law enforcement has gotten the word that they're being investigated, all on the hush, hush. Can you find out?" She paused, gulped some tea. "They have government contracts, and I doubt they're for camping supplies. If they are selling arms, to whom are they selling them?"

"You're suggesting they may be selling to--"

"I'm not suggesting anything. I just need to know. This may all be tied to the murders during Civil War."

"How?"

"According to the document from 1865, the owners of Concord Armaments hired Booth to kill the agents. Let's suppose they also hired him to kill the President to cover their crimes of treason."

"You mean Lincoln's assassination was a murder for hire?"

"Booth may also have killed Joseph because he could identify him. Possibly even Baxter."

"What you're implying is that Concord *Provisions* may be committing the same crimes today as their ancestral company a century and a half ago. Selling arms to the enemy."

"I know it sounds far-fetched, but before I go public with any of this I want to know."

Fitz gazed at a place over her shoulder. "I'm not sure I can find out--"

She put her hand on his. "Please Fitz, if anyone can find out what's going on, surely

you can."

They stared at each other.

"I'll see what I can do," he said.

*

Dumbarton Street

Saturday, June 13, 7:00 a.m.

Maggie's phone rang early the next morning but she was already up, showered and dressed.

"What are you doing?" Frank Mead opened.

"That's an inappropriate question to ask a woman at seven in the morning." She smiled. "As a matter of fact, I'm making coffee right now. Why don't you--?"

"I'm on my way."

"Jeez," she said to herself, "you'd think the man can't get his own coffee." Then she remembered Mead's dimples and smiled.

Twenty minutes later, Maggie sat across the kitchen table from the homicide lieutenant and poured him a cup of Verona. For a minute, the silence was awkward, and she wondered about it. About him. She knew very little about Frank Mead. Bits and pieces that she'd gleaned from conversations. His wife had died only a few months ago. Suicide crossed her mind, but she wasn't sure. Also, didn't he have a daughter who lived in New York City?

She carried the pot back to its cradle.

"Something wrong?" he said.

She turned to find his intense pale blue eyes on her.

"No." She cleared her throat. "But you're here for a reason, right?"

"You invited me, if I recall."

She pulled the chair out and sat. "You have news about the DNA, don't you?" She drum-rolled her fingers on the table.

"I do. Amazingly, there was enough viable material in the body to get a match."

"Well?"

"First, the date of the mummy does fit the time frame we're considering. The mid-1800's. However . . ."

"However?" she said.

"The body in your basement was not related to you."

"What? You're not serious? There must be a mistake."

She inhaled the breath she should have let out and choked. When she could speak, she rasped out, "It has to be Joseph."

"DNA says it's not Joseph, nor any other Thornhill."

She flopped back in the chair, almost tipping it over.

"Who else could it be? This was his house in 1865. That's when he disappeared."

"What do you know about his disappearance?"

"I've been trying to find any snippet of information about his death. I searched through the attic and found nothing." She looked at him. "I guess if he did disappear, there would've been something in the papers, right?"

"Look, Maggie, I'm a cop. I'm into irrefutable evidence. DNA says he's not Joseph. Now the question is who is it? Who would bury someone in this house and why?"

Mead stood and poured some more coffee for them.

"How did the body come to be mummified?" she asked.

"Under certain circumstances, bodies that are abandoned indoors will mummify naturally, but generally in dry conditions, not a damp basement. From what the ME told me," Mead said, "as long as the temperature is moderate and there is sufficient air circulation, preservation is a race between dehydration and putrefaction."

"Obviously in this case, dehydration won."

Mead watched her. "One thing we do know."

She raised an eyebrow.

"John Wilkes Booth wasn't involved with this killing, whoever it was. The timeline doesn't match."

Maggie frowned.

"Booth killed Lincoln on April 14," Mead said, "then made his escape. They finally captured and killed him on April 26."

"The day before Joseph vanished. And the same day Baxter died."

"Booth was already dead."

Maggie hugged herself, at a loss for what to do with her arms.

"I'll buy this," Mead said. "Booth was hired by the owners of Concord Armaments to silence the four agents on the battlefield. I'll even allow that he killed Lincoln for the same reason. To protect these traitors from hanging. I doubt we'll ever prove it." He paused. "But I don't believe he killed Joseph and Baxter."

Maggie pushed back from the table and rose. "We're missing something."

Mead stood. "Hey, we solved four murders. I'd say that's a damn good solve rate."

Maggie watched him head to the door.

He turned. "Let's hope it doesn't take another hundred and fifty years to close the case."

*

That evening, Maggie helped make dinner at T.J.'s apartment, a man's space with thick wood paneling, heavy Persian rugs and Post-Modern art on the wall. Over the mantel hung a Van Gogh, one of her favorites, but unlike his father, T.J. wouldn't spend that kind of money on the real thing. This was just a print.

In the black and white kitchen, Maggie poured olive oil and balsamic vinegar in the large bowl of greens and tossed, sprinkling in garlic salt and pepper. T.J. hovered over a boiling pot of spaghetti.

"Man, I think I'd starve to death if not for spaghetti," he said as grabbed two mitts. "Ready."

"So's the salad."

Maggie shoved two plates under T.J.'s colander and he served up the hot pasta. She poured the sauce.

We're like an old married couple, she mused. Comfortable with each other. Is that a good thing? Her brain flashed to Frank Mead and what he might be doing for dinner.

As they went about these ordinary chores, Maggie filled him in on the latest findings of the body in her basement. They sat down to dinner.

"Jesus. So it's not Joseph. Who the hell can it be?"

"Frank also thinks Booth couldn't have been involved with the body in any case since he was already dead." She explained the timeline.

"I still can't believe this Booth thing. Him being a hired killer and all," T.J. said. "What are you going to do? Write a paper, go to the textbook companies, history Gods, what?"

"First, I want to find out who the mummy is and who killed him."

"How will you do that?"

"I'm not sure. Yet."

She pushed back her plate and drank some wine. Then she stood.

"Leave those for now," T.J. said, referring to the dishes. "They'll keep."

They brought their wine glasses into the living room. Maggie walked over to a beautifully lacquered credenza near the fireplace and studied the photographs on top. She'd seen them many times but had never really looked at them. In the back, she noticed a sepia-toned photo in a large walnut frame. The picture was of three men, dressed in three-piece suits, with long frockcoats, vests and cravats. Each was topped in a dapper derby.

"Who are these guys?" she asked.

"I don't know," T.J. said. "Mom had it in her study and I liked it, the historic look and all, so I stole it."

"You stole it?"

"Yeah. She has so many, I figured she'd never miss one."

"Are they relatives?"

T.J. settled an iPod in his Bose docking station. With the soft sounds of New Orleans pianist Alain Toussaint in the background, Maggie continued to stare at the photo. Finally, she turned it over, unfastened the tabs that held the cardboard in place and slid out the photograph.

"Just make yourself at home," he said.

"Don't you want to know who they are?"

"I guess. Go ahead."

She flipped the photo over. On the back were the names of three men.

T.J. leaned in. "Who are they?"

"Harlow Knox, Porter Hobbs and Samuel. . ."

"Yeah? Samuel who?"

"Samuel Lindsey."

"Lindsey is my mom's maiden name. Maybe he's an old relative, old meaning ancestor." He looked at her face. "So what's the big deal?"

"These men. Harlow, Hobbs and Lindsey. They were the owners of Concord Armaments that Colonel Baxter mentioned in his report."

"You mean the sealed report?" he said.

She just kept looking at the photograph.

"Wait a minute," he said. "These men. They were the profiteers, the traitors who sold guns to the South, weren't they?"

"Had you ever heard of Concord Armaments?" she asked.

"Not before all this happened. You told me about them. What does it mean? That I've got a nefarious great, great grandfather?"

Maggie had no answer. Her mind was pondering a more sinister question. Why didn't Fitz mention the connection?

Chapter 39

Arlington, Virginia

Sunday, June 14, 9:30 a.m.

Maggie was determined to find out what Fitz knew and why he'd lied to her. It was an uneasy feeling, to know that the man who would perhaps be her future father-in-law could do such a thing. Deliberately. Without calling ahead she found herself standing on his doorstep. The day was hot and humid, and sweat began to drip down the back of her blouse. Even the birds were hovering in the shade. She knew her emotions contributed to some of her discomfiture.

She raised her hand, almost changed her mind then knocked. This time Fitz didn't answer. Dorothy Wade did.

"Maggie," she said, her smile lukewarm. "Come in. I was expecting you."

Dorothy spun around and strode into the library, her flowing skirts and scarves swishing in her wake.

Maggie hurried after her, puzzling her remark. "Why were you expecting me?"

"Sit down." Dorothy realized she'd been abrupt, added,

"Please, dear."

Maggie lowered herself on a soft loveseat. Dorothy remained standing by the dead fireplace and gazed out the French doors, profile to Maggie. Her silvery blond hair drooped and her makeup was off-kilter, the blue shadow too deep, the rouge too pink.

Maggie felt a tickle of unease snake up her arms.

"Fitz told me about your interest in Concord Provisions."

Maggie waited.

Dorothy turned to face her. "It's not Fitz you need to speak to. It's me."

"I don't understand."

"Of course you don't," Dorothy said, avoiding Maggie's eyes.

Maggie leaned forward, her nerves like taut wires.

"The body at Dumbarton Street wasn't Joseph, was it?" Dorothy said.

"Who told you? T.J.?"

The older woman shook her head. "T.J.? No." She fixed her pale, watery blue eyes on Maggie.

"How did you know?"

Dorothy didn't respond.

Maggie grasped at the threads that were beginning to weave a pattern in her mind. "You said it's you I should talk to about Concord Provisions. Why? What do you know about them?"

Dorothy's soft blue eyes were now icy chips. "I know everything you are here to find out. I know the truth."

She sat across from Maggie at the edge of the sofa cushion. "A much over-rated concept, I might add. The truth.

"To set the record straight," Dorothy said, "it's *my* family, the Lindseys, not Fitz's family, who own majority stock in Concord Provisions today. Just as they owned Concord Armaments during the Civil War." Dorothy looked over Maggie's shoulder at some point beyond. "Concord Armaments, as you have learned, produced cheap and defective weapons to make a profit. What's more, they sold them to the highest bidder, whichever side they were on." She darted a glance at Maggie. "My great, great grandfather, Samuel, kept a journal too, you see."

Maggie feared interrupting, so she barely blinked.

"When the government found out about the deficient guns and munitions and sent investigators out in the field, Samuel and his partners hired a man to dispose of these agents. This killer did just that. Of course, it was easy to commit murder on a battlefield already soaked in blood."

At this, Dorothy cocked her head to the side and a tiny smile curled her lips. "Oh, they made so much money. Even today, it would have been a lot of money. Back then . . ." She trailed off.

"And Joseph?" Maggie dared to ask.

"Yes. Joseph Thornhill turned out to be a very meticulous and stubborn man." Dorothy rotated her head toward Maggie. "Perhaps that's where you get your obstinacy." She smiled and Maggie went cold.

Maggie reflected on her words. T.J. accused her of being stubborn too. What did T.J. know? Was his mother just protecting him? Nausea began a slow ascent into her throat. She tamped it down with sheer willpower as Dorothy continued to talk.

"Joseph became a problem. As a photographer he was traversing the battle theaters at will. Then, of course, he reported to Pinkerton." Dorothy stopped, stood, walked over to a coffee table and lifted a lid on a silver box. "Pinkerton, a dangerous man." She took out a cigarette, picked up a lighter and puffed.

Maggie couldn't recall ever seeing Dorothy smoke in the twenty years she'd known her.

“Joseph was becoming a threat. When he visited the factories in Concord, in the foolish guise of a newspaper reporter, Samuel knew he had to be dealt with.” Dorothy flicked her ashes into a glass dish on the table as she sat down again, this time on a Queen Anne chair. “So Samuel had him abducted aboard one of his gun-running ships.”

"The Blackhawk," Maggie said.

Dorothy’s eyes rounded. "Yes, you know that from Joseph’s diary. Well, he escaped. You know that too. It was Joseph who brought documentation to Lincoln’s attention. Documentation which would have been devastating to my great, great grandfather and his partners. So the assassin was brought back, this time to eliminate the President himself. Lincoln, the last remaining hazard to them."

“My God,” Maggie uttered in dismay.

"The hired gun was John Wilkes Booth. But you already know that, don't you?" Dorothy didn't wait for an answer. She stubbed out her cigarette, jumped to her feet and paced like a panther.

“Why Booth?” Maggie asked. “How did he get involved?”

"He was the quintessential choice for this job,” Dorothy said. “As an actor he could take on different roles, assume various disguises and slip around unnoticed for the most part-- anywhere, North and South. Ahh, they loved him in the South. Especially in Richmond. And he loved that city better than his home state of Maryland.

"Booth was perfect. A zealot, a white supremacist and a southern sympathizer who hated Lincoln and the Republicans. It wasn’t hard to convince him what needed to be done."

"He wasn't a madman, then, bent on killing the President so the South could rise again?" Maggie said, already knowing the answer.

"Oh no. That’s the textbook Booth, the Northern textbooks, in fact.” Dorothy patted her bubble of blond hair. “Booth wasn't mad.

Passionate, fanatical, most arrogant. But he knew right from wrong, and he knew exactly what he was doing and why. He even understood the consequences. Although, my guess is, he was so egotistical he never believed he could get caught."

"Samuel Lindsey and his accomplices were extremely lucky, weren't they?" Maggie said. "Booth's associates knew about them and Booth himself could have turned against them at any time."

"True. But their names never came up in the conspiracy trials." A smile touched Dorothy's lips. "I bet old Porter Hobbs sweated bullets around that time, though, wondering whether any of the other assassins could point the finger at them. At him."

Maggie sat silently, anger replacing shock and twisting a tight coil in her belly.

"After the assassination, Samuel and his partners met with President Johnson, Secretary of State Seward, and Secretary of War Stanton to discuss the documents and photographs that Joseph and Baxter had uncovered. They all agreed it would be in the best interests of the Union to bury the information for a period of time to allow the country's wounds to heal. The war was over, Lincoln was dead, and so were his assassins. Let it be." She folded her arms.

"Did the new administration know about Concord Armaments' role in the President's assassination?"

"No, of course not. They only knew about the government investigation, nothing more."

"And they agreed to bury it? All those murders?"

"Samuel became, of necessity, good friends with the new President. Johnson agreed that, in the best interests of the country the documentation would be kept secret. And it was. . . for a century and a half." Dorothy shot Maggie a scornful look. "Until you dug it all back up. Literally."

"Tell me," Maggie said. "Who was the body in my basement?"

"John Wilkes Booth." Dorothy sat again, ramrod straight. She inhaled deeply on the cigarette, and blew out a long breath.

"That's impossible. He was already--"

"It wasn't Booth they cornered in the Garrett barn on April 26th," Dorothy said. "Samuel hired another man, a simple, retarded man, who happened to look very much like him. He also bribed the soldiers, the guards to let the ruse be played out." She sighed. "You can see where this is going."

"Booth escaped. There have been theories about that . . ."

"Indeed. He escaped from Garrett's barn and should have made his way out of the country if Samuel's plan had worked."

"It didn't?" Maggie said.

"As the fake Booth was being captured in the barn, the real man was in Washington, tying up the loose ends for Lindsey and his comrades."

"Baxter and--"

"Joseph Thornhill. Yes. He went back to Washington to kill them both. He killed Baxter with a simple poison, made to look like he had a heart attack. He made a fatal mistake, however, with Joseph."

Maggie tried to absorb this news into her already churning gray matter. "Booth didn't kill Joseph, Joseph killed Booth."

The two women looked at each other for what seemed to Maggie an eternity.

Then Dorothy spoke. "According to Samuel's diary, Joseph should have been dead on April 26. He was, however, still alive on the 27th when Samuel watched his house and saw him leave. Booth was the one who had vanished."

"My God," Maggie whispered. "It's Booth's body in my basement? That doesn't make sense. If Joseph killed him in self-defense, why would he bury him in the basement with his own family living right upstairs?"

"Perhaps he planned on moving it when he had time." Dorothy shrugged. "But Joseph ran out of time."

"What do you mean?"

"Someone had to take care of the last threat to the company."

"Samuel Lindsey killed Joseph?"

"He had no choice."

"What did he do with the body?"

"His diary is vague on that point. He buried him with the help of his cohorts in some obscure cemetery. It's not clear where, Virginia or Washington proper, or even Baltimore."

Maggie stared in mid-space. When she finally could speak she asked, "What about the satchel? If Joseph buried Booth in the basement, why would he place the satchel with all its evidence with him?"

"I can only guess but I imagine Joseph did not want the evidence discovered for several reasons. One, he had just murdered a man. Two, the country was healing its wounds. Perhaps he didn't want to undermine the new administration's plan for reconstruction at the time."

Maggie shook her head, not able to believe this.

"And," Dorothy went on, "if Joseph planned on moving Booth's body, perhaps he assumed he'd retrieve the satchel later and in the meantime he'd keep it hidden in a safe place."

"How could he know," Maggie said, "that later would mean a hundred and fifty years."

Chapter 40

Arlington, Virginia

Sunday, June 14, 11:00 a.m.

The women looked at each other for a moment, not speaking, until Dorothy said, "The final irony is that Booth tied himself to Samuel irrevocably and enduringly."

Maggie turned her gaze to her.

"Booth had a child."

"What?" It came out as hoarse whisper.

"That's right. Booth had a child with Samuel's daughter, Rebecca. My great grandmother." Dorothy looked at Maggie with a rueful smile. "John Wilkes Booth is my great grandfather."

The room fell silent except for a ticking grandfather clock in the adjoining room and the pounding of her heart trying to break free of her chest."

"If you test my DNA, you'll see I'm telling the truth."

Maggie finally found her breath. "Does Fitz know? Or T.J.?"

Dorothy's expression took on a faraway gaze. "T.J. knows none of this. I don't think he's even heard of Concord Provisions. I made sure none of this ever reached him."

"Fitz?"

"Fitz knows. He's the one that told me what you've found out." She held up a hand. "But no, he's not involved. It's always been me. I'm the Chair of the Board of Concord Provisions. It's a privately held family business. My family. As a Lindsey, it's up to me to steer the company in certain, er, directions."

"Like to al Qaeda?"

"Sometimes the enemy offers more money than our friends, Maggie."

"That's it? It's about money?"

"And power. Guns can make you very powerful. It's quite the rush to chair a board meeting and quote the financial gains. You should try it."

Maggie jumped to her feet, unable to sit still any longer.

"Where are you going?" Dorothy said.

Maggie didn't answer. Where was she going? Who could she tell? What could she do? The police? The FBI, CIA, Department of Defense?

"Maggie," Dorothy said. "Maggie, it's done. It's all in the past. Nothing can change that now. All the characters are dead. Who cares about a mummy in your basement."

"What about you?" Maggie said. "What about Concord Provisions? What about treason, Dorothy?" She spun around the room. "Do you think you can keep this secret? This completely changes history, for God's sake. And it's still going on today. The same ruthless, treasonous acts. No, the world has to know."

"Maggie, please. Listen to me. How long have we known each other? Fitz has been a father to you. Can you really do this to him?"

"What do you mean, to *him*?"

"This controversy would kill his chances of running for President."

"Running for President?" Maggie rubbed her forehead.

"Of course he's going to run. Who better qualified for the job? That sniveling Governor from California?"

"Tell me, Dorothy." Maggie's voice was strangely quiet. "How many lives have you been responsible for? Are your guns defective too? Like Concord Armament's? You don't really give a damn about Fitz and his future, do you? This is all about you. Your name is attached to the company and once it's exposed, you're the one who will go down." Her voice rose in volume with each word. "That's really what this is about."

"What about Fitz and T.J., then? Don't you care about them?" Dorothy stood now, face contorted in anguish.

"It's because I care that I have to do this."

"Oh yes," Dorothy said. "The truth will set you free. Bullshit. The truth will kill us all, bury us." She stopped. "I can't let you do it, Maggie."

"You can't stop me." Maggie started for the door at the other end of the room.

Dorothy rushed at her and grabbed her by the arm. "No, you can't."

Maggie ripped Dorothy's hand off her arm, but the older woman was surprisingly strong. She grabbed her by the shoulders. Maggie squirmed to get out of her grip and Dorothy pulled back her arm and hit her in the face. Not a slap but a full-on right punch to the chin. Maggie went down.

Dorothy darted away.

Maggie massaged her jaw and struggled to sit up. She heard the other woman fumbling in a drawer. Maggie tried to grab her cell phone in her pocket but Dorothy was already back.

"Stand up. Now." Dorothy stood over her, a 9mm Glock pointed at her chest.

"You're crazy," Maggie said. "Dorothy--"

"No more talk. We're done," Dorothy said. "Stand up."

The look on Dorothy's face and the hardness in her voice caused Maggie's throat to close. Her breath came in short fits and she needed to urinate badly. She must be dreaming. This couldn't possibly be happening. She loved Dorothy. Dorothy loved her. Surely she wouldn't, couldn't, kill her so matter-of-factly.

Maggie found it excruciating to swallow, let alone speak.

"Give me your phone," Dorothy said. "Go on. It's in your pocket. Did you think I didn't notice?"

Maggie reached into her pocket and slowly pulled it out. If it wasn't locked, she could try to press 9-1-1, but that was impossible.

"Throw it on the floor."

She did.

"Now move back toward the couch."

Maggie backed up. Her eyes caught movement behind Dorothy. The library doorknob was turning. Then it cracked open and a figure entered silently behind them.

"Put the gun down, Mother."

Dorothy whirled about, howling a scream and firing a shot at the same time. T.J. clutched at his shoulder and went down to his knees.

Maggie rushed to pounce on Dorothy and knocked the woman onto her face. Dorothy lay there, crying softly but not attempting to get up.

Maggie seized the gun and backed away. Her eyes met T.J.'s.

"I'm okay, okay," he said.

She snatched up her phone and this time called 9-1-1. Then she curled on the floor next to him, cradling him in her arms. Blood dampened her blouse.

"I heard everything," he said, wincing in pain as he spoke. "I can't. . . believe. . .I'm so sorry, so--"

"Don't talk," she said. "Don't. There's nothing to say."

"There's everything. . . to say."

"Joseph's waited over a hundred and fifty years for justice," Maggie said. "He can wait a few more hours."

Author's Note:

This is a work of fiction. Many of the scenes and characters, however, are based on historical fact. Mathew Brady and Alexander Gardner were actually prominent Civil War photographers. Gardner emigrated from Scotland and did, indeed, work for Brady before setting up his own Gallery. During the winter of 1861-1862, Gardner became attached to the "Secret Service Corps" (then under Allan Pinkerton) as chief photographer under the jurisdiction of the U.S. Topographical Engineers. The Secret Service, as it is known today, was officially created in 1865 as a bureau under the Department of the Treasury to combat counterfeiting.

Joseph Thornhill did not exist and the partnership between Gardner and Thornhill is purely fictional. Jeb Reilly is another fictional photographer, but Timothy O'Sullivan, mentioned briefly, did exist, and took some of the most famous shots of Gettysburg. The scenes that Thornhill photographed on the battlefield were very real, however, and many were actually recorded by Gardner or O'Sullivan.

As far as the photographers dragging corpses and "setting up scenes" on the battlefield: this was a rare occurrence. Alexander Gardner did drag the body of a dead young Confederate infantryman a number of yards and rearrange it slightly to set up the scene for "A Sharpshooter's Last Sleep." However, in most cases, the dead soldiers on the field were usually in horrific condition -- bodies in advanced stages of decomposition -- and it would have been an unpleasant task to move them for any reason other than burial. In fact, there was little need to "contrive" more poignant or dramatic scenes than what the photographers could obtain merely by creatively positioning their cameras.

The changeover from the daguerreotype to the new wet collodion process began around 1855-56 in the major cities (earlier in Philadelphia). By 1860, most studios used this new process, as well as paper-print photographs, ambrotypes, tintypes, and the carte de visite, which quickly became a fad. The details regarding the photographic processes of the time are based on writings by experts who study them, and by the masters themselves.

Neither Concord Armaments nor Concord Provisions exists. However, details regarding artillery, guns, and ammunition are based on actual weapons of the period. The military used a hierarchy of specific names to distinguish the various categories of long arms during the Civil War. Rifles had 33" barrels; rifle-muskets were manufactured with *rifled* barrels usually 39" in length; muskets were smooth-bores, also with 39" barrels. In keeping with the colloquial usage of the time, the author refers to the rifle-muskets as muskets.

Many of the officers mentioned were based on actual men who actively fought in those battles: Colonel Joshua Chamberlain, General George McClellan, General Irvin McDowell, General Joseph Hooker, General George Meade, General Ambrose Burnside, General James Longstreet, and General Ulysses S. Grant.

Sutlers were civilian merchants appointed by the government and were considered a necessary evil by both the North and the South. They rode from camp to camp selling various goods and services at inflated prices. There is no evidence that John Wilkes Booth posed as a sutler during the War, however, he did, on occasion, smuggle drugs and medical supplies to the Confederacy.

The information recorded in Thornhill's diary and letters to Sara are based on actual facts relating to the battles in question, the living conditions that the men endured, and the statistics regarding casualties. In Edward Redburn's letter to his father, Otis, he refers to a friend that got "whomped to smithereens" by cannon debris. Daniel Crooks was a Union soldier with the 25th Infantry Regiment, Ohio. In truth, he managed to survive the Civil War intact.

Most of the battlefields described are preserved reasonably well as national monuments or parks and the author visited each site in order to recreate the landscapes more vividly. In many cases the locations mentioned were real: The Ebbitt House exists today as it did during the Civil War, although its original location is not known. It is now called the Old Ebbitt Grill. The Union Hospital was indeed a hotel turned hospital during the Civil War. Louisa May Alcott, actually from Concord, Massachusetts, Mr. Walt Whitman, whose excerpts from *The Civil War Poems* begin the historic chapters, and Miss Dorothea Dix each served their country as nurses at the time.

During the Civil War period, Washington D.C. was known as Washington City. The term *White House* did not actually come into use until Theodore Roosevelt's administration. Rather it was referred to as the *President's* or the *Executive Mansion*. This author chose to keep the *White House* to avoid confusion for the contemporary reader.

Maggie Thornhill's digital photography techniques are based on a blend of fact and fiction. Old photographs can be scanned electronically and enhanced, enlarged and clarified. With a great deal of work, a partial face can be re-constructed into a full face, but since faces are not symmetrical, considerable assumptions must be made. New software has since been developed that allows the user to infer three-dimensional information from a two-dimensional image. With this software one can construct a computer model of a face from a few separate photos of that face taken at different angles. There is also software used in forensics that will apply certain algorithms to an image to synthesize aging.

Assuming the full face is reconstructed with reasonable accuracy, can Maggie program in data of other faces and find a match? There are quite a few software programs that match objects -- fingerprints, retinal prints, faces, manufactured goods, etc. But have thousands of Civil War photographs been painstakingly digitized into computer files? Not to this author's knowledge.

And, lest we forget, John Wilkes Booth did, indeed, kill Abraham Lincoln. Did he kill others? There's no evidence to support that premise. History records that he was killed at Garrett's Barn. Could he have escaped? Was he a madman or a hired gun? This author will let history have its way. For now.

Lynne Kennedy

About the Author

With a Master's Degree in Science and more than 28 years as a science museum director, Lynne Kennedy has had the opportunity to study history and forensic science, both of which play significant roles her novels. Including TIME EXPOSURE, she has written three other historical mysteries, each solved by modern technology. Her most recent novel, THE TRIANGLE MURDERS (formerly called TENEMENT) was a finalist in St Martin's Malice Domestic Competition, 2011 and Winner of the Rocky Mountain Fiction Writers Mystery Category, 2011.

Visit her website at www.lynnekennedymysteries.com.

Made in the USA
Middletown, DE
03 September 2016